BECAUSE
I COULD
NOT STOP
for DEATH

BECAUSE
I COULD
NOT STOP
for DEATH

An Emily Dickinson Mystery

AMANDA FLOWER

BERKLEY PRIME CRIME
New York

BERKLEY PRIME CRIME
Published by Berkley
An imprint of Penguin Random House LLC
penguinrandomhouse.com

Copyright © 2022 by Amanda Flower
Penguin Random House supports copyright. Copyright fuels
creativity, encourages diverse voices, promotes free speech, and
creates a vibrant culture. Thank you for buying an authorized
edition of this book and for complying with copyright laws by
not reproducing, scanning, or distributing any part of it in any
form without permission. You are supporting writers and
allowing Penguin Random House to continue to
publish books for every reader.

BERKLEY and the BERKLEY & B colophon are registered
trademarks and BERKLEY PRIME CRIME is a trademark of
Penguin Random House LLC.

LIBRARY OF CONGRESS CATALOGING-IN-PUBLICATION DATA

Names: Flower, Amanda, author.
Title: Because I could not stop for death: an Emily Dickinson mystery /
Amanda Flower.
Description: First Edition. | New York: Berkley Prime Crime, 2022. |
Series: An Emily Dickinson mystery
Identifiers: LCCN 2022012436 (print) | LCCN 2022012437 (ebook) |
ISBN 9780593336946 (trade paperback) | ISBN 9780593336953 (ebook)
Subjects: LCGFT: Novels.
Classification: LCC PS3606.L683 B43 2022 (print) |
LCC PS3606.L683 (ebook) | DDC 813/.6—dc23
LC record available at https://lccn.loc.gov/2022012436
LC ebook record available at https://lccn.loc.gov/2022012437

First Edition: September 2022

Printed in the United States of America
1st Printing

For Isabella "Belle" Flower

I see Emily in you and cannot wait

to see your impact on the world.

You are loved beyond measure.

Because I could not stop for Death—

He kindly stopped for me—

The Carriage held but just Ourselves—

And Immortality.

—EMILY DICKINSON

BECAUSE
I COULD
NOT STOP
for DEATH

CHAPTER ONE

ICY RAIN SLAPPED the dirt road, turning it into mud. I did my best to protect my skirts, holding them as high as I dared above my ankles. It wouldn't do to go into my interview covered in mud. I had a feeling that Miss O'Brien would not look kindly on me for that.

A shrill whistle broke into my worried thoughts. "Move aside!" called a man who was driving a wagon loaded down with barrels and crates bound for the market uptown.

As the wagon rolled by at a fast clip, one of its rear wooden wheels fell into a rut in the road and splashed mud onto my side. I stopped in the rain and stared at my soiled skirts and cloak. My head hung low. Was there any purpose in going to the interview now? Miss O'Brien would never hire me to be a maid when I arrived in such a state. How could I claim to be able to clean anything when I was a mess?

I watched as the wagon lumbered down the mud-covered street. The rain fell in earnest then, so much so that I couldn't even see the stately homes that sat on either side of the street or the two-story brick primary school that I attended off and on as a child. I yanked at the hood of my cloak, pulling it farther down over my eyes. I couldn't turn back. It would be far worse to show up late than dirty. I marched ahead in soggy boots.

Through the rain, the great house came into view, and I realized that it was just across the street from my childhood school. It was a two-story white clapboard home that loomed above me. I had never been inside a home so large before. If I got the position, I would be able to live there. Possibly. It seemed to be a very far-off chance now.

With shaky hands, I removed the note I had received from Miss O'Brien. In delicate script, *Come to the back door at half past noon. Do not be late. Mr. Dickinson does not abide tardiness.* And then she signed her name, *Margaret O'Brien.*

Rain smeared the ink. I patted it and only managed to transfer the ink onto my hand. Mud-covered skirts and now ink-stained hands.

The worst part was I didn't need to read the letter. I had memorized it. It was only my nerves that made me remove it from my pocket to read it once more. Yet another mistake I made that day. Only I could have made such a mess of things.

There was no one at the front of the house, and the gardens, which stretched far into the backyard, were empty too. No one was silly enough to be out in this cold January rain. Ice slapped my face. The rain was beginning to freeze. It seemed fitting for the state that I was in.

I slipped and skidded on the cobblestone path around the grand home until I came to a plain door painted black with a brass handle and knocker. I swallowed and lifted the knocker.

Tap, tap, tap. It fell against the door. No sound came from inside the house. I waited a moment, wondering if I should knock again. Would knocking again aggravate Miss O'Brien and show that I was not only covered in mud but impatient? I knew she would already be dubious of me due to my appearance.

There was no cover outside the servants' entrance. The rain droned on, soaking me to the skin. I worried about the puddles that I would carry with me into the majestic home. I lifted my hand to knock a second time, and the door opened. My pale hand was suspended in the air. I dropped it to my side.

A thin woman with curly dark hair that was smartly tucked under in a knot on the back of her head stood in the doorway. "Miss Willa Noble?" She had an Irish accent like the men who worked in the warehouse with my brother. Although hers had a much gentler lilt to it than the men at the warehouse.

I nodded. I opened my mouth to speak, but no words came out.

"Come in, then."

I stepped over the threshold into a dark hallway. Two sets of stairs went up in either direction from this spot. I imagined one led to where the family lived and the other to where the servants worked.

"Don't stand there and drip," Miss O'Brien said in a voice that was firm but not harsh. "Take off your cloak there." She pointed at the wall. "There's a peg where you can hang it."

I did as I was told. Still, I hadn't spoken a word. I prayed my ability to speak would return before the interview began.

She looked down at my feet. "You can't walk through the house in those muddy boots. I will have to spend days scrubbing the carpets. Wait here."

She left me standing in the entryway and disappeared down the hallway. I dripped on the floorboards. She returned a minute later with a pair of old black shoes in her hands.

"These belonged to the previous maid. She left them when she took a new post. I have been meaning to mail them to her, but I am glad now I have not." She set the shoes in front of me on the floor. "Take those boots off and put these on."

I again did as I was told. The shoes were a size too small and pinched my toes, but I didn't say a word about the discomfort. "Thank you," I murmured.

"Good, you can talk. I was afraid we would have to pantomime this interview. Now, follow me, and I will take you to the room where we can discuss the position. Lift your skirts as we go, so as not to soil anything. Mrs. Dickinson prides herself on a clean home."

I lifted my skirts and followed her up the left staircase. I assumed this was the way that led to where the servants worked. She opened the door at the top of the landing, and I was astonished to see I was wrong. Instead of walking into a servants' hallway, we were in a large sitting room. Everything in the room was so elegant! A fire crackled and snapped in the hearth. The furnishings were fine. A velvet brocade sofa was on one side of the fire, and two matching chairs were on the other. A modest yet sparkling chandelier hung overhead, and a petite desk stood by the window. I didn't think I had ever been in a room this lovely before.

Miss O'Brien perched on one of the two chairs. "I hope it's all right that I ask you to remain standing. Please know it is only to spare the furniture from the state of your clothes."

I nodded.

"You must look such a fright because of the storm outside, so I won't mark you down too much for that. January is such a horrid month. It rains or snows or both almost every day. More weeks of foul weather lie ahead. I suppose that's why summer is so precious to us. The spring is unpredictable and can be ripped away by a whim of the wind." She said this all in her Irish lilt like she was trying to coax me to sleep with a bedtime story.

I nodded again.

"Where are you working now?" Her tone told me that pleasantries were over and she was getting down to business.

"I clean at Mrs. Patten's Boarding House on South Pleasant Street. I have been there for two years," I said, grateful that I had been able to utter the words so clearly.

"Do you not like working at the boardinghouse?" she asked. "Is that why you applied for this position?"

I swallowed. "No, it's fine work. Good work for a girl like me to find, but I saw the advert in the paper for this position. It's an opportunity to move into a new challenge. I believe working for a family that is so vital to the community would be quite an honor."

"You are right in thinking that working for the Dickinson family would be a new challenge. They are an exacting family and hold a very high standard. Mr. Dickinson especially so. He is finishing his term at the United States House of Representatives," she said with pride. "He served his country, the Whig party, and the great Commonwealth of Massachusetts well. It would be your privilege to work for him and his family, if you're granted the position. When he finishes his term he will be here overseeing the renovations of the family home on

Main Street. He is in the process of buying it, and renovations will begin as soon as everything is finalized. It is right that the Dickinson family would move back to the home that Mr. Dickinson's father built. They have been away from it far too long."

"The Dickinsons are moving?" I asked.

"Yes," she said in a crisp voice. "It has been Mr. Dickinson's goal to return to the homestead for many years. His father ran into a bit of financial trouble and lost it. He fled to Ohio in disgrace." She looked around with bright red cheeks. "Don't repeat that."

"I won't," I promised. My hands began to shake. I clasped them in front of me and pressed them into my skirts.

"Was the boardinghouse your first position?" Miss O'Brien asked, getting back to the task at hand.

"No, I've been in domestic work for the last eight years."

She frowned. "Eight years. You can't be more than sixteen."

"I am twenty, ma'am. I started work when I was twelve."

"What made you work so young?" She eyed me. "Should you not have been in school? The Dickinsons put great value in education, even in the education of girls such as yourself."

"My mother died, ma'am, and I had to provide for my younger brother and me. I had to go to work. Our mother taught us to work hard, so it was no trouble to take over that role."

"Haven't you got a father?" She narrowed her eyes.

"Not that I know of," I said and pressed my clenched hands deeper into my skirts. My father was not a topic for conversation even if it cost me the position at the Dickinson household. I would not speak of him, ever.

"How much younger is your brother than you?"

"Two years, ma'am," I said. "He's an adult now, too, and works just as much as I do. He works even harder, I should say, because of the physical labor required for man's work."

Miss O'Brien stood up. "I'm interviewing several more girls for this post. I will let you know by mail by the end of the week if we choose you." She looked at my wet, muddy skirts again.

My heart sank. If there were several young ladies applying for this position, what chance did I really have at winning the spot? I was the girl who came to the interview covered in mud and who was too young without the proper experience for the post. Why did I think I was the only one who would have been interested in the ad? As I told Miss O'Brien, the position was a chance to move up—this was true not just for me but for anyone in domestic work. There were many young women in my place that would want to do so.

"Thank you for your time," I said. "Would you like me to let myself out?"

Before Miss O'Brien could answer, a breathy voice said, "There will be no more interviews. Margaret, you have found the right maid."

I turned and a small woman stood in the doorway. She was petite and wore a brown dress that was cinched around her small waist. Her chestnut red hair was pinned back in a fashionable knot and her dark eyes shone with interest, but there was a faraway look about them too. She was a very pretty woman, but there was something birdlike in her movements as she stepped into the room. Her hands fluttered like the tips of wings.

Miss O'Brien jumped to her feet. "Miss Dickinson, can I help you with something?"

"You have helped. You have found our new maid. I'm very grateful to you for that. Mother wants us to keep a clean house, especially when she is in the middle of one of her episodes."

Episodes? What does she mean by this?

Miss Dickinson studied me with an exacting gaze. "She looks like she has a strong back too. It's something that we will need if Father insists on pulling us up and moving us back to the place of my birth." She said this like she wasn't very keen on the idea.

"Very well, Miss Dickinson." Miss O'Brien dipped her chin.

"Thank you, Margaret." The small woman looked me in the eye. "I like someone who would sacrifice herself for her family and duty. That's just the kind of person I want on our staff. I think there have been enough questions. Margaret, please show the young maid to her room and cancel the rest of your interviews for the position."

Miss O'Brien pressed her lips together as if she were unsure. "If you are certain, Miss . . ."

"Very certain. I like her, Margaret. If I like her, Father will agree."

Miss O'Brien nodded. "Please follow me, Miss Noble. I will show you to your room."

I blinked; it was all happening so fast. I glanced back at Miss Dickinson, but she was no longer there. She was gone.

"Do not be surprised that she seemingly disappeared. She comes and goes through the house in silence. She's so small and light she floats from room to room. The only time I do hear her come is when Carlo is with her."

"Carlo?" I asked as I hurried to keep pace with her in my too-tight shoes.

"Don't tell me that you haven't seen Miss Dickinson walking through Amherst with that beast of a dog. He's big and brown and has curls just like a woman. He weighs nearly as much as she does."

"He's a beast?" I asked with a slight tremor in my voice. I wasn't very keen on dogs. The only ones I knew guarded the warehouse where my brother worked and took their position of protecting the property quite seriously.

"I just say that because of his size. He's a kind dog, but we have to mind any paw prints on the carpets. That will be something you will have to contend with as a maid in the house. All paw prints must be removed immediately, if they are from the dog or from Miss Lavinia's cats. Mrs. Dickinson does not abide by them." She continued walking. "You will see Carlo soon enough and understand."

I shivered at the thought of running into Carlo unprepared. "Who is Miss Lavinia?" I asked.

She looked at me. "What do you know about this family?"

I bit the inside of my lip. "What you have told me and that Mr. Dickinson is an important man for both the town and Amherst College."

She nodded. "They are a family of five. There are Mr. and Mrs. Dickinson, of course, and Emily, Miss Dickinson, is the oldest daughter. She is the one who gave you this position with very little thought." She pursed her lips when she said that. "She has an older brother, Austin, who is away in Cambridge studying at Harvard to be a lawyer, and Miss Lavinia, the younger sister, is your age. The family calls her Vinnie, which between you and me is not a proper name for a young lady."

"And she has cats?" I asked.

"Yes. Several. They always seem to be coming and going. I believe Miss Lavinia has four at the moment. You will find them lounging about the house and garden. They go where they please."

I might have been a bit afraid of dogs, but I very much liked cats. I had always wanted one, but I had never been in a position where I could care for one. Mrs. Patten didn't allow animals in her boardinghouse. I had high hopes that Miss Lavinia and I would get along on that fact.

Miss O'Brien led me back the way we came and down the stairs and up the second staircase. This one led me into the servants' corridor. There were only four doors there. "The staff is small," Miss O'Brien said. "Mr. Dickinson is not one for extravagances. In the house, it is you and me."

I blinked, wondering how the two of us could keep such a grand house.

She opened the second door. "This will be your room."

I followed her inside.

"Does it suit?" she asked.

I looked around at the tidy bed, washbasin, shelves, and even a small desk for writing letters. It was the nicest place I had ever lived. "It will suit just fine. Thank you."

"Good." She nodded. "I suggest that you get yourself cleaned up. You begin tomorrow." She went through the door, pulling it closed behind her, and it shut with finality.

CHAPTER TWO

I REMOVED MY SHOES with a groan and sat on the edge of my bed. It was dark outside, and I had been up and working since before dawn. Although kind in her own stern way, Miss O'Brien put me through my paces on the first day on the job. She had me dust every room in the house top to bottom. She had said, "Spring is right around the corner and our cleaning must start now to welcome warmer days."

The only room I did not dust was Miss Dickinson's. I went to it with my feather duster ready, but when I peered inside she sat at a small writing desk bent at the waist, scribbling on a piece of paper with a kind of concentration I had never before witnessed.

I placed a hand to my back where I felt a dull ache. I wished that I could take a warm bath to soothe it. Even if that had been an option for me, I don't know that I would have had the will to draw the water.

I thought back to my day of dusting. At times while I

worked, I caught glimpses of the family. Miss Dickinson and her sister, Miss Lavinia, for the most part. I never spoke to them, just carried on with my dusting. They nodded to me when our eyes met.

I desperately wanted to see the gardens. I loved plants so well, but it was another late January day of gray and rain, so all I saw through the windows was a sheet of water and ice. Snow would be better at this point. At least it wouldn't be as dreary.

I prayed that Henry would have the wherewithal to be inside on a night like tonight. I wished that my brother had a bit more common sense.

Rain continued to hit the small window. *Tap, tap, tap.* And then it came harder. *Tap, Ratata, Tat.*

In my exhaustion, I stood up straight. That wasn't rain on the glass.

On shaky legs, I went to the window. A watery face appeared on the other side of the glass. I stifled my scream by covering my mouth with the hem of my apron and biting down hard. I hurried back across the room with my hand on the door handle. I needed to tell Miss O'Brien.

I stole a glance back at the window. The figure waved at me from the other side of the wet windowpane. As much as I wanted to run from the room and hide, I looked at the face, concentrating so that I could make out the features. "Henry?"

I hurried to the window, unlocked it, and pushed it open.

Henry tumbled into the room in a spray of water. I closed the window. "Henry, what on earth are you doing here?"

Henry bounced to his feet like a jack-in-the-box. A puddle spread in the middle of the floor where he had landed. "Look at this place! You're living high on the hog, dear Sister. My, now I can see why you wanted to chuck your job at Mrs. Patten's Boarding House. I would give my left foot to live in a place this nice!"

"Henry, shh. You will wake the housekeeper or the family dog and I will surely be fired for having someone in my room!" I glanced at the door, afraid that Miss O'Brien would throw it open at any second and tell me to leave.

"You worry too much." He pushed his straw-colored hair that was the same color as mine out of his eyes. At the moment, his hair was two shades darker from being wet. He shook his head like a dog, and water hit me in the face.

I held up my hands. "Henry, please."

"I feel like a drowned rat."

"You look like one, too, and that doesn't mean you have to share the rain with me," I said hotly.

He laughed. "Is it true that the mother of the house is insane?"

"Henry, that is unkind."

"Is it unkind if it's true?" His green eyes that were so much like our mother's sparkled in the candlelight. My own eyes were a dull brown.

"Have you seen her?" he asked.

"No, I have only seen the housekeeper and two sisters."

"Spinsters, are they? Could they not find a man who suited them? They probably think they are too good for marriage."

"They are young yet. The youngest sister is my age. Do you think I should be married at twenty?"

"No, not if it was going to be to—"

"Hush!" I cut him off. Henry knew very well that I didn't want to speak of that man.

He lifted his chin. "When I marry I want a wife who will look up to me."

I groaned. My brother with all his confidence thought that everyone should look up to him, even President Pierce and all the learned men in Washington. He thought he was equal to them all.

"Have you seen anyone else?"

I shook my head.

"Not even the father of the house? I heard he's quite severe."

"He's in Washington at present on business," I said. "Now, I am happy to see you, but you must go. I will be in trouble if you are caught in the house. They have a dog. He could sense you are here."

"They won't catch me." He put his hand on his narrow hips. "I'm like a cat with nine lives."

I sighed. "Please, Henry, go. If I lose this position, I can't return to the boardinghouse. Mrs. Patten was angry when I turned in my notice. She won't take me back."

He marched around the room, taking everything in. Had he not been taller than me, I might have been tempted to take him by the ear and force him out the window. However, I hadn't been able to do that since Henry was in long pants.

"You have done well for yourself, Willa. Quite well," he said.

"It's not just for me. The money I make here will help both of us."

"I think of us both too. I have a plan that will make us rich. You will no longer have to clean up after people like the Dickinsons. You will have you very own home."

I suppressed a sigh. This was not the first time that my brother had made such a pronouncement. In the end, nothing good came of it. He spent a night in jail over his last great idea to make money. I would have never been able to get him out if it hadn't been for Matthew Thomas, an old friend of our family who was a police officer. Matthew put in a good word for Henry. Without that, I feared my brother might still be in prison to this day.

"Henry, you know what happened last time. We can't ask Matthew to help you again if you find yourself in trouble. We have indebted ourselves to him too much already."

"You say that because you don't want to fawn over him if I need his assistance." He mimicked a woman swooning.

I folded my arms. "I do not fawn. I have never fawned."

He laughed. "Believe what you must, but Matthew cares for you. You could do worse. Do you want to end up a spinster like the Dickinson girls?"

I had had enough of this. "It's time for you to go." I pushed him lightly toward the window.

"No, not yet. I haven't been able to tell you what I came all this way in the driving rain to say."

I stepped back. "Very well."

"You left your old job and I left mine too," he said with pride.

"You left your job? But the warehouse let you sleep there. Where are you living now?" I squeezed my hands together. "Do you have a place to stay? I won't be paid for another week. I can give you money then to rent a room."

"Don't worry about me, Sister." He jumped onto the only chair in the room. "I always come out on top."

"Henry, shh," I hissed. "You're being far too loud. Someone will come."

He grinned and it showed off the gap in his front teeth. "I came here to tell you the good news, Sister."

"Fine, fine." I watched the doorknob, certain that Miss O'Brien would turn it and come through the door at any moment. "Tell me and then leave. I will see you on Sunday when I have the day off."

He hopped off the chair and pulled it toward me. He straddled the chair and leaned on the back. "I have found work too."

A breath of air went out of me. "You have?"

He nodded. "And Sister, I will make more money than you can ever imagine. You don't have to be in this house and clean for people. Why should you be a servant when you should be a queen?"

"I'm not a queen."

"Mother told us that we were royalty, a prince and princess."

"Henry, that was a fairy tale to make us sleep at night."

He leaned forward. "It was not."

I closed my eyes for a moment. I couldn't get into an argument now. If I did, Henry would only become louder. He always believed that the way to win an argument was to be louder and more obstinate than your opponent. "Perhaps there is royalty in Europe, but there are no queens in America."

"There may be someday," he said. "Mark my words, Sister, this country is about to tear itself apart. I have heard rumblings. The British will come back and pick up the pieces of it all. We will be like Canada, forever tethered to the monarchy."

I swallowed. "Those are just people that want to make trouble."

He shook his head as if he could not believe how naive I was being.

"Tell me about the job," I said, refusing to get into another argument with my brother about politics. I preferred to leave such debates to the officials in Washington. They knew what they were doing; they would not be there otherwise.

He narrowed his eyes and seemed to consider my request. I knew my brother well; he would rather continue the argument than put it to rest. There were days when I wondered how we could even be flesh and blood. I ran away from confrontation, not toward it like he did.

"I have work at the village livery as a stable boy. Then I will move up to apprentice and coach driver. I have been there nearly a month."

"A month? And you are just telling me now?"

"I knew how you would react," he said with a smile. "You would worry, but you have no need to. When I'm a coach driver, I can set my own fare and have my own business. I won't have to work for a rich man any longer."

"But how will you afford your own team and carriage?" I asked.

"Do not worry over that now." He waved away my question as if it meant little.

"But where are you sleeping?" I asked.

"I don't have a room yet but am allowed to sleep in the stables with the horses. It's dry and warm. There's not much else a lad like me can ask for."

I frowned. "I don't want you sleeping in a barn. We have not worked this hard since Mother died for you to sleep with animals."

"It's much nicer than any room we slept in as children."

I shook away dark memories that threatened to cloud my

mind. "Even so, the money I make here will be saved up so you can rent a room. You should be in a proper bed. Working in stables is hard on the body. If you do not rest properly, you may be hurt. You need your wits about you when you are working with all those horses. You don't know yet how they will behave."

He snorted. "I'm not worried about working with horses. I understand them and they understand me."

I wanted to argue more, but before I could speak, he said proudly, "By the time I'm done with this job you will have a proper house, a house all your own where I can be my own man."

"Yes, but that is years away."

He grinned again. "No, it is not. I have a way to speed up the process. When I do, I will come into the money I need to buy my own carriage and team. Then we will be as fancy as the Dickinsons and their friends."

I frowned. "I don't understand, Brother. How can you come into that much money at a livery starting as a stable boy?"

He grinned again. "You will see."

I took a step toward him. "Please don't get entangled into another scheme that might land you in trouble. Tell me exactly what your plan is. I need to know."

He went to the window and opened it. It was raining as hard as ever. There was a flash of lightning and a clap of thunder. "Come to the livery on Sunday, and I will show you." My brother put one leg out the window and began to climb. "I will tell you all then." With that he was gone.

I put my head out the window, and rain pelted it. Henry

shimmied down the side of the house like a sure-footed squirrel. He jumped to the ground, waved, and then ran away.

There was another flash of lightning, and I spotted a small form and a large beast walking through the garden in the driving rain. It was a woman and a large dog. The woman's pale face turned toward me. I gasped, jumped back, and slammed the window shut.

CHAPTER THREE

FOR THE NEXT two days, I worried Miss Dickinson—for I knew it was she who stood in the garden that rainy night with her dog, Carlo—would tell Miss O'Brien that there was a young man in my room. On the third day after Henry's visit when I still had not heard any word of it, I began to relax a little. I knew from past experience that some prefer to hold on to scandalous information until it could be used best as a weapon later. I prayed Miss Dickinson wasn't one of those people.

I saw Miss Dickinson around the house, but she never spoke to me or even looked at me. If she was curious about the man who had been in my room, she did not show it.

On the fourth day, I was feeling much better about it all. I believed if I were to be in trouble for Henry's behavior I would have known by now. And if Miss Dickinson was waiting to use that against me later, well, then, I would be on my best behavior to cause her no reason to.

I went about the day first cleaning the kitchen until it sparkled and then I moved onto the family bath. I had happiness in my step. I liked my new position. Miss O'Brien was firm but kind, and in the evening, she and the market woman, who also was Irish, would sit in the kitchen and swap stories about their homeland. I loved to stand in the hallway and listen to them. I found their accents captivating. I could almost imagine myself sitting by a warm fire listening to their tales. I never let on that I was listening though. I didn't know how they would like it.

It was Friday, and I would be able to visit my brother in two days' time. That brought me great cheer as well. I wanted to see with my own eyes that Henry was in a good spot. If I didn't approve—and I would be very surprised if I did—I would encourage him to find another position. He could be stubborn, so while I scrubbed the bath until it shone, I practiced my speech to my younger brother. "Henry, you need to find a position where you can sleep in a real bed and can save money. Sleeping in a barn is no way to live. Think of what Mother would say if she knew." I muttered this as I polished the pewter feet of the bath. "It's best for your health to be in a real bed in a room of your own. You're young now, but you won't be always. Your back will ache as you age. You don't want to have a crooked spine, do you?"

Two of Miss Lavinia's cats, one ginger and the other gray, stood in the bathroom and watched me work. They seemed to be listening to my speech too. I had learned that the cats liked to watch me when I worked, and I enjoyed having them around. I didn't feel as alone with the cats near.

"Do you two think my argument will work with him?"

They studied me with their amber eyes.

"Willa," Miss O'Brien said from the door. "Can I have a word?"

I jumped. "Yes, Miss O'Brien." I started to gather up my bucket and rags.

"No, leave that," she said. "You can come back for it later and finish."

The cats ran out of the bathroom.

My heart sank. Had she heard me talking to myself? I had heard of girls being dismissed from domestic work for far less. She might think talking to myself was some sort of mental failing. I could see the Dickinsons, who were so learned, not wanting such a person in their home. Or worse, had Miss Dickinson finally told her about Henry's visit? Here I was practicing a speech to Henry about finding new employment, and I would have to do the same for myself in a matter of minutes.

She led me out of the bath and down the main stairs that the family used to the same sitting room where she had conducted my interview.

"Willa, will you please sit?" She pointed at the sofa.

I blinked and did as I was asked. She was asking me to sit? This was bad. Perhaps even worse than I first thought, but what could be worse that losing my position? I didn't have any fallback. I needed the money so that Henry could rent a room and not be sleeping in what I imagined was a filthy barn.

It was then when I noticed that Miss O'Brien fidgeted with her hands. It was as if she didn't know what she should do with them. She held her skirts, let them go. Squeezed her hands into fists, let them fall to her sides.

I cleared my throat. "Miss O'Brien, is everything all right?"

She looked at me then with tears in her eyes. She blinked them away, and I wondered if they had been there at all or just a trick of the sunlight pouring in through the window. After a week of cold rain, we had a beautiful winter day before us, and from where I sat I had a clear view of the gardens that I so desperately wanted to explore. Even in their dormant state for the winter, I looked forward to seeing them, of glimpsing the promise of what might be, come spring. I had always loved growing things. My mother had a small window garden in our rooms growing up. At least for a while until things became more difficult. I dragged my thoughts to the present. Today was a beautiful day. It was the type of day on which nothing bad could happen. It wasn't possible for such a fine day to be marred by bad news.

"I'm afraid that everything is not all right, Willa. When was the last time you saw your brother?"

I stared at her. I had been right after all. Miss Dickinson had told her about Henry's visit, but then, how would either of them know it was my brother who came through the window?

"I ask you this because there has been an accident." Her eyes were sad again. "Your brother was killed last night."

I didn't say anything. I didn't scream. I didn't cry or react at all. What she said didn't sound like it could be real. What did she mean that Henry was killed last night? Did she mean that Henry was dead? But that couldn't be. I had just spoken to him four days ago. He climbed up the side of the Dickinson house like the monkeys I had read about in books. He could not be dead. A dead man could not do such a thing. He was well. He'd always been well. Yes, he got caught in scrapes from time to time, but like a cat, he always landed on his feet. I was the one who didn't land on my feet, but Henry did! I had witnessed it hundreds of times.

Miss O'Brien peered at me. "Willa, are you quite all right?

Do you understand what I have said? Your brother is dead. He was found this morning in the livery stables where he worked. The police said he was trampled when one of the horses became spooked. It seems that he tried to calm it and went into the stall and was crushed," she said.

Henry was dead? Henry was dead and they were blaming his death on him? Because he went into the stall to calm a horse? That wasn't his fault. He did the right thing, didn't he? He worked in the stable. It was his job to calm the horse.

"Willa, are you all right?"

I stared at her. It was such a strange question for her to ask. Did she not see the oddity of the inquiry? Did she not see the giant pit before me about to swallow me whole? Did she not know that if I could, I would jump into that pit and disappear?

My mouth felt dry and I opened it. "Who told you this?" It was the only question I could manage.

"A young officer came to the house this morning. He said his name was Officer Thomas. He wanted to tell you himself, but I told him I would."

My chest tightened. Matthew. Matthew was the one who told her my brother was dead. Of course, it would be Matthew.

The tears came then as if a well had opened up in my heart. They gathered in my eyes and spilled over. My chest heaved up and down. I wasn't conscious of any sound because I felt like someone had rolled up balls of wool and stuck them in both of my ears. I couldn't hear myself. I couldn't hear anything.

Miss O'Brien stood and moved to stand in front of me. Then she perched next to me on the sofa and patted my hand. "Take care, child. Wipe away your tears. When you're struggling so, you must rein in your emotions. You mustn't let them take you over like this. What's done is done. This life has many hard moments. We cannot dwell in sadness. There's not the time."

Numbly, I nodded, but I had no idea how to do what she was asking me to do. How could I not dwell, how could I not drown, in this sadness?

"It is time to move about your day. See, the fire in this room needs tending." She pointed at the cold fireplace. "Working with your hands will drive your hardship away. Tears will make it worse."

How could I move about my day and tend the fire like she asked? My brother was dead. I was utterly alone in the world. The hardship of that could never be driven away. I had no one. No one. And more than that, my brother, who had so much promise, was gone. I knew his schemes were crazy. I knew that he had wild ideas, which, frankly, scared me most of the time, but I think in the deepest place in my heart, I believed him. I believed that he would strike it rich one day. I believed him that he would pull us out of our station in life. That dream was dead. As dead as my little brother, who I loved so dear.

"The police said they would be back in the afternoon to talk to you. Since we don't know how long that will take, it is best to finish your chores before they arrive."

I looked at her, and tears so big that they could drown a man rolled down my face. "Why would the police want to talk to me? I wasn't at the livery when he died."

She shook her head. "I do not know. They would have talked to you right away, but I told them that you'd need some time. It's best to resolve whatever you are feeling before they arrive. You can't let the police see you weak. That's when you will find yourself in the most trouble."

I bit my lip. I was grateful to Miss O'Brien for that kindness more than she could ever know. She was tough, maybe harsh even, but I knew that she was trying to protect me. She was right not to show the police weakness. I knew this firsthand. I would not want Matthew to see me as I am now.

She patted my hand a second time and rose from her seat. "I have work to do, and so do you. Let's get on with it." She pointed at the coal bucket and shovel by the fireplace. "You will see that I have already brought up the bucket so you can clean the fireplace. Distraction is the key for surviving grief, my girl." She lowered her voice. "Trust me. I know this acutely well. I will finish the bathroom for you." With that she left the room.

After she was gone, I remained on the sofa. How long I stayed there, I didn't know. It could have been mere minutes. It could have been days with the sun and moon rising and falling without me even being aware of their journey across the sky.

All I could think about was the scheme that Henry alluded to the night he broke into my room. Was this way to make money what got him killed? He had been known to be in trouble before. Could I assume that his death was merely accidental like Miss O'Brien said? To me, it did not seem the way in which my brother would die. He knew horses: how to care for them and how to be careful around them. He'd worked with them in the stockyards every day, and he loaded and unloaded wagons and carts of goods. He would not put himself in a position where a horse could harm him. I didn't doubt he would want to calm an agitated animal, but he would be vigilant while doing it. He would not have entered that stall without a very good reason. Rightly or wrongly, everything he did, he did with purpose. It was difficult to believe he would die without it.

I let out a breath and stood. What good did it do me to have these thoughts? They would not bring my brother back. Nothing would.

Miss O'Brien was right. I needed to work, and when the police came, I needed to be ready, because I had many questions for them.

I spread a white piece of muslin in front of the fireplace so that when I cleaned, the soot would not mar the carpets. I knelt on the fabric, picked up my stiff-bristled brush, pulled the bucket close, and began to move the grate. That was as far as I went before tears overtook me again.

One of my giant tears landed on the remains of the last fire, creating an inky black puddle that I wished would swallow me whole. I didn't know if I could go on without Henry. I never thought I might have to.

I sat back on my heels.

"Why are you crying?" a breathy voice asked me.

I spun around on my knees and found Miss Dickinson standing behind me. I had no idea she'd come into the room or how long she had been watching me.

I scrambled to my feet and wiped the tears from my face. "I am so sorry, miss. I—I—"

"Please don't tell me that you are tearful over cleaning the hearth. Is Margaret working you too hard? I know the woman is exacting, and she's quite right that my mother and father expect a clean home. However, it should not bring you to tears. It's just a fireplace."

"No, miss, it's not the fireplace or anything Miss O'Brien said to me." I stepped to the middle of the white sheet. "She's been very kind to me."

"Then why are tears falling from your eyes and dripping from your nose?" She cocked her head, and again I was reminded of a bird. She was like the small herons that I had seen at the marsh with my brother, thin, almost frail-looking, but with a determined and keen eye that did not miss the slightest movement. They could also stab a fish with their beaks and eat it in one second.

I squeezed the bristle brush more tightly in my hand.

"If you are not crying over the fireplace or something your superior said, why are you crying?" Her voice was soft but direct. I knew right away that she was asking because she truly wanted to know, not for the sake of nicety.

"It is my brother, miss," I said, wishing myself that I could stop the words from coming out of my mouth. "I just learned that he died last night."

She studied me even closer. "Why are you working, then? Should you not be grieving?"

I didn't want to cause trouble for Miss O'Brien by blaming her for encouraging me to work. "All I have now is work, miss. Henry was my only family. It's best if I get on with it."

"I do not know what I would do if my brother Austin died. I would not be able to get on with it. I would crumble like a centuries-old retaining wall and be nothing but a pile of dust."

That was because she was in a different class than I was. It was because she lived in this grand house and had a father who had wealth and prestige. In the lower classes, like mine, we didn't have the option to crumble. I was proud of myself when I didn't say any of this aloud.

"Who told you of your brother's death?" Miss Dickinson asked.

"Miss O'Brien. She said the police came to the house this morning to tell me. She asked if she could be the one to break the news. I am grateful to her for doing that. It was hard enough to hear from her."

"Why would it be the police? I have not heard of the police telling of someone's death if there was not a crime or accident involved."

"It was an accident. He was trampled by a horse at the livery where he worked." I swallowed as the words threatened to choke me. "He hadn't been employed there long. He had always been gifted when it came to animals, but every creature is different. Perhaps he thought the horse would behave differently than it did. It's the only explanation that I can imagine."

She placed a finger on her cheek. "It is not."

I opened and closed my mouth.

"It is not. You have another possibility in your head. I can tell by the look in your eyes. You wish to bury the other possibility and hide it deep in your heart. You wish to hide it from all, even your inner self."

"I—I do not know what you mean, miss. With all respect, I do not know what you are saying."

"You do," she said in a matter-of-fact tone.

I didn't say anything, and she looked at me, waiting for a

reply. I swallowed. "My brother . . . he had a way of finding trouble. He had a good heart," I added quickly. "But he was always looking for a way to get ahead."

"An illegal way."

"He would not call it illegal."

"Would the police?"

I nodded.

"So you are wondering if your brother—" She paused.

"Henry. His name was Henry." I choked on my brother's name.

"So you are wondering if Henry got in some kind of trouble that led to his death."

I squeezed the brush even harder, and the bristles dug into my skin. "Yes," I whispered.

"So is his death a crime?"

"I—I don't know." I knew in my heart I should have said no. I was wrong to admit to any member of the Dickinson family I was possibly attached to a crime let alone murder. It was grounds enough to have me dismissed from my position.

"It seems to me that's what we need to find out, then." She folded her hands in front of her.

"We, miss?" I asked, confused.

She nodded. "Yes. We."

CHAPTER FOUR

"MISS NOBLE, WHAT is your brother's experience with horses?" a thin-faced police detective asked me. He wore a threadbare suit, and his top hat rested on his knee. When he came into the house, Miss O'Brien asked to take his hat and coat. He handed over the coat but kept the hat with him. Every few seconds he touched the brim as if it brought him some comfort.

Over his shoulder, Officer Matthew Thomas stood with his arms folded. He wore his dark blue officer uniform and held his flat-topped officer cap in his hand. I could feel his sympathy from where I sat on the floral settee in the Dickinsons' sitting room. I didn't look at him. I didn't have to look to know that his handsome face would be a mask of concern, his dark hair would be neatly trimmed, and his dark eyes would be turned down in sadness.

It was both odd and expected that he would be here when the detective came to question me about Henry's death. He always seemed to be there when Henry was involved, but I never thought we'd be discussing Henry in such a grand room, nor did I expect it would be about my younger brother's death.

I met Matthew the first time the police questioned me about my younger brother. It was the first time Henry got caught breaking the law. I did not say it was the first time he broke the law. He had broken the law many times before getting caught. My brother took a cavalier Robin Hood view of rules. He stole from the rich to give to the poor. It was not lost on me that the poor were strictly he and I.

After our mother died, Henry would come to the room that we had managed to rent with our meager wages carrying cookies and cakes for our meals. I would ask him where those treats came from, and he refused to tell me. I was hungry, and the sweets were good. I ate them, praying that I wasn't condemning my soul for all eternity for a mere tea cake.

As I found steady work, I begged Henry to stop stealing, and I thought that he had until I was eighteen and the young Officer Matthew Thomas brought him home. Henry had been caught stealing honey from a local farm stand. After that, we saw Matthew often. He said he came around to make sure that Henry stayed out of trouble. Often he brought us fruit and treats that I knew he had purchased with his small wages. Again, I didn't want to eat those offerings, but I did because I was hungry.

Over time, Matthew became our friend, but when Mrs. Patten threatened to fire me because I had a "gentleman caller," I asked Matthew to stay away. I could not lose my position at the boardinghouse, and I could not seem to make Mrs. Patten understand that Matthew was just a friend. I knew Matthew was hurt by being dismissed. I did not explain well why I asked him to stay away. I had not told him what Mrs. Patten said. It was far too embarrassing, but I knew that to save myself from embarrassment, I had hurt a man who was my friend and was kind to my brother when Henry didn't always deserve it.

Matthew did stay away for a time. Until last spring when he stopped me on my daily walk from the boardinghouse to the post office. He stopped me there on the sidewalk and proposed marriage to me. He told me that he could care for Henry and me, give us a safe place to live. I refused. My mother married because she thought it would give her protection. It only hurt her. I would not marry without love. But now, I realized my mistake. If I had taken Matthew's hand, would Henry still be alive? Had my pride cost my brother his life?

"Miss Noble?" the detective asked for what was clearly not the first time.

I looked at him closely. He'd said that his name was Detective James Durben. He was tall and thin with a nose so straight I wondered if it could cut paper.

"What's your brother's experience with horses?" the detective asked.

My throat felt impossibly dry. "Good, I believe. He worked with horses many times. Henry was a jack-of-all-trades. There was not a single thing that he couldn't do."

"You seem to be proud of him," the detective observed.

"I am. He works—worked very hard." I folded my hands in my lap and stared at them. I wasn't a small woman, and my calloused hands weren't small either. Many people marveled at my height at five feet eight inches—as tall as many men. It was helpful when I was cleaning, as I could reach more places with less effort, but not at a time like this when I wanted to make myself as small as possible and disappear. At times like these, my height was a burden.

"But this was the first time he worked with horses in a livery setting," the detective said.

I looked up from my hands. "Yes, as far as I know."

"So it stands to reason that he could have died in an accident. He did not have enough experience to work in the stable. He made a mistake and was killed."

His words made some of the numbness leave my body. "Henry didn't make mistakes." That wasn't true. Henry broke rules, which could have been thought of as mistakes. I shook my head. "Henry didn't make mistakes by accident."

The detective opened his mouth. I was faster and said quietly but firmly, "I do not appreciate that you are implying that his death was his fault. Anyone could have made a noise that spooked that horse. Horses are unpredictable animals. Accidents happen all the time with skilled men and horses."

Detective Durben pressed his lips into a thin line. It was clear to me that he was not used to a young woman contradicting him, but I could not stand what he was saying about my brother. Henry would not have done something that would cause a horse to trample him. He simply would not.

"So if you're saying that your brother was not at fault for his own carelessness, are you implying someone may have wanted to hurt him? Do you know if he was in some kind of trouble?" the detective asked.

"Sir, if I may," Matthew interjected.

The detective shot an irritated glance over his shoulder. "What is it, Thomas?"

Matthew swallowed. "I have known Miss Noble and her brother a very long time. Henry would not tell his sister if he was in some kind of trouble. He would not want to worry her. With all due respect, sir, I don't think it is helpful to torment her in this way."

"That may be your assessment, Officer, but I must ask these questions." The detective's voice was sharp and intended to remind Matthew of his place.

Matthew dropped his head. "Yes, sir. I am only saying that Miss Noble would not know what her brother knew or was up to at the time he died."

I glared at Matthew. "I knew Henry better than you think. He told me of his new job at the livery and that . . ." I stopped myself. In my frustration, I had almost said that Henry told me he had a new scheme to make money. What a grave mistake that would have been.

Detective Durben narrowed his eyes. "Miss Noble, if you know something else about your brother's circumstances before he died, you must share it."

I opened my mouth, thinking quickly for what else I could say when Miss Dickinson's large brown dog, Carlo, galloped into the room.

Detective Durben jumped to his feet and looked as if he wanted to leap to the seat of his chair as well. "What is this?"

I stood. "Carlo."

The large Newfoundland dog looked back at me, and his tongue hung out of his mouth as he smiled. He looked around the room as if he had come into a gathering of brand-new friends.

"Carlo?" the detective asked.

"He is my dog, sir." Miss Dickinson came into the room. While Carlo bounded into the sitting room, she quietly stepped inside, but somehow her presence took up more space.

I stood. "Miss Dickinson, I'm so sorry. The police are here to speak to me about my brother."

She nodded. "I know." She looked back at the detective. "I hope that you are not making this situation more difficult for Willa than you have to. My father would not want his employees to be harassed."

Detective Durben swallowed. "Miss Dickinson, anything that I ask of Miss Noble is to have a greater understanding of her brother's death."

She studied him with a discerning gaze. "I thought that it was ruled an accident."

The detective shifted his feet and looked down at the large brown dog just a few inches from him. Carlo glanced up at him as if waiting for the detective to throw a stick for the dog to chase.

Miss Dickinson snapped her fingers. "Carlo, come."

The dog whipped around and stood at her side. Standing so close to Miss Dickinson, the dog seemed even larger in comparison to his small mistress. She snapped her fingers again and pointed at the carpet. Carlo lay down. The dog surely weighed more than Miss Dickinson, but he lay on the floor and looked up at her as if asking when or if he could ever move again.

Detective Durben relaxed slightly. "It was ruled an accident, but I believe it's important to follow up on all cases that result in death. These are uneasy times in which we are living, and I don't like to come to conclusions too quickly."

"Even if that means coming to my father's door?" Miss Dickinson asked, arching one eyebrow.

He swallowed again. "Leads must be followed, miss. It is the way of police work. I don't expect a woman of your stature to know or need to concern herself with any of it."

"I am more curious than you give me credit for, Detective," she said evenly. "Furthermore, as you know, my father is a prominent man in Amherst and in the commonwealth. I do not believe that he would like you treating one of his employees as you have been."

"How have I been treating her?" the detective asked.

"I have overheard the conversation, and it's clear to me that you believe Willa knows more than she is telling you. It is shameful to imply that an individual whom my family trusts and who is working in my father's home is dishonest. That is a judgment on the Dickinson name as well as on Willa herself."

"I was making no such judgment on your family, miss." He pulled on his collar. "But she has only been your servant for few days. That's certainly not enough time for you to give her this level of protection and have such certainty in her honesty."

"It is, sir, for I'm a great judge of character. I can see into a person's very soul and find what others cannot." She snapped her fingers again, and Carlo stood, pressing his large body against her leg. "We accept the condolences on the death of Willa's brother, but if that is all, I believe it is time for you to leave."

Detective Durben looked back to Matthew, who shrugged. Miss O'Brien appeared holding the detective's coat. I hadn't even known she was close by.

"Perhaps I will return when Mr. Dickinson is here," Detective Durben said.

"Then you will have a long wait," Miss Dickinson said. "My father is on important business in Washington as a United States Representative for the commonwealth completing the duties of his term. We do not expect him back for weeks."

The detective frowned at this announcement. "I will be speaking to you again, Miss Noble," he warned.

My stomach tightened.

"When you do, we will be ready," Miss Dickinson answered for me.

Miss O'Brien cleared her throat. Matthew and the detective left the house, but I knew this wasn't over. They would be back.

CHAPTER FIVE

WHEN SUNDAY, MY one day off of the week, came, all I wanted was to hide in my small room and cry. I didn't see much reason for going to church. In my mind God had forsaken me by taking away everyone I loved, first my mother and now my brother. Unfortunately, Miss O'Brien would not hear of it.

"This Sunday more than any other, you need to pray. You need to pray for your brother's soul and your own," she said to me when I wouldn't get out of bed that morning. "Now hurry, the family is about to leave for church. You do not want to make a poor impression on your new employer by appearing to be a heathen, do you?"

I got up and dressed. I only had one somewhat good dress, and it wasn't much. It was the same brown gingham dress that I wore to my interview with Miss O'Brien. With diligent scrubbing, I had been able to get most of the mud off the skirt. I was grateful that it was a brown dress and hid a multitude of stains. I prayed that no one looked at it too closely because it was my mother's dress and as such it was quite out of fashion. The bodice was too high, the buttons were too broad, and the skirt was too narrow.

I met Miss O'Brien at the servants' entrance. She wore a red merino wool dress, black shawl, and bonnet with a green ribbon. I could tell it was her one good dress as well. At close inspection there were signs of wear from many brushings and mendings, but she wore it proudly as I would have if I had a dress so fine.

"The family has already left for church," she told me. "I usually allow them to walk a bit ahead before I follow."

"Why's that?" I asked.

"I'm not a member of the family and cannot be viewed as though I believe myself to be."

We walked around the house, and to my surprise, I saw Miss Dickinson sitting in the front window reading a book. "Is Miss Dickinson unwell?" I asked. "Is that why she is not on the way to the church?"

Miss O'Brien pressed her lips together. "The eldest Miss Dickinson does not attend service. She is not a member of the church."

My eyes went wide. "But aren't we going to the First Congregational Church? Her family is very involved in the church, is that not true?"

"The Dickinson family is. Miss Dickinson is not." Her face was pinched. "If it were up to me, I would make her go, but Mr. Dickinson has other ideas about what to command his daughter to do." She started down the sidewalk. "Now let us go."

I glanced back at the house and saw Miss Dickinson watching

me from the window. How peculiar was the Dickinson family. I felt I was going to learn more on that topic in the coming days.

The walk to the church, which was on Main Street, was pleasant enough. I realized whether I wanted to go to services or not, being outside was the best way to soothe myself even if it was on an overcast February morning.

Up until this point, I had attended First Baptist Church on the same street as the Dickinson home, North Pleasant Street. However, Miss O'Brien told me now since I worked for the Dickinson family I would have to go to and eventually join First Congregational. I wondered why that was a rule for me, but clearly not a rule for Miss Dickinson.

There was a line to enter the church as the minister, Reverend Edward S. Dwight, greeted each and every parishioner. I knew the head pastor through my brother, and not in the best way. I hoped that he would not remember me.

I shuffled into the church next to Miss O'Brien and was grateful he didn't seem to notice me. The entryway was crowded as parishioners made their way through the front doors and waited in the small room outside of the sanctuary's double doors as the church members in front of them found their seats. Through the double doors, I saw the pews in neat rows across the room with a center aisle that led to the altar and the pulpit. The floor was polished wood, and the windows that marched up either side of the nave were clear glass. A single wooden cross hung on the wall behind the altar.

The line began to move forward as a large family of seven found their seats. I let out a sigh of relief as I thought I had made it by Reverend Dwight without being seen. That relief was short-lived as a hand grabbed my arm just as Miss O'Brien was to step through the double doors. I was one step behind her. I turned to see Catherine Dwight, the minister's daughter, standing in front of me. She wore a lovely blue plaid dress with a full skirt made with a minimum of three petticoats underneath it. Her bonnet could not hold back the beautiful curls that framed her delicate face. "Willa, is it true?"

I stared at her. I didn't believe that Catherine Dwight had said a single word to me since I left the village school to work. She stayed on from what I heard and went to finishing school to learn how to be a good wife and mother. These were lessons that I would learn someday merely in practice, not in the classroom, but not a day too soon if it could be helped.

"Is what true?" I asked.

"About Henry?" Tears gathered in her eyes. "Is it true that he's dead?"

A man behind us coughed as I was blocking the doorway. I stepped through the double door with Catherine still attached to my arm and slid to the right and pressed my back against the rear wall of the sanctuary.

She pinched my arm. "Tell me the truth. What has happened?"

As people made their way to their pews, they glanced back at Catherine and me at the back wall. It felt like all the eyes in the room were on me, and those eyes wanted answers. It reminded me so much of the time after my mother's death. There were questions. There was a macabre need to know exactly what happened, when in fact it would make no difference to the asker's life if they knew or not. However, the torment it caused me to repeat the story time and time again was close to unbearable. With Henry's death, it was worse because of course it was different. He was young, a young man in his prime. He was a fixture in town and liked by all who met him from street sweepers all the way up to the faculty of Amherst College. And it was the way he died, which was so sudden and so unexpected. There was no long illness like that of my mother's. One day he was perfectly healthy; the next day, he was dead.

Her fingers dug deeper into my arm. "Please tell me. I heard rumors, and I must know."

I twisted my mittens in my hands. I glanced across the large room and saw her brothers watching us. Urschel and Ernest Dwight were twin terrors who ran through the village doing whatever they pleased as they were the sons of the most powerful minister in town. As of yet, they had done nothing more than upset the garden at the college, but they always looked as if they were up to much more. I held them at a distance. Now that I was speaking to their sister, I knew they were taking note. They had at some point assigned themselves as Catherine's guardians. I knew what they thought about her affection for my brother. I knew what their father felt as well. None of them approved, and they held Henry in disdain because of it. It did not matter then that Henry had never returned Catherine Dwight's feelings; they still held him accountable for them.

"He is dead. There was an accident at the stables where he worked." The words sounded wooden to my own ears. I tried hard to keep it like that, so all emotion was held back. Tears were for the privacy of my small room in the Dickinson home, not in the church.

She covered her mouth. Tears spilled over her eyes. "I—I can't believe it."

I didn't know what to say to that. I didn't want to force her into believing it. I didn't even want to believe it myself. I wanted to wake up tomorrow and have Henry tapping on my window in the rain talking about grand schemes to make a better life for both of us.

"People are saying that it was his fault."

I narrowed my eyes. "They are wrong."

"You said it was an accident."

I scowled at her. "Yes. That doesn't mean it was his fault." There was so much more I wanted to say to her, but I held my tongue. I knew my place in society when measured against the minister's daughter, and I was at a disadvantage.

Without another word, she covered her face and ran out of the church. I could feel the twins' eyes boring into me as she fled.

Miss O'Brien came down the side aisle and grabbed me by the arm. "Willa, what are you doing back here? Come sit down." She pulled me into a row in the back of the church.

The organ began to play and the service began. The ushers guided the last few parishioners to their seats. From my seat in the back of the church, I saw Mrs. Dickinson and Miss Lavinia in the front row of the church. They were the only members of the family there, as Mr. Dickinson was still in Washington and Austin Dickinson was in Cambridge. Miss Dickinson was at home.

Reverend Dwight took his place at the pulpit and led the congregation in prayer and a reading of the scripture. I tried my very best to pay attention, I did, but my mind wandered. Memories of going to the country church outside of town with my brother and mother flooded back to me. The congregation was small and happy. The people welcomed us. I enjoyed going to services then, but it stopped when our mother had to take on seamstress work on Sundays to make ends meet.

Henry and I would walk to the country church close to home while our mother worked on her mending, but I always thought the congregation pitied us as we never came with a parent.

Miss O'Brien poked my side. "Willa, stand up. We are on the closing hymn."

I blinked. How could the service be over already? It felt like it had just begun.

The organ droned on as the minister and the congregation processed out of the sanctuary.

Miss O'Brien gestured for me to leave the pew.

"I'm going to slip out the side door. I'm feeling a little light-headed."

Before Miss O'Brien could say a word, I slid out of the pew and went to an exit near the front of the church. I went down a short staircase, through the door, and found myself on the right side of the church. I gulped air. There was something about being in that building that was suffocating to me.

I drew in another breath much more slowly this time. Miss O'Brien would be cross with me for running out of the church like that. I just didn't want to be trapped and have to greet Reverend Dwight. I knew how he felt about Henry, and I wasn't able to hear it at the moment. There was no telling what I'd do if I had to listen to him berate my brother now.

I planned to tell Miss O'Brien that I had been overcome at the service because of my brother's recent death. It certainly wasn't a lie. I hoped that she would accept that and not think less of me because of it.

"Willa Noble, what makes you think you are welcome at our church?" a nasal male voice asked.

My chest tightened and my fingers were suddenly cold. I knew that voice.

"You made our sister cry," Urschel Dwight said, or perhaps it was Ernest—I could never tell the two apart. I hadn't been able to when we were all in school together, and I certainly couldn't now. They didn't make it easy as they wore identical Sunday suits all the way down to their neckties and shoes.

I started walking toward the front of the church.

The other twin jumped into my path. "Where do you think you're going? Urschel is talking to you."

I looked up at him. "That might be true, but I have nothing to say to him or to you. Now, I have to leave. A colleague is waiting for me."

"It's not your brother waiting for you," Urschel said. "We know that because he is dead."

Ernest remained in my path. "I say good riddance."

"Get out of my way," I snapped.

Ernest got into my face. "You can't speak to me like that. I'm the minister's son and am superior to you in all ways."

Fear gripped my heart, but I didn't step back.

Just when I thought Ernest would strike me, Catherine walked around the meetinghouse with tears streaming down her face. "Leave her alone, brothers."

"We are your elder brothers," Urschel said. "You have to listen to us."

I inched away from them.

Catherine threw out her hand and grabbed my arm. "Willa, don't leave. I want to hear what happened to Henry. You said there was an accident. What kind of accident?"

"I heard that a horse trampled him because he was cruel to it," Ernest said.

I glared at him. "Henry is—was not cruel. He was the kindest person there could possibly be. He was even kind to people who were undeserving."

The twins stepped on either side of me, and I realized my miscalculation. I should have known better than to speak so sharply to them. No matter how much I might hate to admit it what they said was true, they were superior to me, at least in society's eyes.

"Willa." Miss Dickinson walked around the building with Carlo at her side. The great dog's back was tense as if he was unsure of the Dwight twins. Carlo was very observant just like his mistress.

"Willa," Miss Dickinson said again. "I thought you would have gone straight home after church to help with the Sunday meal. Miss O'Brien is waiting for you on the corner. You know how seriously she takes making sure each meal is perfect."

My brow was up because it was Miss O'Brien's and my day off. We weren't responsible for feeding the family today, but I saw it as Miss Dickinson's way of offering me an escape from the Dwight siblings. I was happy to take it.

Ernest bowed to her. "Miss Dickinson, what a fine day to see you out and about." He glanced at Carlo. "With your dog. Did you enjoy this morning's services? My father did a fine job, did he not?"

Miss Dickinson looked at him down her petite nose, which was quite an accomplishment seeing how she was a foot shorter than the twins. "I did not go to church. I am not a member of this church as you well know. Carlo and I were just out for a morning walk. That's our means of worship."

The twins looked at each other.

"Surely, that is just an oversight," Urschel said. "You have not taken the time to finish your membership. Our father would be happy to welcome another member of the Dickinson family into his flock."

"You are assuming that I intend to. My god is not there." She pointed at the white meetinghouse with its peaked steeple.

The twins were confused. "If he is not there, where is he?"

"If you must ask, you will not understand the answer. Therefore, there is no purpose in answering a question that does not need to be asked." She looked to me. "Willa, Carlo and I have finished our walk. We will accompany you home. Since you ran into me on the way home, it will explain the delay to Miss O'Brien."

I nodded and started to follow Miss Dickinson.

"Willa," Catherine called. "I just want you to know that I cared for Henry. He was a good man."

I nodded and left the church grounds. As Miss Dickinson and I came around to the front of the building, Miss O'Brien came down the church steps. She wasn't waiting for me at the corner of Main Street, but the truth was I never thought that she had been.

"Miss Dickinson," Miss O'Brien said when she came upon Miss Dickinson, Carlo, and me. "I did not expect to see you here. Is everything all right at home?"

"Everything is quite all right. Can you run ahead of Willa and me to the house and let my sister know that I will be there as soon as possible to help with Sunday dinner?"

Miss O'Brien glanced at me. If she was wondering why she was told to go home while I was to walk with Miss Dickinson, she didn't ask it. She merely nodded and headed down the sidewalk.

Miss Dickinson looked over her shoulder to me. "Why were you talking to those two troublemakers?"

I paused. I was still so new in the Dickinson household; I did not know what was acceptable and not acceptable in the eyes of the family. I imagined speaking to young men in any regard was unacceptable. "Their sister, Catherine, stopped me and asked about Henry. She wanted to know what happened. Her brothers poked their noses into the conversation."

She nodded. "As impetuous young men often do. The fact they are twins makes it that much more unsettling. And, I know Catherine. We went a year together at Amherst Academy before her father moved her to a finishing school where she learned to be a proper wife and mother. I am happy to say my father never considered that fate for me."

"She cared for my brother deeply. I believe that it was always her hope that the two of them would one day marry."

"And what was Henry's opinion of this?"

"He wasn't interested. Marriage wasn't something on his mind. He was only eighteen."

She tilted her head to one side, reminding me of the chickadee I had seen on the bird feeder early that morning. "She is a wealthy young woman. Why wouldn't he be thrilled to have a wife that comes with such a large dowry?"

I shook my head. "Henry, he was different from other young men. He craved adventure. Many times he talked about making a life for us out west." I stared into the late-morning sun as if it could absolve me somehow. "I was afraid to go. I thought there were too many dangers, and I had heard too many stories of men who were lost or lost their fortune in the wilderness. I insisted that I stay here." I took a breath. "I never once told him not to go, but I knew that he would never leave without me because of the vow we both made to our mother."

"What vow was that?" Miss Dickinson asked in studied interest.

"That we would always take care of each other and look out for each other. That was our promise to her." I took a shuddered breath. "Henry kept that promise to the very end. I was the one who failed."

"You have not failed him yet." She scratched Carlo's head as she walked.

"What do you mean? He is dead, isn't he?" I heard my voice rise. "I'm sorry. I haven't the right to speak to you like that."

"You're grieving. In grief some of the worldly rules do not apply. Grief is like a deep pool." Her gaze turned inward. "A deep pool. I can wade grief. Whole pools of it." She shook her head and looked at me. "And so can you. You have before. Is that not true?"

I nodded. "Have you grieved?"

"Friends, yes. I have lost dear friends in my life, but I have not yet borne the loss that you have. I fear that day when it is to come. I hope I will be able to bear it."

"You appear strong to me." I snapped my mouth shut, afraid that I overstepped my place and said too much.

"Appearance is quite a powerful gift, but it is not always the full picture. When I wade through grief, it will not be in the way expected. It will be the way I can manage it," she said. Then she clapped her hands and encouraged Carlo to run with her all the way back to the house.

CHAPTER SIX

"W ILLA," MISS DICKINSON said as she came into the sitting room one morning a few days later.

I jumped. I was in the process of washing the windows. A tedious chore because I knew that they must be perfect with no smears or streaks for Miss O'Brien to find. She was a particular and exacting housekeeper. I tried to concentrate on the task as much as I could. I knew I wasn't doing as well as I normally would have. My thoughts kept traveling back to Henry. His smiling face, his grand plans, his youth that would always be. I was alone in the world now. Completely and utterly alone.

I dropped my rag into the bucket at my feet. "Yes, miss."

"I would like it if you would accompany me on a walk to the village."

Carlo stood at her side and seemed to smile at me. He was such a sweet dog even if he was built like a wild bear. I don't know why I was nervous about meeting him on my first day in the Dickinson home. Well, perhaps that question answered itself. The dog was *quite* large.

I cleared my throat. "I would enjoy that very much, miss, but I'm not sure that Miss O'Brien would like it. She gave me a list of chores for the morning, and I know that she expects them all to be done before the noon meal."

"I have already spoken with Margaret, and she has given you permission to go. Grab your cloak." She left the room, effectively ending any debate. Not that I would argue much with her on that point. I was eager to leave the house and get some fresh air. A walk might just be what I needed to clear the thoughts that plagued my mind.

A little while later, I found Miss Dickinson and Carlo standing in the front of the house. She was staring up at the building as if in deep thought. I glanced back at what Miss Dickinson was looking at, and saw her younger sister Miss Lavinia staring at us from the upstairs window. When Miss Lavinia caught my eye, she moved out of view.

I had not spoken with the younger Miss Dickinson yet, and as much as I hoped we would be friendly because of our love of cats, she made no effort to speak to me.

Without a word, Miss Dickinson turned and made her way to the sidewalk. I hurried to follow behind her. Carlo was in front of her on a leash. She glanced over her shoulder. "Why are you back there? I told you that I wanted to go on a walk with you, not for you to walk behind me."

I stepped around her and walked at her left side to block any mud that might hit her from the road by a passing cart. As I was much taller than she was, I had to measure my stride, cutting it in half to match her short yet quick steps. "It was very kind of you to ask me on a walk, miss. I have barely left the yard since I began working for your family. It is a lovely winter day. I do love the change of season. I don't think I could live in the South where there is no snow at all."

"I could never live anywhere else," she mused. "I pray that I never will."

"I suppose that will be up to your husband one day. He might want to move to a faraway place."

"That won't be my fate," she said in such a way that I knew the conversation was over.

I bit the inside of my cheek afraid I had been too forward. I didn't know if I had upset her by suggesting someday her husband might make her move.

"It is good to get out," Miss Dickinson said, breaking into the silence. "I make myself walk every day. Carlo helps with it. I think if it were not for Carlo, I would never leave home. I go out because he needs the exercise. Sometimes you can make yourself do things that are good for you when you believe you're doing them for someone you love. The benefit comes without selfishness then. The best part of having a pet is having someone to think of other than yourself, having someone who depends on you. No one depends on me but Carlo. He's the only one in this life that truly needs me. This makes me both grateful and sad. Every person needs to be needed, but being needed takes away from thoughts of yourself. This may sound selfish to your ears, but I do not think it so. I know I am unable to be needed like others are. I know that my inner world would be jealous."

I didn't know what to say to that. As we waited to cross the street, Carlo leaned on her leg as if he was providing not just warmth but support.

"Carlo is so loyal to you. I've never seen a dog so loyal to one person before."

Miss Dickinson smiled at Carlo. "He was a gift from my father. Father knows how much I enjoy long walks, and as I am slight, he felt that a dog would be best to have at my side. I rarely leave the house without him. Everyone in town knows him, too, if not personally by sight."

I glanced at the large dog. "He would be quite hard to miss."

She chuckled at this.

We walked in silence for few minutes, as I did not know what to make of her earlier comment about being needed. The only thought that came to my mind was with my brother's death, I no longer had anyone who depended on me or who I depended on. I could see why that would make a person want to hide away. I certainly did. But I wished that someone needed me. Without that I was adrift. Before, even when I was poor and lost, I had Henry to hold on to like an anchor in the Massachusetts Bay that I saw once when I was younger. It's the farthest I had ever been from home. Henry, my anchor, had been there, and our mother. I shook the memory from my mind. I knew if I dwelled on it for too long the tears that I had barely contained would break loose in a tidal wave.

When we reached the corner, I expected Miss Dickinson to turn toward the center of town. I thought perhaps that she wanted to stroll through Amherst and look into the shopwindows. Maybe I would hold her bags while she made purchases.

She was smartly dressed, so I knew she must have had a clear eye when it came to such things as fashion.

To my surprise, she went in the opposite direction, away from the shops and the houses.

"Do you not want to go to town?" I asked.

"We are going to the livery," she said.

My throat felt tight, and we walked half a block in silence before I could find my voice again. "The livery?"

She adjusted her grip on Carlo's leash. The dog pranced ahead of us like he was the grand master of a parade.

She did not look at me. "Yes, the livery where your brother died."

I stopped in the middle of the path. "Why would we go there?"

She looked back at me and also stopped. She tugged on Carlo's leash, and he turned and stood at her side. Miss Dickinson studied me with her discerning gaze.

I licked my lips. "Miss Dickinson, I am sorry if I spoke out of turn, but I'm not sure what good it will do me to go there. It will be difficult."

"I do wish you would speak frankly to me, Willa. Also, please, when we are away from the confines of the house call me Emily for I do like the informality of my given name."

"Emily," I said as if I were testing the word.

She nodded. "See, that wasn't so hard." She began to walk again, and both Carlo and I fell into step just like we had been trained to do. I did not like the image in my own mind that I was as obedient as her dog.

After a few steps, she said, "We are going to the livery

because we agreed that the two of us were to discover if there was some sort of crime tied to your brother's death."

"Yes," I said unable to make myself say "Emily" again so soon. "Yes, but Detective Durben has ruled his death as an accident since then."

She shook her head as if she were disappointed in me for some reason. "Yes, it was ruled an accident almost immediately, but why was he questioning you if that was the case? You were not there when your brother died. You did not witness the horse trampling his body."

I sucked in a gasp at her description.

As if she did not notice my dismay, she went on, "The detective asked you those questions because he thought that there was something more to all of this. He believes that foul play was involved. He might even believe that you had a role in it."

"*Me?* I would never want to hurt my brother. I loved him. He was all the family I had in the world."

She nodded as if she finally approved of my reaction. "Then you will want to know the truth."

The livery came into view. A large arch with a hand-painted sign hung over the long dirt driveway. The sign read "Amherst Carriage Company and Stables."

Carriages, wagons, and carts lined the driveway to the stables and shone with fresh black paint. To our right was a large paddock with a dozen horses wandering around the pasture plucking at the grass with their wide teeth and swatting their tails. Since it was winter, some of the horses wore blankets on their strong backs and the grass was little more than tufts of brown peeking out from crushed snow.

I opened and closed my hands at my sides. They were impossibly cold, and I wished that I had thought to bring my mittens. I rarely carried them until it was below freezing for fear of losing them. It would take me such a long time to make another pair, not to mention to afford the yarn. I didn't feel like I could risk it. Henry used to tease me about this and say, "What is the point of having mittens if you don't ever wear them for fear of losing them?"

Henry had lost dozens of pairs of mittens that I had knitted him over the years. He went through at least three pairs each winter when I had had my one pair for many years. All my yarn money and knitting skill had been spent on making more mittens for Henry, at least up until now. My brother had never feared losing anything, not even his life.

As we drew closer to the stable, which was the largest building that I had ever seen up close, I noticed a house to the left of it. Miss Dickinson—no, Emily—noticed my gaze. "That's the home of the livery and stables owner, Mr. Elmer Johnson."

"Have you met him before?" I asked.

She wrinkled her nose. "Yes."

I thought she would say more than that, but she didn't utter another word and walked toward the stable. Carlo looked as happy as he could be every time he saw a horse.

"Don't you want to go to the house and tell Mr. Johnson that we are here? Shouldn't he be told?" I asked.

"No." She continued on the gravel path. As we drew closer, I started to see young men move around the stables. Some were raking, and others were hooking horses up to wagons and carriages as if they were preparing to go into town.

We were the only women there, along with a giant dog, and

surely stuck out, but no one stopped us. No one asked any questions at all.

The giant barn door stood open. The sunlight made it difficult to see inside. I caught flashes of movement before I saw anyone, and then a person appeared.

A young Black man with close-cropped hair and glasses met us at the door. "I'm Jeremiah York. You must be Henry's sister, Willa. I've been waiting for you to come."

CHAPTER SEVEN

"Y OU HAVE BEEN waiting for me to come—to come here?" I asked in disbelief.

He held on to his suspenders. He wore a white work shirt, brown trousers that were a bit too long and rolled up several inches to keep them out of the mud, and a pair of worn black boots. Leather gloves stuck out of the pocket of his trousers. "I have. Henry said you would."

My heart was in my throat. "You knew my brother?"

He cocked his head. "I did. He was the best friend I've ever had."

I frowned.

As if Jeremiah could read the confusion on my face, he said, "I worked with Henry at the warehouse for a few months before leaving and working at the stables. We stayed in contact after I left and remained friends."

Why had I never heard of him?

"I'm Emily." Miss Dickinson—I mean Emily, as she wanted

me to call her—removed her wool mitten and thrust her hand out to the young man.

Jeremiah stared at her hand. "I know who you are, miss."

"Aren't you going to shake my hand?"

His eyes widened and he gave her hand a firm but quick shake.

"Willa is my companion."

I tried not to show my surprise. Companion was quite a leap up from housemaid.

"And," Emily continued, "she wanted to see the place where her brother died. I thought it would be best to come with her and lend my support."

Jeremiah nodded. "It might be hard to view."

I swallowed. It wasn't until I was there at the livery that I realized that Emily was right. I did want to see where my brother had died. I hadn't enough money to give him a proper burial. A kind, anonymous soul paid for his coffin, which was laid to rest in the potter's field away from town. The Calvinist minister said a few words demanding repentance and it was done. I had been the only person in attendance. That wasn't completely true. Matthew was there too. He stood ten yards away from Henry's graveside. He did not speak to me, and I was grateful for that. Speaking on that day would have been impossible, and I certainly didn't want to answer any more questions about my brother's death.

But now, I wondered why I was at the grave alone. Since Jeremiah claimed to be my brother's close friend, I wondered why he hadn't been there.

"Come with me," Jeremiah said and walked into the stable. As soon as I stepped into the large building, the smells of horse, manure, hay, and animal feed hit me like a brick wall. I glanced at Emily to see if the scent bothered her, but it did not seem to. This wasn't the typical place for a young lady such as herself to be.

Horses hung their large heads over the stall walls and studied us with hopeful eyes. Maybe they wished that we had carrots in our coat pockets.

In one stall, I heard the *bang, bang, bang* of a hammer on metal. As we walked by, the local farrier with his white shirt-sleeves rolled up was shoeing a dark brown horse with a blond mane and tail. He didn't even so much as glance in our direction.

I took care where I stepped. There was hay on the dirt floor, and I didn't know what it might be covering. A ginger-colored cat walked the length of the stables with us at Jeremiah's side.

Carlo's body tensed at the sight of the cat, but Emily snapped her fingers and said a fierce, "No." The big dog remained at her side.

"That cat doesn't seem to be afraid of my dog," Emily said. "My sister has many cats, and they all scatter when Carlo is near."

Jeremiah glanced over his shoulder. "Oh, that's Caesar. He's been a fixture in the barn longer than I have worked here, and I have been here for a year. I started as a stable hand just like Henry was and worked my way up to apprentice." He said this last part as if he was proud of his advancement, as he should be.

I could understand why. I would have great pride if I worked for the Dickinson family for as long.

"You can tell a lot about a person by the way an animal

reacts to him," Emily said. "It seems that Caesar approves of you."

"We have been friends from the start."

"How did he get the name Caesar?" I asked, happy for the distraction to get my mind off what we were about to see. "It's a grand name for a small cat."

"I don't know, to be honest. It was his name when I met him. It certainly fits him. He's the boss of this place and lets everyone know it. I saw him once chase a new stallion into the pasture. The horse was petrified of the little cat." He laughed at the memory.

Jeremiah stopped walking when we reached the back of the barn. There was a large stable, and when I peeked inside, I saw mats on the floor. Men's clothing hung from pegs on the wall. He glanced at me. "This was the stall that I shared with Henry."

My heart sank as I saw the straw just covered with a wool blanket that my brother or Jeremiah must have slept on. Despite being a horse stall, the space was neat. It was clear that the boys tried to make it as homey as they could. There were even illustrations from magazines of horses and grand buildings tacked to the wooden walls.

"Now, I can tell from your face that you don't like your brother living here, but it's actually very clean, and we received extra pay for staying in the stables. If there was ever a problem with the horses in the night, we were there to care for them. Mr. Johnson was very firm on the fact that anyone who boarded their horse here would have the best care possible. We have always tried to do that."

I tore my eyes away from the straw mat on the floor. "Was that what happened with my brother?" I asked. "Was there a problem with a horse and he was trying to care for it when he died?"

"I would guess that is what happened." Jeremiah pushed his glasses up his nose. "I do not know for certain."

"Why not?" I asked. "Where were you when he was killed?"

Jeremiah's Adam's apple bobbed up and down. "I—I wasn't here that night."

"Why not?" I asked a little more harshly than I intended to. "If the two of you received extra payment to stay in the stables all night, why did you leave him?"

Emily placed a hand on my arm, and I let out a breath. Jeremiah was staring down at his scuffed and worn boots, which were likely too small for his feet based on his height.

"Was anyone here when Henry died?" Emily asked.

Jeremiah looked up from his boots and shook his head. "No, not that I know of. I was . . . out . . . I was out that night, and I came back around five in the morning."

What could Jeremiah be doing until five in the morning? Nothing good in my opinion. Who was my brother living with? What kind of mess did Henry get himself into this time, the last time?

"When I came home, I was the one who found him."

"What did you do then?" Emily asked.

He broke eye contact with her. "I ran to the house and woke Mr. Johnson. He was not happy about it, but it couldn't be helped. Most of the servants were up at that time. The day begins at four here."

"Was anyone else in the stables when you found the body?" Emily scratched Carlo's head as she asked her questions.

I was grateful that Emily was there to make the inquiries. I couldn't comprehend what had happened. I couldn't even comprehend my brother sleeping on a mat on the floor. When our mother died, we had promised ourselves we would always have a bed to sleep in. It wasn't a lofty goal, but to two motherless children, it was a difficult goal to reach, and one that could only be attained by hard work. And my brother's final bed was the floor.

"No, not yet," he said. "By the time Mr. Johnson and I reached the stables and he sent a house servant to get a doctor and the police, many of the stable hands had reported to work. They were all standing around the stall where Henry died. It was a gruesome sight."

My stomach twisted into a knot. However, Emily said calmly, "I imagine that it was. Did any of those men or did you touch anything?"

"Touch anything?"

She nodded. "Yes, in the stable. Did you touch anything?"

"No, I didn't. I didn't notice if the other men did."

I looked around the stall that Henry and Jeremiah had used as their room. "Is this the stall where he died?"

"No." Jeremiah shook his head. "If it had been, I would not be able to sleep here at night. I just thought you would like to see your brother's final home."

I was glad to have seen it and also sorry that I had. It was good to be in the final place where my brother had walked and lived.

"The stall where he died is not far." He stepped out of the stall and walked to the back of the barn.

A large black horse blew hot air from his nostril when we walked past.

I shivered.

"It was in the very last stall here," Jeremiah said. He pointed at the closed stall door. "We don't have a horse in there now. None of the stable hands want to go in there. Partly because Henry was well-liked around the stables and partly because they are afraid that it is haunted."

Emily studied him with her appraising eyes. "You believe in ghosts."

He put a hand on his chest. "Me? No, no, I don't. Not really."

It wasn't the most confident denial that I'd ever heard.

Emily nodded and gave no indication as to whether she thought there might be ghosts roaming this world or not. I personally did not believe it. The only ghost mentioned in the Bible was the Holy Ghost, and that was very different.

"It won't matter for much longer," Jeremiah went on to say. "Mr. Johnson says that we have to start putting horses back in it next week. As spring grows closer, the stables will be almost full. Mr. Johnson rents his stalls to some of the wealthiest men in Amherst. Many of them don't have the land to keep a stable or a barn of their own on their property."

"My father had boarded our horses here before, I know," Emily said. "When we move, that will no longer be an issue, as we will have plenty of land to house them."

Jeremiah nodded and then looked to me. "Would you like to look inside?"

I swallowed hard.

"It's been cleaned the best we can," he said.

I wondered what "the best we can" meant. Would there still be blood on the walls? Or worse? However, my mind didn't have the capacity to think of much worse than that.

"Yes," I whispered. "I would like to see it."

Jeremiah opened the stall door without a word. The first thing I noticed was the dirt floor, which had been raked over. It had new dirt and straw laid down over it. My gaze traveled up from the walls, and there were deep dents in the wood at the back of the stall. One was so deep that it broke through to the outside of the stable. There was a piece of wood on the outside to keep the cold and rain out of the building.

I nodded to that mark on the wall. "That is where he fell." I said it as a statement. It wasn't a question.

Jeremiah nodded.

Emily stepped into the stall and walked up to the indents in the wall. She held her small hand up against the hole. The hole was larger than her hand. "The horse must have been very upset, almost crazed, to kick through the wall like this. Was the animal hurt?"

Jeremiah shook his head. "Not seriously. He had a few splinters and scrapes, but nothing that put his life at risk. When I first saw everything, I thought the horse would have to be put down. One broken leg can fell a horse. They are actually quite fragile animals for their strength and size."

Emily tilted her head, and her face fell under the shadow of her navy blue bonnet. "Was it the large black horse that we passed that made these marks? He looks like a creature large enough to cause the damage to the stable wall."

Jeremiah tugged on the sleeves of his white work shirt. They were an inch too short from his wrist. "It was," he finally admitted.

"And the horse's name?" Emily dropped her hand from the broken spot on the stable wall.

Jeremiah shifted back and forth on his feet. "Why does the horse's name make any difference?"

"I believe in a case like this, it's best to gather all the information no matter how insignificant, including the name of the horse that killed Willa's brother," she said evenly.

He pulled on his sleeve again. "His name is Terror."

My heart clenched when I heard the name. I don't know if I might have felt better if the horse had a more subdued name like "Sam" or "Sunset" or something. Terror sounded like a name that the horse felt obligated to live up to, and it seemed that the animal had no choice in the matter.

"The horse is still alive," Emily said. "You didn't have the horse destroyed after killing a man? I find that to be very surprising. Masters put down dogs for less."

Carlo looked at his mistress in concern, as if he knew what she was saying.

"No," Jeremiah said, looking increasingly uncomfortable. "He's a champion racehorse, and Mr. Johnson wouldn't hear of it. He believes that it's not the horse's fault, and the horse should not pay the price for the accident."

"How can it not be the horse's fault when Henry is dead?" I blurted out.

Jeremiah glanced at me with sadness in his eyes. "Mr. Johnson believes Henry was to blame, not Terror."

I felt like he had reached into my chest and squeezed my heart in a vise. My breath became shallow. If Emily noticed how I struggled in that moment, she gave no indication. Carlo, however, walked over to me and leaned against my side. He might just make me into a dog person yet.

"What will happen to the horse now?" Emily asked.

"He is being kept away from the other horses in the barn. A veterinarian came yesterday and examined the animal and said that he would be well enough to race again by the time the season begins in spring."

"Did the veterinarian find anything out of the ordinary that would indicate why the horse had such a terrible reaction?" Emily loosened the ribbons on her bonnet, and it fell to her shoulders. She then removed the bonnet.

Out of habit, I stepped forward and took it from her hands. As her servant, it was my duty to hold and carry anything that she wished.

"Yes," Jeremiah finally said.

Emily crossed her arms, and the fabric of her cloak brushed across the stable floor. "And what was it?"

Jeremiah didn't look her in the eye. "There is a burn mark on his left flank. A number of burn marks, in fact. The veterinarian said that none of the burns were too severe that Terror would not recover. They are superficial burns—in his words. However, they would be painful enough to upset the horse and cause him to fight back. They would have caused him to kick through that wall like he did."

I drew in a breath. "Who would be so cruel to do that to an animal?"

Jeremiah had my answer, or I should say he had the accepted answer. "It is believed that Henry did it."

I gasped. "He would never! Henry had a very soft heart for all creatures. He would—"

"And this is what you believe?" Emily interrupted me and asked with a raised brow.

"No, miss, but I learned what I believed does not hold

much bearing with the men who make the rules in our society." Jeremiah studied my face. "I do not believe Henry hurt that animal. I think . . ." He trailed off.

"What do you believe?" Emily asked.

There was a banging sound of a door hitting a wall in the back of the stables. "Jeremiah!" a man shouted.

"I must go. You can wait here for me. Do not make much noise. It would be best if you did not gather more attention than you already have." He stepped out of the stall and disappeared around the corner.

Emily looked at me for the first time since we entered the building. "What do you think, Willa?"

I stared at her. Emily was quite different from other women of her station. It was not that often that I was asked to give my opinion, and I certainly had never been asked to give my opinion on a matter as vital to me as the circumstances surrounding my brother's death. I held tight to her bonnet in my hands. The satin was smooth against my palms.

"I do want to know what you think, Willa," she said in a quiet voice. "Do not assume because I am from another class that I don't value the opinion of my servants. In truth, you know more about the real circumstances of the world than I ever will. You are in it, while I will always have some level of separation from it."

I looked her in the eye. "I think—I think it's all a lie. Henry would never burn a horse. He wouldn't. When he was a child, he would carry spiders from our rooms and release them outside. He gave a portion of his meal to the mouse family that lived in the walls. He was kind. Yes, he had a way of finding trouble, but his motivation was kindness and doing what he believed was right. Maybe that didn't follow convention and maybe it made his life more difficult, but he did not care. He was a free spirit with a good heart. No matter what Jeremiah, Mr. Johnson, the police, or anyone says, I know my brother. I know him better than anyone else. He would not be so vicious." I took a breath as I finished my speech and was amazed that I had been able to say all of that without bursting into tears.

Emily gave a curt nod. "Then it seems to me we have a real mystery on our hands."

CHAPTER EIGHT

"WHAT SHOULD WE do?" I wiped my sweaty palms on my cloak. Moments ago my hands had been close to frozen, and now they felt like the rest of me, which was burning up.

"Just what we are doing," Emily said. "Asking questions and learning what we can about what happened the night Henry died. I believe our next step will be to examine the horse."

I swallowed. "But that could be dangerous."

Emily didn't appear to be concerned by this. "We have to see these burns with our own eyes." She stepped out of the stall and began walking back in the direction of the black horse.

I followed. I could not let my mistress be hurt by this animal on my account.

Terror hung his head over the stall wall and blew hot air out of his nostrils. He tapped his front hoof on the dirt floor. I saw the large and powerful hoof under the bottom of the gate to his stall. *Thump, thump,* the hoof hit the earth. I shivered as I imagined the floor as my brother's head.

Emily walked up to the stall with her small, pale hand outstretched to the animal.

"Emily," I warned.

Carlo whimpered next to me as if he agreed with my concern.

"Do not be afraid, Willa." She let her hand rest on the bridge of the horse's nose, and he stopped kicking at the ground.

I stared at her. "How did you do that?"

She looked over her shoulder. "Every creature most desires comfort when in pain. Now," she continued in a firm voice, "since you are much taller than I am and will be able to see inside of the stall, peer into it and look for the burn marks on his left flank."

Holding on to the wall, I perched on my toes and peeked over the stall door. I couldn't see the horse's flank from my angle. If I had been a foot higher, I believed I would be able to spot it. I dropped my heels back down onto the ground and looked around the stables. Across from Terror's stall there was an empty gallon bucket. I grabbed it, turned it over, and stood on the bottom of it.

From my high vantage point, I could now see Terror's left flank, and my heart ached at what I saw. There was a cluster of five red welts on his side. They shone in the light coming in from the stable window behind his stall because there was some sort of salve covering the top of each wound to soothe it.

"You poor thing," I whispered.

"What do you see?" Emily asked from below me, and I described the gruesome sight as best as I could.

Terror turned his head then and looked at me with his left eye. His eye was round and brown, and I was so close I could see every eyelash that fringed his eyelids. I knew he was not a person, but there was sadness in those eyes, and I knew whatever may have happened to Henry, it was not this great beast's fault. He had been tormented to kill.

"What are you doing?" a harsh man's voice asked.

I jerked in surprise and the empty gallon bucket wobbled below my feet, causing me to hop off to the ground. Emily dropped her hand from the horse's nose and stood straight. "Who are you?"

A large man with gray curls and suspenders that were pushed to the breaking point over his round belly scowled at us. "I'm Louis Masters, and I am the foreman of these stables. This is no place for a couple of women." He said the word "women" like being such a creature was a fate worse than death.

Emily took her bonnet from me and put it on her head. "Well, Mr. Masters, we were just leaving."

He glowered at us. "Why are you here?"

Emily lifted her chin. "I am Emily *Dickinson*," she said, putting special emphasis on her surname. "I'm sure you have heard of my father."

Masters blinked. "Yes."

"Well, Father had asked me to visit the stables to see if it was a suitable place to board our horses while we are in the process of moving to the old family homestead on Main Street later this year. Of course, we would not want the horses to be disturbed by the move, but now I wonder with your harsh greeting if there is not a place we would be more comfortable storing our animals during that time."

Masters paled. "Oh, Miss Dickinson, I am so sorry about how I spoke to you. The last few weeks have been strained here at the stables. We are low on staff, and I am desperate for more help. However, I can assure you that it will be all rectified soon. We would be honored to assist your family in any way."

Emily tilted her head to the side. "Are you low on staff because Henry Noble was killed in these stables?"

Masters opened and closed his mouth. "It— It was a terrible accident. And we feel awful over what has happened, but anyone working for us must know how to control these large and powerful animals."

"Have you spoken to his family?" She raised her brows.

"Miss, a young man like that never has any family to speak of," Masters said.

I bristled and wanted to yell at the man that Henry was my family. Emily put a steadying hand on my arm.

"It was a horrible thing to happen, miss," Masters went on. "But not something that we will ever allow to happen again. Please know that your horses would be well cared for in our stables."

"If it was an accident, how do you explain these burn marks on this horse's flank?"

Masters pulled on his suspenders. I prayed that he not pull too hard because the suspenders looked like they were moments away from snapping.

"I don't know, miss, but we have the very best veterinarian from the county here, and he cared for the animal. Terror is to make a full recovery. Now, I know you are here on an assignment from your father, but it would be best if you cut your visit short. I would be happy to plan a tour for your father at a later date."

Emily wasn't done yet. "Were you here when Henry died?"

Masters swallowed hard. "No. I live with my family on a small farm on the other side of the college. Henry died in the middle of the night. I was home with my wife and children."

"Who was here?"

"There was no one inside of the stables when he died." Masters's voice had a slight edge to it as if he tired of Emily's questions.

"But who would have been on the grounds?" She was relentless.

Masters clenched his jaw, and I thought for a moment that he wouldn't answer. However, he finally said, "The stable apprentice, Jeremiah, and the Johnson family and their servants who live in the big house."

I wondered what Emily would ask next because I had a dozen more questions spinning around inside my head. But to my surprise, she nodded and said that it was time for us to leave.

Jeremiah appeared then, and his eyes stared when he saw Emily and me there speaking to Masters.

"Oh, Jeremiah, you're here," Masters said. "Please show Miss Dickinson and her companion out of the stables." There was something in his tone that said he didn't wish us to come back anytime soon.

"Yes, sir," Jeremiah said with a nod.

Emily followed Jeremiah in the direction of the entrance, but before I left, I took one more glance back at Terror. He forlornly hung his head over the stall gate again. In my mind, I promised him that I would find the person who hurt him and killed my brother.

Jeremiah didn't say a word until we stood by the entrance. "You are lucky that Masters didn't throw you out of here. He doesn't like visitors."

Emily sniffed. "He was not going to throw a Dickinson out if he knows what is good for him. Willa and I wanted to see Terror's injuries for ourselves. He is a remarkable animal."

Jeremiah nodded. "He is, and I hope he can pull through this. Despite his name, he has always been a good horse and he was especially fond of Henry. Every day, he would neigh until Henry scratched his nose and gave him an apple or carrot. It didn't matter if another person was willing to give him a carrot; he would only take it from Henry's hand. It does not make sense to me that Terror would hurt anyone, especially Henry. He loved Henry. Since Henry has . . . has been gone, Terror won't eat. Masters is at his wit's end over it, and Mr. Johnson is furious. He has great hopes for Terror on the racetrack. I'm afraid if the horse continues to refuse food and decline, Mr. Johnson will put him down."

"Henry would not want the horse put down," I said in a quiet voice. "His heart was too big for that. He would be upset at Terror's sadness. Someone hurt the horse so he would attack my brother. That much is clear."

"But who would do that?" Emily glanced at me. "Someone injured Terror, and if it was not Henry, who was it? If we answer that, we find the real killer and absolve the horse and Henry for being blamed for Terror's injury."

Jeremiah's eyes went wide. "You think he was murdered too?"

Emily turned to him. "You believe Henry was murdered?"

Jeremiah chewed on his lower lip and pushed his glasses up his nose with his index finger. "I do."

Those two simple words sucked all the air out of my lungs, and I felt faint. The next thing I knew I was being lowered on a straw bale outside of the barn. It was starting to snow and the cold snowflakes fell on my face.

"Take deep breaths. You need to bring air into your lungs and heart," Emily said. Her face was just inches from mine, and her intelligent brown eyes were studying every detail of my person. "There you go. Deep breath."

I did as I was instructed. "I'm sorry. I don't know what came over me."

Emily stepped back. "It was shock. I don't think anyone ever expects to hear a loved one has been murdered. I do not know what I would do in your place if it were my brother, Austin." She turned slightly green at the thought.

I looked up at Jeremiah. "Why do you think my brother was murdered?" I could hardly choke out the words, and I wrapped my cloak more tightly around myself like a cocoon.

"Yes, Terror killed Henry in the fact that he delivered the fatal blow to Henry's head, but it was not his fault. And . . . you would think I was out of my mind if I said it."

"Sometimes the most outlandish things are the most truthful," Emily said.

Jeremiah glanced at me and then focused back on Emily. "I think Terror was brokenhearted over what happened. Before I ran and got Mr. Johnson, I moved Terror from the stall. He—he was lying down next to Henry's body like he was trying to keep him warm. He was protecting him. Horses rarely lie down. Maybe no more than an hour or two when they are in a deep sleep. Terror was awake. Wide awake. He was guarding Henry's body."

I began to shiver and wrapped my arms around myself. The wool of my black cloak felt scratchy again the palms of my dry hands. I focused on that feeling, because the picture that Jeremiah had painted in my mind was too painful to imagine.

"I have no doubt that Terror kicked that hole in the wall," Jeremiah said. "But I think he wasn't kicking at Henry. He was kicking at someone else."

"And he kicked and killed Henry by accident?" Emily asked.

Jeremiah nodded. "Yes, this is what I believe. The horse was defending him. It was an accident."

"Did you tell the police any of this?" Emily wanted to know.

"They did not talk to me. They spoke to Masters and Mr. Johnson, but I don't believe they spoke to anyone else at the stables."

"Why not?" I asked. "You are the one who spent the most time with Henry."

He glanced at me. "Mr. Johnson didn't want me speaking to the police."

"But you were the one who found Henry and Terror. I would think the police would want you to speak to them," Emily said.

"He said the police wouldn't listen to a—they wouldn't listen to a person like me."

"Because you are Black," Emily said in her blunt way. There was no emotion in her voice as to the fairness of this pronouncement. Like many things that she said, it came out as fact. This was the way of the world.

"Yes, and to be honest, Miss Dickinson, I was not keen on speaking to the police. If they determined that it was not the horse that killed Henry, then in their minds, who is the next most logical person?"

"They wouldn't think that you were the killer," I protested. "You said you weren't even here when it happened."

"I wasn't, but would I be believed?" He looked at me. "Trust me when I say, Willa, I wish that I was here. I wish that I had been here with my whole heart. Then I might have saved Henry." His voice caught. "He was a good man. I wish I could tell you all the good he did, but I cannot."

I wanted to ask him what he meant by that, but Emily spoke up. "You can still tell them what you know. The police may listen if you have the Dickinson family support."

"You said *may* listen. Not even you are confident that they would take my word as truth—even with your family name as backing." He dropped his gaze and looked out over the grounds.

It snowed in earnest now. It was the time in winter when there were hints that spring might someday arrive but it was impossible to believe it. Any hope that spring was just around the corner would be dashed by the next blizzard to blow off the coast.

"I don't blame you for your fear," Emily said. "It is valid."

"Can't you just tell them that you weren't there when it happened?" I asked. "Surely, there is someone who can speak for where you were."

"There is not," he said with an air of finality. "There is not."

"But—"

He cut me off. "I can't tell them where I was when Henry died."

"Why not?" I asked.

He wouldn't look at me. "I can't. There are more important things to be concerned with."

"More important than finding out what really happened to my brother?" My voice was pained.

"Yes," Jeremiah said. "And I know that Henry would agree with me on this. He knew what was most important about his position."

"What was most important about his position? What do you mean by that?" I asked.

"Nothing. I misspoke." He broke eye contact with me then.

I knew he hadn't misspoken. He was lying about that part, at least. It made me wonder what else he might be lying about. Could I really trust what Jeremiah was saying to Emily and me? I didn't know him. He claimed to be my brother's closest friend, but Henry never spoke of him. I never once heard the name Jeremiah. How close could they really be if I had never heard of him? I couldn't see any reason that Henry would hide him from me unless—unless they were involved in something illegal.

"Willa," Emily said and pulled my mind away from my worries about Jeremiah and Henry. I looked at her.

She smiled. "We should go back to the house. Vinnie will have noticed that we have been gone far too long. She does tend to worry." She turned to Jeremiah. "I'm sure we will speak again before this is all over."

He swallowed as if he heard a threat in those words, not a promise.

Emily began down the path with Carlo without waiting for me. I glanced back at the stables one last time before I followed her.

"Willa," Jeremiah said. "Before you go." He reached into his barn coat and pulled out a small package wrapped in brown paper. He put it in my hand. "This is for you from Henry. He told me to give it to you if anything bad happened to him."

"Why would he believe anything bad was going to happen to him? Was he in some kind of trouble?" I studied Jeremiah's face.

"I can't tell you. I've divulged too much already." Behind his glasses, tears gathered in the corners of his eyes. "Just know that Henry Noble was a good friend to me. His friendship was a gift I will always cherish." With that, he turned and went back into the stables where my brother took his last breath.

CHAPTER NINE

I TUCKED THE SMALL package into my deep cloak pocket. I would open it, but not now. It would have to be done in the privacy of my own room back at the Dickinson home. Alone.

And to be completely truthful, I didn't have the energy to open the brown paper–wrapped package at the moment. With everything that I had learned from Jeremiah, my brain was awash with information. I didn't know what to believe, and I guessed that whatever was in the package in my pocket wasn't going to help me on that point.

A large man in a suit and black wool coat glared at us as we walked down the path away from the stables. He had long sideburns that were full and dark and would be the envy of any young man who aspired to the fashion. His skin had a pasty quality to it like he spent even the summer months inside. He did not speak to us. Emily didn't speak to him. She continued to walk with Carlo at her side.

Carlo, for his part, tensed and pressed his warm body

against Emily as we walked by the man, to the point that he almost toppled her over. She placed a reassuring hand on his head.

When we were a good bit away from the stables, I asked, "Who was that man?"

She glanced at me. "Oh, I thought you knew. It was Mr. Elmer Johnson, of course. He is the owner of the livery of whom Jeremiah and Masters spoke."

I swallowed. "He doesn't look like a kind man. Why would my brother choose to work for him?"

"That's a very interesting question. Do you typically pick an employer based on his kindness?" she asked archly.

It was a fair question. Not all my employers had been kind to me over the years, but I had not left, because my brother and I had to eat.

Before I could say anything more, she added, "Let's walk to town before heading back home. It will give you time to gather your thoughts, and I have a letter to post at the post office."

I walked quietly beside her. She was right—all of my thoughts were jumbled together in my head. I didn't know what was happening. What was in the package? Could Jeremiah be trusted? He seemed like a kind young man, but I didn't know him or the true nature of his relationship with my brother.

The walk into the village was pleasant. The snow stopped and the sun came out as if to remind us that it existed. The shops in the center of town were doing good business. The barber stood outside of his parlor and smoked a cigarette. Mrs. Cutter from the bakery next door squinted as smoke wafted in her direction and she swept snow from the front walk of her shop. Out of habit, I peered in the bakery window. Breads, cakes, and muffins filled the display. My stomach rumbled at the sight of them, especially when I saw the two-tier chocolate cake that sat proudly on a glass cake holder. The only times that I had ever had treats from the bakery had been when Henry and I had been much younger and he stole a few cakes for us to eat. Of course, he did not tell me that he took the cakes without paying for them. I hadn't asked. I knew that he had because I was sure we would never be able to buy them. I had eaten them with a twinge of guilt, but I had eaten them all the same.

Mrs. Cutter gave me a kind smile and glared at the barber again.

Young women came out of the dress shop with the olive green awning showing one another the new ribbons that they had bought, and young men likely from Amherst College walked about the town as if they didn't have a care in the world. I could not imagine what it must be like to go to college or to sit in classes inside the stately stone buildings that made up the campus. To me, it was such a grand place.

The college men weren't much more than my brother's age. I know that he would never have received the schooling that they had, but nor would he ever laugh and joke with his friends again. I had to look away.

The post office came into view. It was a brick building painted white with black-framed windows and black shutters. The front door, which seemed to always be open no matter the weather with so many people coming and going, was a colonial blue. "United States Postal Service" was hand painted above it.

Emily and I waited as a woman with a stack of packages shuffled out of the post office. She wore a burgundy velvet bonnet that matched her coat and gloves. Peering over the packages, she said, "Oh, Miss Dickinson. We have missed you at church services as of late. Have you been unwell?"

Emily cocked her head. "Did my father or mother tell you that I was unwell?"

"No," the woman said. Her face turned a pink shade that clashed with the burgundy. "I just don't understand why a young woman like you wouldn't want to be involved with the church. There are many young men that attend with us, as you know. Many walk down from the college. You might be missing a golden opportunity. A young lady of your age and rank should be thinking of an attachment and the future."

"Thank you for the advice, Mrs. Huddleston, but I have no need of it." With that, Emily walked into the post office.

Mrs. Huddleston opened and shut her mouth in dismay. Then she saw me standing there. "Move along, girl," she snapped as she pushed her way past me and down the sidewalk. As she went, she knocked into an elderly man walking a small dog. She didn't even stop to see if he was all right.

I rushed over to him. "Are you hurt, sir?"

He smiled at me, and I saw that three of his front teeth were missing. "No harm done. As long as Junior is fine, so am I."

"Junior?" I asked.

He nodded to a dog that looked like a mop with paws. "Thank you for your kindness."

I acknowledged him and went into the post office. As soon as I stepped into the room, I inhaled the post office scent. It was a mix of fresh paper, old books, and lavender. The lavender came from the wreath on the door. Mrs. Milner, the postmaster's wife, loved lavender, and in the summer, half of their yard was dedicated to the plant. She made potpourri satchels and wreaths like the one on the post office door. She sold her wares at the local farmers market in season. I would guess that Amherst's was the only post office in the entire commonwealth that smelled so much like lavender.

Mr. Arthur Milner was at the desk. He handed the man just in front of us a package. "Be careful with it," the postmaster warned. "It says fragile on the side of the box."

"Oh, I will," the man assured him. "It's a new mirror for my wife. I don't want seven years' bad luck for breaking it. Even more than that, I don't want to anger my wife. This is her birthday gift."

"Good luck to you then," Mr. Milner said with a smile.

After the man carefully went through the door with his fragile package, Mr. Milner turned to us. "Emily Dickinson!" the postmaster cried. "To what do I owe this great honor of your visit?" He glanced at Carlo who had followed us into the post office. Mr. Milner didn't appear to mind the dog's presence as he said, "And the same goes for you, Carlo."

Carlo gave a slight bark and grinned from ear to ear. This made Emily smile.

"Oh! And who is that behind you but Willa Noble?" the postmaster exclaimed. "I have not seen you in many days."

"Willa is working for my family now," Emily said. "She's been an invaluable help."

"Is that right? I have been wondering what became of you, Willa, when you stopped coming to collect the mail for Mrs. Patten's Boarding House. When I asked Mrs. Patten about you, she said I was being nosy." He laughed. "Well, of course I was. A man doesn't become the postmaster if he's not curious about the people around him."

Emily raised her brow at me.

I took a breath. "In my last place of employment, the boardinghouse, I used to come every day and pick up the mail for Mrs. Patten and everyone who lived there."

"That she did, and it was the highlight of my day. I always liked chatting with you, Willa. I was disappointed that you stopped coming."

I smiled and was flattered by his comment. I hadn't known that the postmaster liked speaking to me at all. I thought he always spoke with me because he was the postmaster and that was part of his job.

I cleared my throat. "I'm sorry I didn't tell you that I left the boardinghouse."

He waved away my concern. "It wasn't your job to inform me. Don't worry yourself about it."

"And how is Mrs. Patten?" I asked. "I haven't seen her since I left."

"Mrs. Patten is the same. I'm convinced she sends someone to collect that mail so that she can look at it herself before she gives it to her boarders. That's illegal, of course. It's a serious offense to open and read another person's mail."

"Can she get in trouble?" I asked with wide eyes.

He laughed. "Most likely not. The federal government has bigger problems than a busybody proprietor of a boardinghouse." He harrumphed noisily. "Enough about Mrs. Patten. She will find a replacement for you and be fine. Women like her always are."

I wanted to ask him what he meant when he said "women like her." Who were the women like Mrs. Patten? In my experience, I had never met anyone else like her.

Before I could ask my question, though, Mr. Milner said, "I was sorry to hear about Henry. He was a kind young man. He had a nose for trouble, but it was all in good fun, I believe."

Tears came to my eyes. "Thank you." I didn't know why I was surprised that he had heard about Henry's death. I shouldn't have been. He was the postmaster after all. He knew everyone and everything that happened in Amherst.

"He will be greatly missed," Mr. Milner added. "It's such a shame to die so young in a pointless accident."

I tried to speak again, but no words came out. I couldn't say it wasn't an accident because I really didn't know. It could have been, or Jeremiah could be right and my brother was murdered. The burns on Terror's flank came to my mind. How could those be accidental?

In either case, I stood in the post office at the age of twenty without a single family member walking the earth . . . that I knew of. I shook the thought tickling the back of my brain from my head. I had no family; no family that mattered, anyway.

Emily cleared her throat. "To answer your earlier question, I am here to post a letter to my young Norcross cousins. I do like to entertain the girls with my verse." She handed Mr. Milner the letter.

He accepted it and studied the address. "I know it will be a treat for the girls to receive it. You must be their favorite cousin with the number of letters you send them."

"I enjoy sending them lines to brighten the days. They are sweet girls."

Mr. Milner nodded. "Austin said you wrote quite often. You must have more letters that should be mailed."

"Yes," Emily said, and there was something in her voice that made it clear she would prefer to leave the conversation at that.

Mr. Milner tapped the back of the letter on his desk. "Well, you can rest assured that the United States Postal Service will deliver this letter and its verses inside with the utmost care."

"I'm glad to hear it," Emily replied.

"I have another reason I'm glad you are here, Willa," Mr. Milner said as he stamped the corner of Emily's letter and set it in a basket to be sorted later. "I have a piece of mail for you. I have been holding on to it because Mrs. Patten told me that you were no longer working for her, but being Mrs. Patten, she would not tell me where you'd gone. I should have known that you would move up and work for a family like the Dickinsons." He nodded at Emily. "You have a good worker here."

Emily nodded. "We know that. We're happy to have her in our home. Miss O'Brien says that she works twice as hard as the last girl that we had in the position. That girl only lasted a week."

I couldn't help but smile at their comments. It wasn't often that I received such praise. It wasn't often that I received any praise, in fact.

"Let me go grab that piece of mail." Mr. Milner stepped behind the partition to the back of the post office.

I had the package in my cloak pocket that Jeremiah said was from my brother, and now, I would be given a letter too. I didn't know the last time I had received so many things.

Emily looked at me. "Were you expecting something in the mail?"

I shook my head. "No, there is no one to write me. Every time I came and collected the mail for the boardinghouse, there was nothing for me. The only person who might have written me was my brother. There was no reason for that since we lived in the same town and saw each other often."

"There is always a reason to write," Emily said. "Words fall differently on the page than they do from the lips. There is more control, more thought, and more possibility."

I frowned. I had never thought of writing in that way. I remembered the first day I worked at the Dickinson home and spied Emily feverishly writing at her tiny desk in her room. It was clear she took the act quite seriously. But what would come of it? Could a woman really be a writer? And support herself doing it? Could a man, for the matter? Other than a man who was already rich?

"Here we are," Mr. Milner said as he reappeared from the back of the post office. He had a plain brown envelope in his hand. He held it out to me.

My name, the name of the boardinghouse, and the boardinghouse address were all written in clear, plain printing across the middle of the envelope in dark black ink. I didn't recognize the writing, and there was no return address.

Emily watched me curiously. Perhaps she wanted me to open my piece of mystery mail right then and there, but I wasn't about to do that. We had learned so much about Henry that day that we hadn't known before. If there were any more surprises to be known, I would like to learn about them when I was alone.

When I tucked the letter back in my pocket, Emily gave a slight nod. I knew she must be curious about it. She was one of the most curious people I had ever met. She reminded me of Henry in that way. He always wanted to know and learn more. He loved secrets and learning all he could about everyone around him. It was a behavior that got him into trouble on more than one occasion. I couldn't help but wonder if it might have gotten him killed as well.

Suddenly, my skin felt very hot as the reality of my brother's death settled over me again. Emily chatted with Mr. Milner, but I couldn't hear them. My ears were ringing.

"I'll be outside," I managed to say, and I stumbled out of the post office.

CHAPTER TEN

IN THE COLD early February air, I was able to breathe again. I bent slightly at the waist and let my breath move in and out of my body. It seemed to me that grief took a physical toll. This wasn't my first loss. I had known this physiological fact from my mother's death, but this loss of Henry was somehow worse.

Carlo walked over to me as if he sensed I needed his warmth and support. He sat on my feet, and I welcomed the weight on my boots.

To my left, a group of old war soldiers sat on the benches beside the post office. It seemed to me that they were there every time I came to the post office, no matter the time of year. It was cold today, but they didn't appear to mind the chill and snow as they were bundled up in coats, hats, and scarves. One of them wore the brightest pair of yellow mittens that I had ever seen, and the vibrant color popped out against the gray landscape around us.

As they usually did, they spoke of the Revolution, the War

of 1812, and things that happened decades ago or good times that had long passed. There was nothing that could change their minds that days gone by were better than the present and the future yet to come.

"There is no unity now," said one of the old soldiers. "The young people don't understand how hard it was to give them the comforts of today."

"Some would not agree that there are comforts. The country is boiling and might erupt," another man in spectacles said.

"They have been saying that for a generation," the first man scoffed. "There will always be those who want to upset the apple-cart."

The man with the yellow mittens agreed. "Even when we were fighting the British, there were those who sympathized with Britain. True unity is an impossibility. People need to learn to live with their differences. Let everyone have their space and peace of mind. That's the true heart of America. We should be showing one another tolerance. Let one man do what is best for him and leave him be."

"You say this even if what the other man is doing is against the teachings of the Bible?" his companion in glasses asked in disbelief. "Are you saying I should be able to stab another man, and others should tolerate that?"

"You are exaggerating. That is much different from what I mean."

"Tell me how when Black men, women, and children are being killed and sold like cattle. How is that different?"

"There is slavery in the Bible," the man in the yellow mittens said gruffly.

"There is also murder in the Bible. Slavery in the Bible was a fact of the time it was written, but the Bible doesn't condone slavery. It never calls it righteous."

Yellow Mittens folded his arms across his chest and hid his mittens under his arms. "The truth is we must keep the peace. Let the states decide what it is they want to do on slavery. The Union must not have a hand in it. It will lead to nothing good."

"That isn't possible when there are runaway slaves and they pour over into Northern states. What do we do when a slave catcher comes for those men, women, and even children who cross our borders?"

Yellow Mittens didn't have an answer for that.

"You see," the man with the glasses said. "You can't leave it to the states to decide because try as you might it will spill over into the free states and always will until it's finally decided one way or another. Mark my words, this will come to conflict in the end. What Congress has done so far is just put a piece of thin linen on a seeping wound. It has already bled through."

Yellow Mittens shook his head. "Americans won't fight Americans. It's just not our way. Every state needs to be left to make its own choices. That's what the country was founded on, states' rights. To take that away now would change everything. The United States of America would be no more. I didn't fight in the Revolution and the War of 1812 to have these fools tear apart what we built."

"Willa, are you ready to leave?" Emily asked in her breathy voice.

I nodded. "Sorry. I suppose you caught me daydreaming."

"Daydreaming is serious business, and I would never interrupt you unless it was time for us to depart." Emily smiled at me. "Mother and Vinnie will be wondering what became of us."

Our conversation caught the old men's attention.

"Miss Dickinson, when will your father be home from Washington?" Yellow Mittens asked.

Emily turned to look at them. "He will be home at the end of March. There are many things that he needs to do to finish up."

"It's a shame that he didn't have another term. I have always liked your father's politics. We need more Whigs in Washington," the man with the glasses said. "They are level-headed men."

Emily thanked him.

"When he gets home, have him come see us. We would love to hear what he has to say about all this unrest that we keep hearing about from Washington. I believe that the newspapers are inflating it for sensation," Yellow Mittens added as he eyed his friends.

Emily nodded but made no promise that she would do that. Without saying goodbye, she walked to the street and waited to cross as two carriages rolled by. Carlo walked over to her, and she patted the dog's head. "At least we have Carlo to lead us home."

I wished I could be that confident just to turn away when I didn't want to speak to someone, but then again, I wasn't a Dickinson. My snubbing wouldn't be as well received.

FINALLY THAT NIGHT, after all the chores were through, I removed the brown paper–wrapped package from the pocket of my cloak. I sat on the edge of my bed and held it on my lap. From the feel, weight, and shape I knew it must be a small book. This would not be unusual for Henry to have had since we both had a love of reading. Perhaps he left a favorite novel for me to enjoy. However, I didn't know if I could read it knowing that it was his last gift to me. When it was read it would be over, and Henry, in heaven I prayed for God's mercy, would be that much more distant from me.

Maybe I should have shared this moment with Emily. She had helped me. Without her insisting that I go to the stables that day I don't know when I would have received the package. If I were in Jeremiah's shoes, I certainly would have been afraid to approach the Dickinson house with a gift for me.

And what would Miss O'Brien think if I had a young man come to the back door asking after me? Nothing good, I wagered.

Perhaps he would have found another way to locate me. I supposed he would have. He seemed determined to keep his promise to my brother.

Inside the brown package was a leather-bound book no bigger than the palm of my hand. A leather cord held it shut. I had never seen it before.

With shaky hands, I loosened the cord and opened the book. I let it lay on my lap no longer tied but still closed. I had no idea what was inside the book, and I was unsure if I wanted to know.

I opened the cover to the inside of the binding. Inside in my brother's neat hand was his name and the word "diary."

I swallowed. This was my brother's diary. I had known that he kept one. Sometimes Henry fancied himself to be a writer. He read anything and everything that he could get his hands on. He told me once that he planned to write his own memoirs someday. He planned to have a life deserving of a memoir. It pained me to remember that. Henry would never have the chance to live that dream.

We were poor, but my mother insisted on one thing: that we both go to school and learn to read and write, skills that she never had. She had said, "Education is the only way you will go anywhere. It will make your life easier, and that of your children. Remember that. I want that for both of my children."

Henry had said, "Why does Willa have to get educated? She's a girl. All she has to do is get married. She does not need to worry about earning money and being able to read."

My blood had boiled when he said that, and had I not been on the other side of our mother at the time, I would have kicked him in the shin for his unkind words. I should have been able to learn to read just as much as he should.

"I will remind you, my son, that I was married once to your father. Where is he now? Willa, just like you, needs to be able to stand on her own two feet. There is no guarantee that the person either of you will marry will be the support that you need. You are your own support. Beyond yourselves, you have each other. Promise me that you will always stick together."

I had crossed my arms. I was still angry at Henry for suggesting that I didn't need to learn to read because I was to get married.

When neither of us said anything, my mother had said in a forceful voice, "Promise me. You must promise. You are blood and must care for each other. Always."

My brother and I promised my mother in unison. I didn't know how much we believed at the time we would keep that promise. Frustrated with my boisterous brother, I hadn't thought that I would put much stock in it at all. Then, years later, our mother died, leaving us alone, and the promise became the lifeline that tethered us together. It was like an invisible string braided by our mother's hand. It was unbreakable.

And I had kept that promise until . . . until my brother was killed. I not only failed Henry, but I had failed our mother too. I should have been more insistent that he not take the stable hand job. I should have kept a better eye on him.

Why did he take that job? Why did he have to push for something bigger and better? Why hadn't he been content where he was? We would never be in a position to have everything we wanted like the Dickinsons or the other wealthy families in Amherst. It was impossible, but we could be content. Contentment had not been enough for my brother. If he was still among the living, it would never be.

I shook the memory from my mind.

I flipped to the first page of Henry's diary and began to read.

I started to keep this diary as a testament of what I learned. What is inside of these pages is truth and should be treated as such. Not everyone will want me to reveal what is found here, but I trust if you read on, you will find truth here.

Willa, if you are reading this diary that means I have failed in my mission. It started as a way to make more money so that I could give you the life you deserve. But it became much more than that. I realized I was doing something that could make a difference for hundreds of lives. I hope you will understand my motives.

You are so much more than a sister to me. You are a sister, a mother, and a friend. You must keep the secrets that are found inside these pages. I will not ask you to join my cause, but I do ask you that out of your love for me, your only brother, you will protect it. Do not share what you find here with the adversary. If you do, the cost would be too high.

Adversary? What was Henry's meaning in this?

I will not mention the names of any guilty parties in these pages, he wrote. *To write the names down would be far too dangerous, but I still wish to a record an account of my experience.*

I sucked in a breath. The words on the page were as if he came back from the grave and spoke them to me himself. They were full of passion and hyperbole. It was the way that Henry spoke. Everything was of the utmost importance to him. It was impossible not to be overwhelmed by it.

I bit the inside of my cheek. Should I read the diary beginning to end or skip to the end? I laid it over my lap and it fell open to an entry for the last day I saw my brother alive.

I saw Willa today. I climbed up the side of the house that she is living in and jumped through her bedroom window. My, was she very surprised! As expected, she scolded me for coming to her employer's house unannounced, but I secretly know she was happy to see me. She's working for the Dickinson family now. They are a wealthy family in Amherst. The father is some kind of politician type. I have no use for politicians myself, but Willa seems to be happy with her new employer, and I must say that it made me happy to see my sister in such a comfortable and spacious room all to herself. She's worried about me as to be expected, and she wasn't happy when I told her I left my job at the warehouse.

What she has to understand is that it will all be worth it in the end. Since I left the warehouse and started my new assignment, we have a real chance of having a home of our own or going out west like I think that we should. I know Willa doesn't want to go. She has never been a great fan of change, and living on the frontier would certainly be a change from the predictable society of Amherst.

But if Willa wants to stay, I will stay. She has been a good sister to me and has saved me on more than one occasion. I would not be here without my sister. She is the person most dear to me in the world. I cannot imagine caring for another soul as much.

I closed the journal then and tears fell from my eyes. How could I read on after reading those words? Henry was the person most dear to me in the world. He would never be replaced in my heart. Knowing that he had felt the same both comforted and pained me.

How could I continue with any of it? Reading this diary? Finding out what really happened to Henry? Life? All three and much more seemed too heavy to bear. I didn't know if I was up for the task.

I stilled as another tidal wave of grief washed over me. As I did so, a loose piece of newsprint fell from the pages of the diary. I set the diary on my bed and picked up the piece of paper.

Unfolding it, I found that it was a map, and not just any map, but a map of Amherst. On the map there were ink dots barely noticeable to the eye. An equally tiny number was beside each dot on the page.

An owl was sketched in the corner of the page. I recognized Henry's hand in that. He loved to sketch when he was a child and still did as a young man.

What did this mean? What was this map in my hands? My heart thundered in my chest. What did I do with this information? Where did I go with it?

I folded the map up, tucked it back into the diary, and wound the leather strap around the diary again. I would have to try to read this later, on Sunday, my day off. Yes, I would read it Sunday when I wasn't as tired.

I changed out of my day dress, which I had worn on our walk to the stables and while cleaning and cooking the rest of the day for the family, and put on my nightgown. I was about to blow out the candle for the night when I remembered the letter that Mr. Milner had given to me.

I would worry about it in the morning, I told myself. I blew out the candle, rolled over, and put my feather pillow over my head as if it would block out my thoughts of the letter.

Tossing and turning for a few minutes, I realized I wouldn't be able to rest until I knew who had written to me and what the letter had to say.

I sat up and fumbled with the matchbox and candle on the small table beside my bed. Finally, the scent of sulfur stung my nostrils as the match ignited. I lit the candle. My bare feet hit the cold wooden boards, and I hurried over to my cloak hanging on a peg on the wall. I found the letter by feel and scurried back to my bed as the air around me chilled me through.

I slid back under the quilt and pressed my back to the wall. I studied the envelope again, and there was no indication of who or where it was from. Other than the postmark being

Amherst. That was just as well. I didn't know a soul who lived outside of the town, so there was no reason for anyone outside of Amherst to write to me.

I opened it carefully, wanting to preserve the envelope as much as possible. Why I wanted to do this, I wasn't sure, since there was nothing telling on the envelope.

I unfolded the letter. The writing was the same utilitarian print that had been on the outer envelope.

Tell your brother to stop poking his nose where it doesn't belong. If he keeps at it, he will come to a bad end and so will you.

That was all it said. That terrifying message was there right in the center of the page, written in those printed heavy-handed letters. The only other writing on the page was the date. "January 23, 1855."

"He will come to a bad end and so will you." That line burned the inside of my head.

My hands shook. The date on the letter was three weeks ago. It had been sent shortly after I left Mrs. Patten's Boarding House. Had I still been at the boardinghouse, I would have received this letter not long after it was sent . . . and Henry might still be alive.

Was it my fault that Henry died because I received this letter late and I hadn't been able to warn him?

I didn't know what to do with all of this. I couldn't carry it alone. I needed to show Emily, and I needed to show her now.

My heart sank. It was in the middle of the night. Now wasn't the time to bother her. But then, maybe she would still be awake and willing to listen to me. I knew there was no possible way that I would be able to sleep with the contents of this letter weighing on my mind.

She was interested in Henry's death. She would want to hear about this sooner rather than later, I told myself. If she was asleep, then I would return to my room and try my very best to rest. But if she was awake, I needed to tell her about the contents of the letter now.

As quickly as I could, I put my dress back on. If I was stopped in the hallway by Miss O'Brien or the cook, I wanted to have some sort of plausible story to share as to why I was wandering the Dickinson home in the middle of the night. Maybe I was up to check the fireplace. It was my job to snuff out the fire in the family room after the family retired. I would tell Miss O'Brien that I couldn't remember if I did that.

I opened my door into the hallway, and the hinges gave the most terrible screech. I froze and waited a full minute before I slipped through the open door. At any moment I expected Emily's bear of a dog to come barreling down the corridor, barking in response to the noise I made. It was a small miracle Carlo didn't appear.

I tiptoed down the hallway. It was drafty, like the winter wind had found a way to penetrate the cozy house.

At the top of the stairs, I looked behind me again at the door to Miss O'Brien's room. There was no sign of movement. She must be asleep. I wasn't surprised that the housekeeper was a sound sleeper. She was one of the hardest-working people I'd ever met. She kept the Dickinson household running. I had on occasion even seen her give Emily and Miss Lavinia directions in the kitchen. I can't say that Emily had put much stock in Miss O'Brien's advice when it came to her baking, but Miss Lavinia seemed to take the housekeeper's words to heart.

The house was like a maze, and I knew it was nowhere as large as the home that Mr. Dickinson was in the process of renovating for the family. I hadn't heard when we were moving to the second house. I only knew it was the house that Mr. Dickinson had grown up in, where the three Dickinson children were born, and had been lost due to some financial troubles in the family.

Finally, I came to Emily's door. I stood outside of it, afraid to knock. I was even afraid to breathe. Who was I to disturb her? I was a servant. I wasn't her friend. Had I thought we were friends? That was a mistake servants made, and it could only lead to trouble for them.

Before I could knock or change my mind and leave, the door opened. Emily stood on the other side of it. Her hair was plaited into a long braid, and her fingertips were stained with pencil. There were pencil marks on her nightgown as well. There were scraps of paper all over the floor. She stared at me like she was a person who was in a very deep hole and was wondering where I had come from.

She blinked at me like she was struggling to focus. "Willa, what are you doing here at this time of night?" She shielded her eyes from my candle as if the light pained her in some way.

"Emily, I'm so sorry to bother you this late. I—I just read the letter that Mr. Milner gave me at the post office. I think you need to see it. It's about Henry."

Her mouth fell open, and her eyes came back into focus as if she was returning from whatever thoughtful place her mind had wandered to. I was starting to recognize the times when

Emily was thinking. She thought so much more deeply than any other person I had ever known, that her outward self appeared blank.

But now when I mentioned Henry, she was fully back with me.

"Come in," she whispered. "I am curious to see this letter. Perhaps it can shed some light onto our investigation."

I stepped into the room before Emily closed the door, and from somewhere behind me, I heard another bedroom door's latch click closed. I shook my head. I must have imagined the sound, or so I told myself. Had anyone seen us this late at night, certainly they would have asked what we were up to.

Emily's room was very fine by my standard. There was a bed, a dresser, and a writing desk. All around the desk there were paper and broken pencils. Emily didn't make any apologies for the mess. It was hard for me not to start cleaning it up, but I suspected that she would find that offensive in some way.

The wallpaper had flowers all over it to the point it appeared that the blossoms would burst right off of the walls.

"My father told me that when we move into the old homestead I can pick the wallpaper."

"And what will you pick?"

"Flowers of some sort, like I have here. I dearly love flowers. Perhaps roses. Flowers on the wall remind me spring will come even in the deepest trench of winter. Flowers are hope, you see." She looked out the window into the night. "I have been working in my greenhouse preparing for spring. I do love growing things. Do you?"

"I do. I would have chosen to be a gardener if that was a good job for a woman."

"And why is it not? If you are good at growing things, you should do that. If you enjoy it, you should do that even more."

I shook my head. "I like my position, miss. Gardening is the work of men."

"But more housewives garden."

"Perhaps it is a different standard when there is money to be made," I said. "I do not know who makes these types of rules, but they are there nonetheless."

"Standards are things I do not expect to follow. I will not be told to believe this or that or like this person or that person. The only person making decisions for me is me," she said. "Now that I know that you enjoy the garden, you can help me when spring comes. It is a busy time."

"I would love to if Miss O'Brien would allow it."

She shook her head. "If I ask her if I can borrow you for an afternoon here and there, she will allow it. By the time spring comes, we will be working on the new old house in earnest. There will be much work to be done in the gardens there. I don't believe the man who owned the property had taken as much care of it as he should. My father is building a greenhouse off of the dining room for my sister and me. He knows how important the gardens are to us." She pressed her lips together. "You have a letter to show me?"

I pulled the letter from the pocket of my apron and held it out to her.

Emily took the letter over to her writing desk and sat down. "You should sit too," she said.

There was the bed, and I didn't want to sit there. It didn't seem right as a maid to sit on my mistress's bed.

There was a small chair in the corner of the room. It looked like it was more suited for a child than an adult. At the very least, it was suited for a woman of Emily's small frame. I didn't think it could hold a woman of my size.

I perched on the edge of the seat and prayed that the chair wouldn't give way under me.

Emily opened the letter and read it. She stared at the page for a long time, a much longer time than she needed to. It was only a couple of sentences, and their meaning was very much to the point.

After what seemed like an eternity, she folded the letter up again and tucked it into the envelope. "This is the proof that we needed."

"Proof of what?"

"That your brother, Henry Noble, wasn't killed in an accident. He was murdered."

CHAPTER ELEVEN

THE NEXT MORNING, I was washing up the dishes from the family's breakfast when Miss O'Brien came into the kitchen. "Willa, you can go help Miss Dickinson in the greenhouse when you are done there."

My eyes went wide. I had no idea that Emily would actually ask Miss O'Brien for me to help with the garden.

"What about my other duties?" I asked.

"Oh, I still expect you to get those done too. If Miss Dickinson really wants your help with her plants, that can't take away from your other responsibilities. I hired you to help with the household, not the flowers," she grumbled.

"I will get all my responsibilities done. It's very gracious of you, Miss O'Brien, to let me help Miss Dickinson in the garden. I know the garden is very important to her."

Miss O'Brien pursed her lips together. "She does like to grow things and is very good at it," she conceded. "It is a good occupation for a young lady to have. It's much more worthy of her time than scribbling on those pieces of paper like she does. Do you know how many times I have to ask her to wash her hands before she bakes the morning bread? Her fingers are constantly stained with pencil lead." She clucked her tongue in disapproval.

After Miss O'Brien left the kitchen to tend to her next task, I made short work of washing and drying the remaining breakfast dishes and went in search of Miss Dickinson.

The greenhouse was a small glass building behind the main house. It was no bigger than the garden shed. Snow was falling by the time I put on my cloak and made it outside. Even though it was late morning, the skies were dark with the promise of more snow. I was grateful that Emily asked me to help with her plants. I longed for the greenness of spring and summer. It seemed now that everything was awash in gray and white.

Through the greenhouse's many windows, I saw Emily and Miss Lavinia moving around inside. When I was just a few steps away from the cracked open door, I could hear their voices too.

"When we move, and we have a new greenhouse, it will be attached to the main house, so I won't have to go outside in foul weather," Emily said.

"As usual, Father granted your wish," Miss Lavinia said in a perturbed voice. "Like he always does."

"Father does not grant my every wish. Far from it," Emily scoffed. "He doesn't do that for anyone."

"Maybe so, but he is much more lenient on you than on Austin and me. He has always treated you differently."

"That is your perception, dear Sister, but it is not true. Father is stern and reserved with us all." Emily must have noticed me standing in the cold. "Willa, come in. I'm glad that you are here."

I stepped into the greenhouse, and the space was tight with all three of us there, not to mention Carlo.

Miss Lavinia frowned at me, and Carlo, who was napping in the corner of the greenhouse on a large pillow, lifted his head just a fraction. When he saw it was me, he set his chin back onto his massive paws and closed his eyes.

"What are you doing here?" Miss Lavinia asked. "Shouldn't you be in the house brushing the furniture?"

I didn't know what to say to that.

"Vinnie," Emily said. "Be kind. I asked Miss O'Brien if she could spare Willa so she could help in the greenhouse."

Miss Lavinia's eyes went wide. "But I am the one who helps you in the greenhouse."

"I know, but you don't enjoy it as much as I do. I learned that Willa loves plants, so I asked her to help. In that case, you can spend more time on what you enjoy, like your music and needlework."

Miss Lavinia frowned. "What if what I enjoy is spending time with my sister?"

"We do that enough, Vinnie. You need your own pursuits. Everyone should have their own singular passion that is unattached to any other person. Without it, life becomes a cycle of serving others' passions. That's not much of a life at all."

"I believe caring for your family is a worthy passion." Miss Lavinia stomped out of the greenhouse. The glass door rattled behind her as she slammed it shut.

"Don't mind her," Emily said. "Vinnie is not happy unless

she is taking care of a problem. If there is no problem to be mended, she becomes lost."

The door had not closed completely when she slammed it, so I quietly closed it until the latch caught. "I don't know what I did to Miss Lavinia to make her dislike me this much. I haven't had the chance to say more than a few words to her in all the time that I have worked for your family."

"Vinnie is protective of me. She always has been. I am the older sister, but both she and Austin treat me like a child from time to time."

"Why would they do that?" I glanced through the wavy glass wall of the greenhouse and saw Miss Lavinia hurry into the house.

"It is hard to stay. I would like to believe that I have proven myself to them by now." Emily pressed her lips together as if she realized that she had said too much.

I wondered if this was what it was like to have a large family. There were so many relationships to navigate. It had just been Henry and me for so long that it had been far less complicated. I had only one person to think about, at least after my mother passed on. I didn't have nearly the number of friends and family that Emily did. How did she manage all of those relationships? I had a feeling that I would certainly have failed at it if I had that many people to consider. Hadn't I failed Henry? And he was my only one.

Emily cleared her throat. "Now is the time that I start the seedlings for spring. I like to have healthy green plants before I place them in the ground. They have the greatest chance of success then. To sow the seed directly into the earth is taking a big risk. I do that for some plants that I know will be able to flourish with the seeds in the ground, such as nasturtium, sunflowers, and cosmos. But my more delicate plants get the utmost pampering in my greenhouse until they are ready to transplant."

"How many types of seeds are you starting?" I leaned over her potting table and stared and the lines of neatly labeled seeds.

"Dozens. In my mind there can never be enough plants in this world. They attract the animals, bees, and birds. All are welcome to my garden. The only thing that makes me happy about moving is we will have ample land for a large garden. I worry about my plants being moved from here to there. I will have to keep an extra careful eye on them when that happens."

Carlo snored softly in the corner.

Emily smiled at the dog. "I like him in the greenhouse with me. When he is here, it keeps Vinnie's cats out. Those rascals."

"I've always like cats," I confessed. "I've never had a pet. I've never lived anywhere where I could have a pet of my own, but I think I would have a cat if I did."

Emily wrinkled her nose. "Well, that's something you have in common with my sister. Perhaps she will start liking you if you tell her about your affinity for felines."

I guessed it would take a lot more than my appreciation of cats to make Miss Lavinia like me.

Emily put me to work setting tomato seeds in small clay pots. "Don't put more than four seeds in each pot. When they come up, we will choose the strongest sprout and thin the rest. When we transfer them to larger pots we will include cow manure. Tomatoes love manure."

I nodded and set to work. I was careful to count out four tiny seeds to each pot. Before long, my fingertips were encrusted in dirt and my fingernails were black. I glanced over at Emily, and I saw she had the same, and there was a streak of dirt on her forehead where she must have brushed a stray hair away. There was another streak on the plaid silken skirt of her day dress. The dress was a lovely navy and orange plaid. It pained me to see it marred in any way. Emily seemed not to even notice.

"I have been thinking a lot about the letter you received and what we have learned about Henry's death. There must be more to the story. There is an important piece that we're missing. I believe Henry knew something or saw something that could get him in a great deal of trouble."

I thought of my brother's diary, which I had hidden inside of my straw mattress in my little room at the top of the house. I opened my mouth, because I believed now was the time to tell Emily about it.

"However, we cannot discount another possibility for a motive."

"What is that?"

"Catherine Dwight, the minister's daughter. What if her brothers or father were afraid that she would marry Henry after all? He was very poor. It would not be an advantageous match for the family. Perhaps one or all of them went to the stables to speak to Henry and spooked the horse, and that's how he died."

"But," I said, "what about the burn marks on Terror's flank? That cannot be an accident."

"Maybe they were brandishing a poker to scare Henry and accidentally injured the horse."

I shook my head. "I can't believe it. Reverend Dwight is a man of the cloth. It would be impossible for him to do such a terrible act."

"Nothing is impossible. Is he not a sinner too? His collar does not remove his humanity."

I didn't know what to say to that.

"I have put out some inquiries in letters to friends who know the Dwights better than me. I asked how serious Catherine was about Henry and what the family's feelings were on that."

"I don't want to cause trouble in your family's church." I started a fifth pot of tomatoes.

"There is always trouble in the church. It does not start with us."

I wanted to argue with her more, but I didn't know if it was much use if she had already sent the letters. I feared the gossip that would come from this.

"My friend Susan Gilbert will be coming over tomorrow." She plucked dead leaves from a potted sword fern. It was clear the plant was many years old, as it was the size of Carlo's head. "Susan is quite brilliant. I think you should tell her what has happened to your brother. She is well-connected in the town, and she might have some theories."

I kept my head down. I wasn't sure that I was ready to share what I knew about my brother's death with another person, and certainly not to share his diary with anyone new.

"You can trust Sue," Emily said as if she could sense my hesitation. "There is no one else that I trust more in this world. She is my dearest friend."

I went to my last tiny pot and gently pressed four tomato seeds into the rich dirt. "If you think that it's the right thing to do."

"I do," Emily said without hesitation.

I decided that I would wait to tell Emily about the diary until after I met Susan Gilbert.

Emily turned to me. "You look like there was something that you wanted to tell me, Willa. What was it?"

I concentrated on tucking the remaining tomato seeds back into the brown envelope to save to be planted later. "Nothing, I had nothing else to share." I didn't look at her, because if anyone could sense a falsehood, it was Emily Dickinson.

CHAPTER TWELVE

THERE WERE CHEERFUL voices in the foyer the next day while I was polishing the silver in the dining room. It was actually a duty that I enjoyed because Miss O'Brien allowed me to do it while seated at the table. As a housemaid, anytime that I wasn't on my feet was welcome rest. I also liked to polish the silver to such a high sheen that I saw my reflection in it.

In that reflection, I saw a sturdy, blond housemaid with dark brown eyes. My eyes in truth were my one vanity. I thought they were well spaced and well shaped and sat behind a clear brow. But that day while I polished the silver, I could not look at my reflection. Henry had had the same blond hair. Despite our differing eye color, my mother said many people thought we were twins and I wasn't two years his senior. I believed it was my larger size and my height that was just an inch shy of my younger brother's and not just my coloring that made them think this.

"Austin! We didn't know you were coming!" I heard Emily cry.

I set the serving fork I had been polishing back onto the table and crept to the dining room door. I was grateful I had left it open a crack. I had done so because Miss Lavinia's cats liked to visit me when I polished the silver. They sat on my feet at every opportunity they could find. They were a comfort to me. If only their mistress would warm up to me as well.

I peeked through the crack in the door and saw a hand-some young man smartly dressed in a black suit and overcoat with silver buttons running down either side. In his hand he held a top hat that appeared to have been brushed free of dust that very morning. I could still see the etching in the wool where the bristles had swept across it.

The young man, who I had taken to be Austin Dickinson, the only son in the family and a person of whom they all spoke with excitement and high regard, was not alone.

Next to him was a young woman. She wore a hunter green morning dress trimmed with black velvet on the double skirt. She held a cloak over her arm and a bonnet in her hand and was smiling brightly at Emily and her brother as if she had never been happier to see two people together in all her life.

"There, there, Sister. There is no need to squeeze the breath out of me. Do you want me to die here at the doorstep to our home so that I can never go back to Cambridge?"

"Do not die," Emily said. "But do not go back to Cambridge either. What does Harvard have that you can't find right here in Amherst?"

"More learned men," he said with a sparkle in his eye.

"I am learned as those men. I am learned in the thoughts that matter," Emily said.

"I see your confidence remains unshaken. It's an endearing quality. And you will note, I had said *more* learned *men*. You, dear Sister, try as you might, are not and never will be a man." He took the woman's hand. "I just so happened to run into my betrothed when I was walking here from the train station. She was like a ray of sunshine on this dark February day. Why is the middle of winter so dreary? Did God create winter to make us appreciate the spring that much more?"

"Your God. I do not—" Emily began, but her mother interrupted her.

"Why did you walk?" Mrs. Dickinson asked as she came into the room. Her hair and eyes were dark like Emily's, but her hair did not have the reddish tint nor the eyes the curious sparkle of her eldest daughter. She wore a plain navy blue day dress and a crocheted gray shawl with a long fringe over her shoulders. She held the shawl tightly at the base of her neck as if it was the only thing that was keeping her warm. "You know that we would have sent the carriage."

"It was all fine. Gave me a few moments to be alone with my love." Austin smiled. "Until we are wed, I won't have much chance of that." He held the young woman's hand. She was beaming.

"And Sue, sweet Sue, I have missed you terribly." Emily wrapped her arms around the young woman. "How can you live such a short distance away and we never meet as much as I like?"

Was this Susan Gilbert? Was she the friend that Emily wanted to speak to about my brother's death and the threat that I received far too late in the mail?

It was odd to me; when Emily mentioned Susan Gilbert to me, she said she was her friend and not Austin's betrothed. Wouldn't her main role be her brother's fiancée?

There were so many aspects of this family that I didn't understand. Their lives were so intertwined. It was clear that there was a deep love there and something else. Whatever that something else was, I couldn't put my finger on it. Perhaps it was because I didn't have a large family so it was impossible for me to understand how it all worked.

"Come in, come in," Mrs. Dickinson said, and she loosened her grasp on her shawl. "Don't stand in the foyer. We have tea waiting in the parlor. Your father is home, Austin. I know he is eager to hear about your studies at Harvard. He arrived just last night. He is here for a quick visit because he has business as the Amherst College treasurer, but he will be leaving again on tomorrow's afternoon train for Washington until the end of this term."

Austin's face clouded over. "He is here for more than college business. He is eager to convince me to work at his law firm. You told him that I was coming, didn't you, Mother? And that is his real reason for being here. It is no accident that our visits have overlapped."

Emily's brow knit together. "I think it would be a fine idea if you worked with our father. The family should stay together as much as possible. You would be here in Amherst for good where you belong. It's where all the Dickinsons belong."

"There are opportunities west," Austin said. "Our grandfather knew that."

"Grandfather died in Ohio away from the place he was born, away from most of his family, away from society," Emily said hotly.

"The school in Hudson, Ohio, where he worked has a good reputation. Not all society is found in New England," her brother argued.

Emily sniffed as if she didn't believe that in the least.

"Let's not argue," Miss Lavinia said as she came into the foyer holding one of her cats. This one was a longhaired orange tabby. His plume of a tail swished back and forth leaving white hairs on the fabric of her black dress. Miss Lavinia didn't seem to be bothered by this. "You don't want Father to hear you arguing already, do you?"

They grew quiet. It seemed that they were all in agreement that they didn't want Mr. Dickinson hearing their quarrel.

The family moved to the parlor, and I ducked back into the dining room before I could be seen. I had just sat down to begin my polishing again when the dining room door opened widely.

Emily stuck her head in. "Eavesdropping is an art form that I also practice." Her face disappeared again.

My heart was in my throat. I hadn't been as silent as I thought when I peeked into the hallway. What did Emily think of me, knowing that I was listening to a private conversation between her and her family?

With a red face I finished the silver polishing.

Just as I was putting the last pieces back into the china closet, Miss O'Brien came in the dining room. "There you are, Willa."

"I was just about to come down and help you with supper, Miss O'Brien."

"Thank you, Willa. Please, when it is just the two of us, you can call me Margaret." She studied me. "I wasn't sure when you first arrived in that mud-covered cloak if you would be the right girl for this job, but it seems Miss Dickinson saw something in you that I could not. I have been pleasantly surprised with your work."

I blushed, surprised by the uncharacteristic praise. "Thank you, Margaret."

She smiled when I said her Christian name. "Before you come down to help with supper, I would like you to go into the parlor to see if the family needs anything for their visit."

I felt myself pale. It would be the first time that I would be seeing Mr. Dickinson since I began working for the family. He had not come down to breakfast this morning. Instead Margaret delivered a tray to his room. I glanced down at my dress and brushed at my skirt. I touched my hair. I wanted to appear as though I had everything in place and was the right person for this position.

"What is it that they might need?" I asked.

"Well, that's what I don't know. I must return to the kitchen and finish the pudding for tonight's meal, and I cannot leave the custard when I begin or it will be at risk of curdling. Go into the parlor, and when it is the right time, ask if there is anything that they require."

"How will I know when it is the right time?" I asked, unable to keep the nervousness from my voice.

She frowned. "Dear Willa, just go and you will know." With that, she left the dining room. I watched her leave with an anxious heart.

After checking my reflection the best that I could in the dining room window, I took a deep breath and went into the parlor. As I stepped through the door, it seemed that I had come into the room in the middle of a tense conversation.

"I am not like Grandfather," Austin said with exasperation in his voice.

"I hope you would not be. I raised you not to be," Mr. Dickinson replied. "My father was a pious man, but he was challenged by managing money. He was impractical and ran himself and the institutions that he served into the ground."

Mr. Dickinson had long sideburns that were turning from brown to gray and a lined, rather stern face. He looked like a man who was used to getting respect. Not only that, but he looked like a man who expected respect.

"The question is, whose fault is that?" Austin, a younger version of his father, shot back.

Mr. Dickinson's dark eyes narrowed at his son. "What do you mean by that, Son?"

"These institutions that he supposedly caused so much trouble for kept hiring him. They knew—or if they didn't, they could have learned—his reputation with money, yet they hired him because they wanted a Dickinson under their employ. It is their fault in hiring him just as much as it is his fault for his own incompetence."

"Do not speak of your grandfather in that way," Mr. Dickinson said in a low and threatening voice. "He deserves your respect. Just because you are a Cambridge man now, it does not mean that you can take such a tone with me."

"And your words about your father were spoken highly?"

"Watch your tongue when you are in *my* home," Mr. Dickinson snapped.

Austin looked like he wanted to say something more, but Miss Gilbert put her hand over his. He looked down at it.

There was a long moment of silence when no one said anything. I wondered if this was the time when I should ask if they needed anything. But in all honesty, they were so locked in their argument, I don't even know if they were aware I was there.

"The Ladies Auxiliary is having a fundraiser for the Sunday school classes," Mrs. Dickinson said out of the blue. "Emily, I hope you will make some of your wonderful rye bread for the ladies to sell."

Emily frowned at Mrs. Dickinson as if she couldn't believe her mother would change the subject. "I can," she said finally.

"Oh, wonderful, I will be sure to tell them at church on Sunday."

"Do you need something, Willa?" Miss Lavinia asked as she pet her cat.

All of them turned and looked at me.

"Oh, yes, I mean no, I am not in need of anything. Was there anything that you all needed before Miss O'Brien and I finish making the evening meal?"

Mr. Dickinson studied me under his dark hooded brow. "Who is this?" It was clear the question was not directed at me, but at the family.

"It's Willa Noble, our new maid, Edward," Mrs. Dickinson said. "If you recall, Margaret asked for more help the last time you were home and you granted it."

He frowned as if he didn't remember this conversation at all. I froze. What if I was sacked? I didn't have anywhere to go. Mrs. Patten was too offended by the fact that I quit the boardinghouse to take me back. I didn't have anything or anyone to fall back on.

Mr. Dickinson's face cleared. "I do remember that conversation. I should have thought of it more. With leaving Congress and the renovations on the homestead, we need to be frugal at this time. There are many things that I know all of you want in the homestead when we move." He frowned at me. "But you are here, so there is no taking it back now."

It took all of my strength not to melt into a puddle right there on the carpet. I had thought for certain that I would be dismissed.

"Willa, that will be all," Emily said.

Her breathy voice snapped me to attention. I nodded to the family and slipped out of the room.

By the evening meal, I hoped that the family had forgotten about what happened in the parlor. It appeared that they had. No one said a word to me as Margaret and I served the meal.

"Have you read in the paper about the slave catcher who is in Amherst?" Miss Lavinia asked. "How terrible that he should be here walking our quiet streets."

Emily stiffened. "I did see that in the paper. What business does a man like that have here? We are a free society."

"According to the law, he is within his rights to collect runaway slaves and take them back to the South," Austin said. "I do not agree with the philosophy behind it, but law is law."

"And the law is a living, breathing thing. As such, it can change," Emily said. "They should not allow slave catchers in the North. They should not allow slavery at all."

Mr. Dickinson cleared his throat as if he was uncomfortable with the direction this conversation was headed. "I will be leaving to return to Washington tomorrow, and Austin, I would like you to bring your mother and sisters to the Capitol for a visit before the end of my term."

"Father, I have studies in Cambridge."

"I know you do, Son, but this is your chance to see the politics and the practice of law in action."

Austin sipped his water.

Miss Lavinia's eyes were wide. "We are going to Washington?"

"You will leave in one week. I have made all the arrangements."

Mrs. Dickinson's face appeared pinched at the very idea, and Emily also looked slightly pained.

"I know you might not want to go, Emily," Mr. Dickinson said more gently than I had ever heard him speak. "But I would like you to see the city."

Emily moved a carrot around her plate with the back of her fork. "I'll go."

Those two simple words made her father smile.

The family finished their meal with a much more genial conversation about plans for the homestead, and everyone seemed at least to be in brighter spirits.

After I cleared, washed, and put away the supper dishes, Margaret came into the kitchen. "Miss Dickinson was asking after you. She and Miss Gilbert are in the parlor."

I wiped my hand on a tea towel and hung it on a hook on the wall. "Did she say what she wanted?"

Margaret pressed her lips together. "No, but when you are finished with whatever it is she wants, I have some extra tasks for you. Even though Mr. Dickinson is home for just a day, there is much to be done."

I told her that I would be back just as soon as I learned what Emily wanted, and I left the kitchen. I found Emily and Miss Gilbert in the parlor as Margaret said they would be. The two young women sat close together and spoke in whispers. I felt like I was interrupting an intimate moment between sisters.

I cleared my throat. "Miss Dickinson, Miss O'Brien said you wanted to see me."

Emily looked up from her whispered conversation with Miss Gilbert. "Willa, yes, come in, shut the door, and sit down. I was just filling Susan in on all the circumstances surrounding your brother's death."

I did as Emily asked, but it always felt wrong to sit on what I had come to think of as Dickinson family furniture. I perched on the edge of a chair across from the two women on the settee.

Miss Gilbert studied me with intelligent hazel eyes. "You are a nervous young woman, aren't you?"

I straightened my back. "I think anyone would be nervous speaking of her brother's death. Wouldn't you be?"

Miss Gilbert smiled at my reply. "I'm glad to see that you have a backbone. I was wondering if you did when I saw you in the parlor before dinner."

I made no comment to this.

"Emily told me everything she knows about the circumstances of your brother's death, and it very much sounds like a fantastical tale. Someone burns a horse to kill a man? It's hard to believe."

"I agree," Emily said. "But it is the only explanation of what might have happened to young Henry Noble."

Miss Gilbert nodded. "It does sound to me like your brother was in some kind of trouble. Did he find trouble often?"

I thought of the many times that my brother found trouble and the many times that I helped him out of it. Or, when it was even more complicated, when Matthew helped him out of it.

I could only guess what Matthew would think if he knew that Emily, Miss Gilbert, and I were looking at my brother's death as a possible murder.

"He did have a way of finding trouble, miss, but I can assure you that he had a good heart," I said.

Miss Gilbert seemed to consider this, and then she said, "What I think is the most interesting piece is the location where Henry died."

"Why is that?" Emily asked.

"I have heard rumors about the town stables in relation to what Lavinia said at supper."

"About the slave catcher?" Emily asked in surprise.

Miss Gilbert nodded. "There are stories that there is something happening at the stables. Mrs. Charles said that she saw a Black man there in shackles. He was held there until the slave catcher came and took him back to Virginia."

"That's horrible," I blurted out. "I can't believe something like this is happening right here in such a learned town as Amherst."

"I heard this whispered at church," Miss Gilbert said. "I don't know if it's true. Elmer Johnson is not well-liked in town, so any rumors about him tend to be harsh. You know how the church ladies like to gossip about anything and everything."

"Another reason not to go to church," Emily said.

"You have reasons enough," Miss Gilbert said. "But it might be easier for your foray into society if you did attend. It would be easier for the family as well."

Emily lifted her chin. "It is not my goal to make my movements in society easier. It was not what I was put on this earth to do."

"And what were you put on earth to do?" Miss Gilbert asked, but she asked it in such a way that I think she already knew the answer.

"To write." She held up her hand as if she were brandishing a pen.

Miss Gilbert nodded approval. "I wish that for you and for myself, my dear Emily. My journey will be more difficult when I have children and responsibilities at home."

A strange look crossed Emily's face, as if she didn't completely approve of Miss Gilbert having a family with her brother.

"We need to find out if this rumor about the stables is true, and if it is, could it be related to Henry's death," Emily said.

"I don't know how to begin," I said.

"We will just have to find out by speaking to people. There are guests, stable hands, and people that board their horses there. It is impossible to believe that a slave catcher could move around the stables so often and go unnoticed. We need to question those people."

"But won't that draw attention?" I asked nervously.

Emily laughed. "We are women. They won't think a thing about us asking questions. They will wonder why we are there, but they won't see us as a threat."

"Even though they should," Miss Gilbert said.

"Precisely," Emily agreed.

CHAPTER THIRTEEN

IT WAS A few days before Emily and I could return to the stables to ask questions. There was much to do to prepare the family for their trip to Washington, and on the way home the Dickinson ladies would be visiting friends in Philadelphia. Emily would be away from Amherst a total of five weeks. I couldn't help but wonder what would happen to our "investigation," as she called it, when she was gone. Should I carry on alone?

There was a light dusting of snow on the ground over the gray piles of frozen slush along the streets. It was just enough to mask the ugliness of the late winter. Carlo trotted out ahead of us while we walked through town to the stables.

"You will have to keep a watchful eye on Carlo for me while I'm gone," Emily said. "I have not been away from him for this long before. He will be lonely."

"I'll make sure that he is well cared for," I replied.

She nodded. "There are the stables now. It is important

when we are there that we act like we belong there. Do not show any hesitation. You will be surprised what people allow you to do when you have confidence."

I nodded. Confidence wasn't something that came to me naturally.

"I say," she went on, "that we start in the main barn again and speak to Jeremiah. I just have a feeling there was more he wanted to tell us."

I knew that Jeremiah had more to say about my brother's death, but I wasn't nearly as sure as Emily that he wanted to share what he knew with us.

We walked down the long driveway that led to the large stable. We went past all the black carriages and carts that sat along the side just waiting until they would be needed again. Carlo plopped himself down on the ground just outside the stable, and Emily and I went in.

The familiar scent of hay, dirt, and horse filled my nostrils as soon as we walked into the stables. A blond mare wearing a blanket over her back hung her head over her gate and blew a horsey breath in our direction.

From what I could see, there wasn't a single person around, just horses. Perhaps this was a good thing. Emily would see there was no one around to question and she would agree to leave. I was very uneasy about being in the stables again, not only because it was the place where Henry died but because I feared that Mr. Johnson or Masters would not be pleased if they saw us here again. I didn't think Emily's story about boarding the Dickinson family horses would go very far with them.

"There is no one here," I said. "We should return home and finish preparations for your trip."

"Not yet," Emily said and waved away my suggestion as if it was nothing more than an annoying fly buzzing around her head. She walked deeper into the stables.

I followed her, and before long, I knew exactly where she was headed. It was back to the scene of the crime, as she called it. Emily went into the stall where my brother died, but I could not go in there again. I waited outside the stall, not looking in. I had seen enough on our first visit. I shifted back and forth on my feet until a puff of hot air was blown into my ear. I turned to find Terror staring at me. I looked into the horse's eyes. There was so much sadness there. I wondered if they mirrored my own.

Turning my back to Emily, I walked over to the horse. His feed trough was full. It looked like he hadn't even touched it. Squatting down, I stuck my hand through the beams in his gate and took a large scoop of feed from the trough.

He watched me closely. I then raised the food to his mouth. At first he turned away, so I could just see his profile.

"Go on. Take it," I whispered. "Henry would want you to be strong. If you can't eat for yourself, eat for him."

He turned his mouth back in my direction, and I held my breath as his thick lips brushed across my hand and he took mouthful after mouthful of feed. We repeated this four times; I scooped the feed in my hand and he ate it. Every time Terror took the food from my hand, I felt lighter. It was as if I accomplished something, or we accomplished something together, and I knew that act would have made Henry happy.

"I don't care if it's difficult. Find a way to fix it," an angry male voice said, and it sounded like it was coming in our direction.

Terror jerked his head back from me and disappeared into his stall.

"Willa," Emily hissed at me and waved from the stall where my brother had died. "Get over here."

I dropped the last of the horse feed that was in my hand into the trough and ducked into the stall with Emily just as two men appeared around the corner. It was Mr. Johnson and Masters, the stable master.

"Yes, sir, I will do my best," Masters said in a much quieter voice.

"You had better. I have a lot riding on this, much more than you could ever understand."

Masters murmured something in reply that we couldn't hear as the two men turned and went down another row of stalls away from us. Emily stepped out of the stall and began following them.

"Emily," I whispered, but she didn't even look over her shoulder to acknowledge that she heard me.

I grimaced and followed her.

The stables were so large that they had four pens of horses that ran ninety feet from end to end of the building. Most of those were rented by local businessmen and merchants who could afford a horse but didn't have the barn or space to house it.

I found Emily peering over the edge of an empty stall. She had to kneel on a hay bale to see over it. Being much taller than she, I could just stand on my tiptoes and look over the wall. On the other side, Mr. Johnson and Masters stood in what I would guess was a tack room with harnesses, bridles, and reins hanging from the wall. Masters was waxing the leather of a giant yoke that looked better suited for oxen than horses. Mr. Johnson stood a few feet away with his arms crossed.

"You will have to be on your toes while I am in Washington, Masters," Mr. Johnson said. "I leave in two days on the afternoon train."

Emily and I shared a look. Mr. Johnson was going to Washington on the same train that Emily and her family were.

"I understand, sir," Masters said. "I know you have business in Washington."

"It's very important that I go. There are men I need to speak to that will help the cause for the South."

Masters stopped moving his rag over the yoke. "I know you sympathize with the South, sir, but . . ." He stopped talking as if he realized that he was making a grave mistake with this line of speech.

"But what?" Mr. Johnson glared at him. "How can I sympathize with the South if I live in the North, is that what you are asking?"

Masters concentrated on the yoke. "It is not my business, sir."

"You are right. It is not. Get back to work." He stomped out of the tack room, and Emily and I ducked below the stall wall to avoid being seen.

When I dared look up again, Mr. Johnson was gone and Masters threw his rag on the tack room floor like he was angry about something. He marched out of the room too.

Emily and I shared a look.

"This proves at least that Mr. Johnson has sympathies with the South," Emily said.

"Yes, but sympathies are much different than actively working with slave catchers," I replied.

She nodded. "Maybe Jeremiah could answer that."

I placed a hand on my cloak pocket and felt my brother's diary there. I had debated all morning if I should bring the diary with me on this errand to the stables. I wondered now if bringing it was a mistake. Perhaps it would have been much safer under my mattress in the Dickinson home.

I hadn't read more than a few pages. I used the excuse that I was caught up in preparing the Dickinson family for their time away, but in truth, every time I went to open the diary and read my brother's words, pain overtook me. Henry wrote himself that he would not be revealing the names of those who had done wrong in the diary, so at the moment, I felt reading it was harming myself with no clear answer in the end. And the end was what I feared. When I read the last words of my brother, he would be at an end.

"I must ask you something, Willa, and I do not believe you will like the question." Emily loosened the ribbons of her bonnet.

I waited.

"You said that Henry told you that he found a way to make money that would allow you to not have to work any longer." She looked me directly in the eye. "Could he have been the one working with the slave catcher?"

Her question took my breath away. "He would never."

"If the slave catcher was giving him a portion of his bounty to catch runaways, he might make the money he wanted rather quickly."

I shook my head emphatically. "Henry would not do that.

You heard Jeremiah when he was here. He said Henry was a good friend to him. How could Jeremiah think that if Henry was helping the slave catcher?"

"Jeremiah is a free man. Perhaps it makes a difference."

"I can't see how." I refused for one second to believe what she was suggesting. Henry would not do any of it.

"What makes a difference to me?" a man's voice asked.

CHAPTER FOURTEEN

EMILY AND I both jumped and turned to find Jeremiah York standing behind us holding two full buckets of water. His shirtsleeves were rolled up, and I could see that his muscles strained under the pressure of holding the buckets off of the ground. His glasses slipped down the bridge of his nose, but there was no way he could fix that without putting down one of the buckets.

"Jeremiah, how long have you been standing there?" I asked.

He set the buckets down and adjusted his glasses. "Long enough to see the two of you spying on Mr. Johnson and Masters. You do realize if they had seen you, it would not have been good."

Emily lifted her chin. "They would never have spied us."

"If they weren't so angry at each other, they would have. Half of Willa's head was sticking over the stable wall." He shook his head as if he couldn't believe we would be that stupid.

I grimaced. It wasn't easy being tall.

"Well, it's lucky they didn't look at us then," Emily said, seemingly unconcerned with the close call.

"What are the two of you doing back here?" Jeremiah wanted to know. "And why are you spying?"

I wasn't sure we should share the answers to his questions. We didn't know Jeremiah could be trusted with our investigation.

Emily didn't have the same qualms as she said, "We are here to find out who is behind the murder of Willa's brother, Henry. We have returned to the scene of the crime."

Jeremiah looked from Emily to me and back again. "You are investigating Henry's death."

I started to shake my head, but Emily said, "Yes, that's exactly it. To do that we need your help."

Jeremiah bent down to pick up the buckets again. "I'm sorry that Henry is dead. He was my closest friend. He was like a brother to me, but I can't help you with this." He turned and walked away toward the horse stalls.

Emily followed him, and I, of course, followed Emily.

Henry poured water into a trough for a pair of large draft horses that were in the same stall.

Then he moved on to the next stall with his bucket.

Emily wouldn't be ignored. "We have heard rumors about this place being involved with a slave catcher. What do you know about that?"

Jeremiah shook the last droplets of water out of his second bucket and turned to her. "I have worked here a year, and I have never seen a slave catcher here."

"Have you heard of any here?" Emily asked. "I assume men of that persuasion keep to the shadows."

Jeremiah didn't say anything, which made me believe that he had heard the rumors about the stables and slave catchers.

"Was Henry involved with that?" Emily asked.

Jeremiah spun around. "No. He was fighting it. He was trying to find the truth."

I gasped.

"And that was why he was killed?" Emily asked.

Jeremiah hung his head. "I am certain of it," he whispered.

"I think you need to explain from the beginning," Emily said.

I let out a breath, grateful she was taking the lead with these questions because my mind raced. What could Henry be searching for? How was he finding the truth? The truth about what exactly?

Jeremiah seemed to consider this. "I will tell you what little I know. Henry didn't share everything with me. He said it was his way of protecting me. He believed the less I knew, the less likely it was that I would become a target."

"A target for what?" Emily asked.

"For the men that Henry was spying on."

I blinked. "Henry was a spy? For who? Why?"

"A wealthy man paid him to spy on Mr. Johnson. That is why he began working here. I didn't know it for some time, but he finally told me."

"A wealthy man?" Emily asked. "Who?"

"I don't know. He wouldn't tell me. Like I told you before, he felt the less I knew, the safer I would be. He didn't want me involved in that part." He sighed.

"In that part. What does that mean?" Emily crossed her arms over her chest.

Jeremiah grimaced as if he realized that he might have said too much.

When he didn't answer her question, she asked another. "Why was he supposed to spy on Mr. Johnson?"

Jeremiah's shoulders relaxed. "Because of the rumors that you said. Mr. Johnson was known to sympathize with plantation owners who lost slaves to the North."

"Why?" I asked. "What does he care about it? Is he from the South?"

Jeremiah shook his head. "No, and I don't know why he wants to help that cause."

"And why isn't he stopped?" I asked. "Shouldn't someone stop him?"

"He's not breaking the law. He's abiding by it. It is the laws that must change. Until they do, there will always be greedy men like Mr. Johnson who want to make a profit off of others suffering."

"If you know that it's Mr. Johnson behind this, why was my brother spying? If you already have the answer then there is nothing that can be done about it."

"There is always something that can be done. I must believe that," Jeremiah said. "I must believe that to keep going."

Emily tapped a glove-covered finger to her cheek as if she was deep in thought. "To learn why Henry was killed, we have to learn what he knew." She looked to me. "The only way to do that is to spy on Mr. Johnson ourselves."

I stared at her. She could not be serious. We were young women. We couldn't be spies. And we didn't even know who or what we were spying for.

Before I could make any of what I thought were very logical arguments against it, Emily said, "And he just so happens to be headed to Washington on my train. We have no choice but to go and find out what his real purpose is for traveling to the capital."

I squinted at her as if I didn't hear her correctly. "We?"

"Yes, you need to join the family in Washington."

"I can't do that. Miss O'Brien has so much work planned for us to do while the family is away. We are cleaning the house top to bottom, and we are organizing the attic and the storage areas, so that moving at the end of the year will be easier. I can't leave. Miss O'Brien would never allow it."

Emily lifted her chin. "You work for the Dickinson family, not for Margaret. It is not her decision. You will be on that train with us." She turned to Jeremiah then as if the conversation was over. "Who else is here that we can speak to about Mr. Johnson?"

"Please don't," Jeremiah said. "I implore you to just go home. If Mr. Johnson knew you were here he would be angry. If you really do plan to follow him in Washington, I think that it is best that you leave here now. You don't want to tip him off."

Emily nodded. "I suppose you're right, and we need to go home to make arrangements for Willa to join my family on the train." Without saying goodbye, she headed for the stable doors.

Jeremiah looked to me. "This is a bad idea."

I agreed with him, but Emily was my employer. If she wanted me to go to Washington with the family, I had to go.

I glanced in the direction that Emily disappeared. "Is there anything you can tell us to help us? Anything at all? If it is dangerous, the more information that we have before we leave, the better."

Jeremiah looked to me. "Did you open the package I gave you?"

"I did."

"And what was it?"

"You don't know?"

He shook his head. "I think I know."

Unsure why I was telling him, I said, "It is my brother's diary."

Jeremiah frowned. "That is what I was afraid it was. I hope that he didn't write anything damning in it." He stepped closer to me. "You have to be careful with it. If the wrong person knew that you had that diary, you would be in danger."

I stumbled back from him. "The wrong person? Mr. Johnson, you mean?"

"You must be careful. Keep it safe. It's more than your life at stake, so much more."

Emily reappeared. "Willa, are you coming? We have a great deal to do."

My chest heaved up and down. I did my best to calm my breathing, so Emily didn't see how upset I was. "Yes, I'm coming. I was just asking Jeremiah about Terror and how the horse was doing."

Without missing a beat, Jeremiah said, "He is on the mend. He's eating a bit of his feed again and drinking water." He shook his head. "He is not himself just yet. He misses Henry terribly."

That made two of us.

CHAPTER FIFTEEN

THE NEXT NIGHT, I stumbled into my small room in the Dickinson home and fell into my bed with my shoes still on. Somehow Emily had convinced her brother to get a ticket for me to accompany the family to Washington. She claimed that she would be more comfortable traveling if she had my help, and without me, she would not go. Since Mr. Dickinson very much wanted his eldest daughter to see Washington, the family agreed.

But not everyone was happy about it, namely Miss Lavinia.

Margaret was upset, too, because she would be left alone to do much of the work in the home. So for the last day, she had put me through my paces and had me work double time before I left with the family on tomorrow's afternoon train. The compromise was, I would not accompany Emily to Philadelphia and during that three-week time would do all the work that Margaret planned for me in the original five-week period.

Even though every muscle in my body ached, my mind would not rest. It thrummed with anticipation over the adventure I was about to embark on the next day. I had never been so far from home before. I hadn't even been to Boston in my lifetime. My whole existence had been within thirty miles of the spot I lay at that moment. Tomorrow, I would be traveling hundreds of miles.

Who would have ever thought that would happen to me? Perhaps Henry had. He'd had the capacity to think that large. He was open to possibilities. I was not, or at least, I had not been until he died.

Thinking of Henry, I sat up in my bed, kicked my shoes off of my sore feet, and reached under my mattress for his diary. As hard as it was to read my brother's words, I knew that I must. I opened the book and let it fall open to an early page. I thought that if I read the entries in random order, it might be less painful for me to "hear" my brother's voice again.

January 2, 1855

Her name was Belinda. She was the first runaway that I met in person. She came to the stables just like I thought would happen. All the signs were there that runaways were being directed to the stables with the purpose of trapping them. They believe it is a safe haven on the railroad, but it is not.

They were being chased into a net. It turns my stomach to think of how many people this happened to before we were made aware of it.

What I don't know is how Johnson was spreading these lies that the stables are safe. No one would believe Johnson. Anyone on the railroad would take one look at him and know he was on the wrong side of this. I hate to judge a man, but he's mean and looks mean. Something evil oozes off that person like a living and breathing sore.

There must be someone else involved, someone that people trust and would listen to. But who?

How many men, women, and children were so close to freedom to be caught this far north and sent back? I try not to dwell on those thoughts for too long or they will overcome me. If I am overcome, I will not be able to keep others from the same fate. When this is all over, I will let the tears fall. Until then, I must hold fast.

My employer is happy with the work I have done and has agreed with me that Johnson is part of all of this, but there is a second man involved. We don't know who that is yet. It is my job to find him. When I do, we will be able to put a stop to Johnson and this man and will have saved countless lives.

I just don't know how to find this other person, but I must.

As for Belinda, I pray she is safe in Canada now, but I can never know for sure what happens to those we help. When I first told her to leave the stables, she did not believe me. I do not blame her. I'm a white man. Why would she believe me? White men had hunted her for weeks. If Jeremiah had not been there to back my story, she surely would have been caught and sent back. I have to believe that she made it. I have to believe that this wasn't all for nothing.

It was the end of the entry, and I was too tired to read on. I set the diary aside, blew out the candle, and fell asleep fully clothed.

I HAD NEVER been on a train before. There had never been any reason to be. I was born in Amherst and lived there my whole life. Everywhere that I had ever gone, I could walk to. The number of carriage rides I had been on could be counted on one hand. Mrs. Patten hadn't believed in me using the carriage or a wagon for boardinghouse errands. And in truth, I had been so intimidated by the stern woman, I had been afraid to ask.

I stood on the platform a few feet from Mrs. Dickinson and her daughters, holding an old carpetbag that had been my mother's. All of my worldly possessions were inside it, except for my brother's diary, which I kept close to my body.

Very early that morning, I woke and had sewn a snug pocket on the inside of my cloak to keep the diary safe.

The Dickinsons' many trunks and cases were already inside the train, as a porter had arrived at the Dickinson home this morning to transfer them to the station.

Steam blew out from under the locomotive, and black smoke billowed out of the engine's chimneys. A conductor stood at the head of the train speaking with the soot-covered man in the engine room. The conductor wore a double-breasted wool jacket and a flat-topped hat. A gold chain ran from pocket to pocket on the right side of his jacket. His hat did not protect his ears from the cold wind, and they were bright red. He nodded at something the train engineer said and started toward the Dickinson family.

"Mrs. Dickinson." The conductor greeted Emily's mother with a smile. "It is a pleasure to have you and your family on the train today. The station is indebted to Mr. Dickinson for all he has done. Without him, we wouldn't have this lovely station right here in Amherst. We will give you and your daughters the utmost care on your journey to show our thanks."

Mrs. Dickinson gave him a nervous smile, and I started to think she wasn't looking forward to this trip at all. "We appreciate your kindness. We are grateful for this station just as much as you are. Travel is challenging enough. It would be made much more so if we had to travel farther afield to meet the train."

Emily spoke up, "You must also know that my father advocated for this station for purely selfish reasons as well. He travels for business often. It is much easier for him to do that with a station in Amherst."

The conductor laughed. "I don't know many young women who would come out and be so blunt about their father's motivations."

"More should," Emily said. "When you understand better why a person does something, you can appreciate it more."

The conductor seemed to consider this and regarded Emily with a peculiar look on his face. It was an expression that I had seen often on listeners when they were around Emily. It was a mix of confusion and awe. It was as if they couldn't believe what she had just said and at the same time, they didn't quite understand it either.

The conductor noticed me then. "And who is this?" He eyed me with suspicion.

I was certain my plain dress and the fraying edge on my cloak, which I had mended countless times, made it clear I was not a relative of the Dickinson family.

"This is our maid, Willa Noble," Mrs. Dickinson said. "She will be accompanying us to the capital."

"Oh," the conductor said. "I would think that the Dickinson family would need some help with traveling. Should I show her to the second-class cabin?"

"No," Emily said quickly. "Lavinia and I would like Willa to stay with us. We don't know when we will be in need of her services."

Mrs. Dickinson frowned as if she didn't like this idea at all, but she didn't want to argue with her daughter in front of a stranger. "Austin and I each have our own cabin. The girls are sharing."

The conductor removed a piece of paper from the pocket of his coat. "Ah yes, I see that right here. Your cabins are prepared if you are ready to board. I know ladies like to get settled before we leave the station."

"I would like to board," Mrs. Dickinson said. "I tire from standing too long."

"Yes, of course," the conductor said and took the small case that she was holding from her hands. "Let us get you settled, and I will come back for the younger Miss Dickinsons."

The family agreed.

When the conductor and Mrs. Dickinson disappeared into the train car, Emily asked, "Where is Austin? If he is not careful he will miss the train."

"He is probably with Susan, spending every last moment he can, until this train must depart," Miss Lavinia said.

Emily looked as if she didn't like this idea in the least.

"He was quite sour that Father didn't allow her to come on

this trip," Miss Lavinia went on and glanced at me. "It is hard for me to understand that a maid is permitted on this trip, but Susan, who will be a member of our family in a year's time, is not."

Before Emily could answer, the conductor reappeared. "Ladies, your mother is all settled. Let us find your cabin on the train as well." He took the cases that the two sisters held from their hands and gestured to them to get on the train.

Both Emily and Miss Lavinia lifted their skirts and climbed aboard.

Before I could follow, the conductor turned to me. "You're last name is Noble, correct?"

I nodded.

He looked me in the eye. "You would not be related to Henry Noble, would you?"

"Henry is—was my brother." I held back a wince, afraid that this man was going to tell me how Henry had stolen or outsmarted him in some way.

He nodded. "He was a fine young man."

I wanted to ask him more about how he knew Henry, but the whistle on the train blew with a warning that it would soon be time to leave.

"Time to board," he said.

Holding my carpetbag to my chest, I climbed onto the train. On the way to the cabin I would share with the Dickinson sisters, the space was close. There was not enough room for two people to walk by each other. If another person wanted to pass me, I had to turn and press my back flat to the wall. This was certainly a time that my large size for a woman was unwelcome.

Emily and Miss Lavinia, both small women, glided through the corridors like they were made for them.

"This is your cabin," the conductor said, pointing at cabin number seventeen. He slid the pocket door open, and Emily and Miss Lavinia went inside.

Miss Lavinia looked around the empty cabin. "And our trunks and cases?"

"Those are in the luggage compartment and will be delivered to your hotel just as soon as we arrive. In all likelihood, they will beat you to your rooms. Porters at the Washington station are as quick as light."

"Thank you," Miss Lavinia said. "Please take care of them." She put a coin in his hand.

"Of course, miss," the conductor said with a nod and stepped out of the cabin.

"Willa, don't just stand there looking like a statue. Have a seat," Emily said, removing her bonnet, tossing it on a shelf, and sitting up by the window.

Miss Lavinia sat across from her sister in the middle of her bench, making it clear that I was not welcome on that side of the cabin.

I sat next to Emily. "Thank you."

Emily studied me. "Look at you. You're as tight as a drum. Have you not traveled before?"

I shook my head. "I've not gone anywhere. Do you travel often?" I asked.

She glanced at me. "No. I have all that I need right here. I do not have the taste for travel."

I didn't know if she meant right here as in Amherst or

something else. When Emily spoke, I always thought there was a second meaning to her words. My understanding of what they meant was never going to be clear, and Emily wasn't one to stop and explain her meaning to me or anyone else. If a person was brilliant like Susan Gilbert, perhaps she would be able to understand all of what Emily said.

I was not brilliant. I was a simple housemaid who had been caught up in something larger than myself, something that was larger than Henry, for it had entrapped him and led to his death. Maybe it was wise to leave it all alone and let the dead bury the dead. Then I thought back to Henry's journal entry that I had read and the woman named Belinda. He had saved a person. Was it that act or ones like it that cost him his life?

Emily's voice broke into my thoughts. "I'm making this trip for my father, and . . ." she trailed off.

I knew her second reason, which was to spy on Mr. Johnson. While we had been on the platform, I looked for him but did not see him. I hoped he was in fact on this train. If he wasn't, I was on the trip with the Dickinsons for no reason at all.

I looked out the window then, and to my surprise, I saw Mr. Johnson on the platform. He wore a long overcoat and a black bowler hat with a brown feather attached to the brim.

The stable owner looked around the platform with a gaze that said he was taking in every detail around him. His mouth twisted in a small crooked line. People on the platform stepped out of the way to let him pass. He gave off an air of someone that you didn't block from his purpose.

I glanced at Emily, and she was chatting with Miss Lavinia. She didn't know that Mr. Johnson was on the platform. I bit my lip. When I looked back to where Mr. Johnson had stood, he was gone.

The train whistled again. The conductor shouted, "All aboard!" The closed window in our cabin muffled his cry, but it could still be heard. People hugged loved ones and waved. The platform cleared. The train jerked once and pulled away from the station.

There was a catch in my heart as I saw Amherst Station disappear. It was as if I lost something in that moment, but I could not for the life of me understand what it was.

The train picked up speed, and the town dissolved completely into farmland and forest. I settled back into my seat. There was no getting off now. At least for the next fortnight, I would be away from home. It felt like a wild thing to be traveling so fast and so far. It would take two days on the train to make it to Washington.

Miss Lavinia removed needlepoint from her case. She was working on a sampler. Shutting the case, she said, "I don't know why you brought that maid with you. We do not need her to make our way to Washington. She's too young for anyone to consider her a chaperone. She's younger than I am!"

"Vinnie," Emily said in a soothing voice, "Willa will be very helpful when we are in the city. She can carry our shopping bags and make arrangements for us. It will save us a great deal of time."

Miss Lavinia folded her arms across her traveling suit. "Did you ask Father if she could come?"

"There was no time to write him about it. When Father is away, Austin is in charge of the family, and he said that it was all right for Willa to come."

It was not lost on me that they both spoke like I wasn't even there.

"Austin," Miss Lavinia snorted. "We will be lucky if he even made the train."

"He's on the train," Emily said with full confidence. "Austin likes to test boundaries, but when it comes right down to it, he wants to make Father proud."

"If that is the case, why is he thinking of moving west after he's done at Cambridge?"

"He's just pushing boundaries again. He and Susan will never permanently leave Amherst. They can't." She sighed. "In any case, I paid for Willa's ticket, so it should be no wonder at all why Willa is here. I had some prize money stashed away from the bread and cakes competitions I won over the years."

"There are much better ways to spend that money," Miss Lavinia grumbled. "Just take note that Father won't be happy with all of this. Father believes that he has to be asked first and needs to approve all things. I thought you would have learned that by the age of twenty-four."

"You say this because you are afraid to push him. I push him just far enough. Believe me, it makes a difference. As for Willa, there is nothing to worry about. Willa barely eats a crumb, and she can sleep on the floor in our room if necessary. Having her with us on the trip will be of no consequence to Father.

One of her statements was wrong. I ate much more than a crumb. I wasn't a small, light thing like the Dickinson girls. I very much hoped that she was only making a point with her sister that I wouldn't have very much to eat.

Miss Lavinia snorted and saw me there open-mouthed. "Have you been listening to us the whole time?" she snapped.

I stared at her. How could I not hear their conversation? "I—I—"

There was a knock at the cabin door.

Emily told the person on the other side to come in.

"Miss Dickinson, Miss Lavinia," the train conductor said when he looked to me. "Miss Noble."

"Willa," I said. "It's just Willa."

He nodded. "Willa. I'm here to let you know that since we are underway, you are welcome to move about the train. There is a dining car to the left when you leave your cabin. Beyond that, we have a lounge car. It's a very popular place and seating is limited. If you would like to sit in the lounge, I suggest you find a spot now."

"I think we are very happy right here for the moment. Thank you," Emily said. "Do you know if my brother made the train?"

"Oh yes, he's resting in his compartment right now. He nearly missed the train; he was the last person to board."

Emily gave her sister an "I told you so" look when the conductor said that.

I cleared my throat and hoped that changing the subject would stop the bickering between the two sisters; in particular, I hoped it would stop the bickering about me.

As Miss Lavinia began to work on her needlepoint, I whispered to Emily, "I saw Mr. Johnson on the platform. I believe he boarded this very train."

"You did?" Emily asked. "Why didn't you point him out at the time?"

"You and Miss Lavinia were having a conversation, and I didn't want to interrupt." I shifted on the leather seat.

"Ah, the conversation about you," she whispered. "Just bear in mind that Vinnie doesn't like anyone at first. She didn't even like Susan when she became my friend. There is a jealousy there."

"Emily, I'm sitting right here and can hear everything that you have to say." Miss Lavinia threaded her needle. "This cabin is too small even for whispers. You had better not be hiding anything from me."

Emily's eyes slanted in her direction. "Oh, I know. I'm not trying to hide anything at all."

That was a lie.

The train whistled, and I jumped in my seat.

"It does that when it makes a crossing," Miss Lavinia said. "You must become used to it."

My heart was pounding, but Miss Lavinia and Emily seemed to be perfectly calm about travel. Emily set her case on her lap and began to look through her books.

"Can you read, Willa?" Emily asked looking up from her case. Perhaps she could feel my tension as I stared out the window.

"Yes. I love reading, in fact. My mother made sure even if Henry and I didn't learn anything else we could read."

"It seems to me that you had a very wise mother," Emily said. "The ride will be long." She handed a book to me. It was *Jane Eyre*. "This one will keep you occupied for a little while. It's one of my favorites."

"It's one that Father didn't want you to read," Miss Lavinia said as she threaded her embroidery needle with a new color. This was a vibrant red.

Emily shrugged. "True, but I did anyway, and you are one to criticize; you read it too."

"Because you read it first and got away with it."

"It is good to know that I can lead you astray, Little Sister," Emily said with a laugh.

I ran my hand along the cover of the book. The spine had cracks in it as if it had been read many times before. I was happy to see that. I didn't want to be the one to break the spine first.

The sisters continued to argue as I opened to page one. Maybe it was just the way they communicated. In any case, I was grateful for a book that would be an escape from Emily's aloofness and Miss Lavinia's prickliness if just for a short while.

CHAPTER SIXTEEN

M Y NOSE WAS buried in the book. My heart ached every time Mr. Rochester appeared on the page. He was so tormented. I thought Jane could help him, but I was starting to wonder why she would choose to. Maybe it would be better if she struck out on a life of her own. I couldn't wait to read what happened next. What would she choose?

"Willa," Emily whispered in a tone that told me that it wasn't the first time she had whispered my name.

I came out of the deep depths of a good story. I had been on the gloomy moors of England in the dreary hallways of Thornfield Hall. It took a moment to remember where I was.

She pointed at her sister across from us. Miss Lavinia was slumped against the window fast asleep. She held her embroidery limply on her lap.

Emily then pointed to the door. I nodded. She wanted us to leave the compartment. I was pained to go. How hard it was to leave a good book behind! I reluctantly put the copy of *Jane*

Eyre down on the bench beside me. I knew we hadn't come onto the train to read.

Outside of our compartment, the rock and rattle of the train was that much more pronounced. I didn't know if it was because the outer part of the train was less insulated or because we were standing upright. I braced my hand against the wall.

"This is much like being on a boat," Emily said. "I imagine we're going to feel like we are still on a train long after our feet hit the immovable ground."

"What are we doing out here?" I asked.

"You said that you saw Mr. Johnson about to board the train, and we are going to find him. We need to know what he's up to. It's time we got to work on the real reason we are here."

"How are we going to find him? We can't knock on every compartment's door," I said.

The train jerked a little on the track, and I braced my hands on the wall again.

"That's easy. I think I know where a man like Mr. Johnson would go." She stepped around me and started to the back of the train.

I could do nothing but follow her. We went through the first-class car, where the passengers were in small yet comfortable rooms behind closed compartment doors, and then went into the second-class passenger cars. People sat in rows throughout the compartment. They were pressed close together as if they were in crowded church pews.

Many of them were sleeping, and their heads lulled to one side or the other. No one said a word to us or even glanced in our direction. It was hard for me to believe that a person like Mr. Johnson would sit in such a crowded place. He certainly had a compartment of his very own. As a stable owner, I assumed he could afford a first-class ticket.

After the second-class car came the dining car, which was all but empty. The evening meal would not be for another hour. Silverware and crystal glistened ready and waiting on the tables covered in crisp white linens. Each table held a vase of flowers and a candle in a glass votive just waiting to be lit. I had to wonder where the flowers came from in February.

After the dining car, we came into the lounge car. It was a room of windows even over our heads. I could see the bright blue sky. The room smelled of tobacco and people packed closely together. I touched a hand to my nose. Neither was a scent I cared for. It seemed that every man in the compartment was smoking either a pipe or cigar. Blue smoke was thick in the air. The compartment went dead quiet when we stepped inside. We were the only women in the space.

A man with a luxurious mustache shook the newspaper that he had been reading rather aggressively, and that seemed to be all that was needed to break the spell. Conversation resumed.

I grabbed Emily's arm. "I don't think many young ladies are welcome in this part of the train."

"Nonsense. The conductor told us about the lounge car himself." Emily stared up as the sky and tree limbs flew above the train. "The world is gone by," she murmured, and then she murmured the same words again as if she were testing them.

I looked around the lounge, and I finally spotted Mr. Johnson on a leather-covered bench. He was smoking and staring out the window.

Most of the men in the compartment were doing the same.

It was as if they were each in their own little worlds, save for the few that resumed lively conversations about politics. I supposed it made sense that politics would be a main topic of conversation among the passengers headed to Washington.

I touched Emily's arm. "He's here," I whispered.

Emily's lips curved into a smile. "Just as I expected. You will find, Willa, that most conventional people are predictable as to what they will do next."

"I don't think anyone would say that Mr. Johnson was conventional."

"Conventional in thinking."

I wasn't sure what Emily meant by that, but I guessed I was quite conventional in my thinking too. I certainly didn't have a mind like Emily, or like any member of the Dickinson family for that matter. Was it because I had been born without it or was it that I was of another class and I didn't have time to nurture it?

"Now what do we do?" I asked.

"It's a very good question," a male voice said. "I was going to ask the same thing."

I turned and gasped as I found Matthew Thomas standing in the middle of the train car. He was out of his policeman's uniform and in a traveling suit.

"Matthew!" I yelped. "I mean Officer Thomas, what are you doing here?"

Emily raised her brow at my reaction.

"I should be asking you the same thing," Matthew said.

Emily spoke for me. "My father asked my brother, Austin, to bring our mother, Lavinia, and me to visit him in Washington before his term in Congress came to a close. I brought

Willa along as my maid. She has been a great help to me already."

Matthew pressed his lips into a thin line. "These are dangerous times for young ladies to be traveling."

Emily sniffed. "That's something a man would say about any time past, present, or future. They will always claim the times are too dangerous for a woman to travel. And my brother is on the train somewhere. We have nothing to fear."

Matthew frowned. To our right, a man stood up from a booth where he sat alone and left the lounge. "Let us sit before we make a scene," Matthew said.

Matthew sat on one side of the booth, and Emily and I sat on the other. I was on the inside closest to the window, feeling trapped.

"Why are you on this train, Officer Thomas?" Emily asked.

He glanced in the direction of Mr. Johnson.

"Are you following Mr. Johnson?" I whispered.

"Shh." Matthew put a finger to his lips. "Don't say names. It is loud in the lounge now, but you never know when there will be a lull in the conversation and he might be able to hear you."

"Are you following *him*?" Emily was sure to emphasize that she didn't use Mr. Johnson's name.

"Yes, and I am only telling you this so that the two of you will stay away from him."

"Why?" I asked. "Why are you following him? Is it because of the rumors?"

He looked from Emily to me. "What rumors?"

"That he might be working with a slave catcher." I said the last two words barely above a whisper.

"No, it's not because of that."

"Then does it have to do with my brother?"

Matthew pressed his lips together and said nothing.

Emily sat up straight in her seat. "Do you think he had something to do with Henry's death?"

Matthew looked out the window.

"So you believe that Henry was killed too?" I asked.

Matthew folded his hands in his lap. "I'm open to the possibility. We have witnesses that have told us that Henry was in over his head, and he took the job at the stables to spy on Mr. Johnson at the request of his employer."

"Whose employer?"

Matthew glanced this way and that as if to make certain that no one was listening to us. "Henry's. I'm to Washington under the guise of a sightseeing trip to keep an eye on him. I have an uncle who lives in the city, so it made the most sense for me to go."

"Is this your uncle Nevin?" I asked. Now that he mentioned it, I recalled that he once told me he had an uncle who was a police officer in Washington. It was why Mathew had wanted to be an officer too.

"Yes, but he is retired from service and is living off his pension. As he has not been well, this trip gives me an opportunity to keep an eye on a suspect and visit my uncle."

"I'm sorry to hear that about your uncle," I said.

He nodded at my words.

Emily's forehead wrinkled, and I knew she had to be wondering how I would know that Matthew had an uncle. She must think that it would be an odd bit of information for me to have about a police officer. I knew Emily would never let it go. She would ask me about it later when I least expected it and was caught the most off guard.

Matthew rubbed the back of his neck. "I wish you both weren't on this train. It complicates things."

"How so, Officer?" Emily asked.

He placed his hands on the table. "I know you have been to the stables at least once. Why?"

I dared not look at Emily for fear my expression might give something away.

Emily leaned back in her seat. "Are you spying on us, too, Officer?"

"No, but when I was there, I saw you."

"Why didn't you say anything to us?" I asked.

"I couldn't risk being seen," he muttered. "So you can see why I'm concerned that you are here now. You need to stay away from that man. Promise me you will."

"Officer Thomas," Emily said. "We are going to Washington at the request of my father. Why on earth would you believe it was anything more than that?"

Matthew covered his eyes and groaned.

CHAPTER SEVENTEEN

A s LONG AS we were on the train, Emily and I agreed to stay away from Mr. Johnson. There was too great a risk of Matthew seeing what we were up to. If he told Emily's father, we would surely be sent on the next train home to Amherst.

After dinner, the Dickinson sisters and I were sitting in our cabin when there was a knock on the door. "Turndown service."

Miss Lavinia stretched and yawned. "Finally, I am ready to go sleep. Travel is exhausting."

"Like she hasn't been napping on the train most of the afternoon," Emily whispered to me.

I looked out the window so no one could see my smile.

"Come in!" Emily called.

A young porter dressed all in white stood in the doorway. "Good evening, Miss Dickinson and Miss Dickinson." He merely nodded at me. "If you wouldn't mind stepping out of the cabin for just a moment, I will turn down your bed."

I looked around the cabin. Bed? What bed? There wasn't any more space in the cabin for a chair much less a bed.

Emily and Miss Lavinia didn't seem nearly as perplexed as I did and stepped out of the cabin, where Emily said, "Come, Vinnie, let us wash up while the porter does his work. Willa can stay here and tip him when he is done." She tucked two coins in my hand before she and Miss Lavinia walked down the corridor toward the washroom.

Through the doorway, I watched in amazement as the porter removed the cushions from the seats where we'd just been sitting. He then released latches that I had not noticed on the wall behind where Emily and I had sat. He pulled down a small bed complete with a thin mattress, linens, and even a pillow. He then tucked the seat cushions into the empty compartment.

He ended the turndown service by fluffing the pillow and setting two pieces of candy on the pillow.

He smiled at me as he left the room. "The world is quite amazing, isn't it?"

I nodded dumbly and handed him the coins Emily had given me, and he handed me a piece of candy in return before he went on to the next room.

In the middle of the night, I got up from the blanket where I slept on the floor. Emily and Miss Lavinia were sleeping soundly in their pull-down bed on the wall. With care, I opened the compartment door and slipped out. I had my coat wrapped tightly around myself. My plan was to run to the privy and back as quickly as possible.

I made it to the bathroom without incident and almost made it to our compartment when a familiar voice whispered my name.

I looked over my shoulder to see Matthew peering out of the second-class car. He wore a white shirt, trousers, and no stockings or shoes on his feet. I was acutely aware of my hair being down over my shoulders and my night dress sticking out from under my coat.

"Matthew, go back to sleep."

"What are you doing up in the middle of the night?" He closed the door to the second-class cabin behind him.

I was relieved that he did that; I didn't want anyone to overhear our conversation. As we were on the platform where the two train cars intersected, we shook and bounced, and the rattling sounds and screeching of metal on metal was almost more than I could take.

"If you must know, I am returning to my compartment after going to the privy."

In the moonlight streaming through the windows in the train doors on either side, I could see Matthew blush. Good, now perhaps he would leave me alone. I turned to go.

I was about to slide open the door into the first-class car when he said, "Why did you ask me to stay away? I thought we were friends."

I closed my eyes for a moment, and then against my better judgment, I turned around. "We were—we are friends, Matthew. You have always been a good friend to Henry and me."

"I have been. Why do you think I'm trying so hard to find out what happened to him? It's for him and for you."

I stared at him, and my heart lurched. "Are you really traveling to Washington as an officer?"

He looked away and out one of the windows. "As far as the police department is concerned, I am going there to visit my ill uncle, which is true. They do not know what else I might be up to."

"Does the department think Henry was purposely killed?" I asked.

"It's been ruled an accident." He looked back to me. "Caused by Henry."

"But—but what about the burn marks on Terror the horse?"

He didn't ask me how I knew about those. I supposed he didn't have to. He saw Emily and me visit the stables.

"Henry wouldn't do that," I said. "He found trouble, I know this, but he would never hurt any living thing."

"I know," Matthew said quietly. "I could have kept a better eye on you both if you hadn't asked me to stay away."

I felt like I had been punched in the gut. Was he saying that it was my fault that my brother was killed?

"Mrs. Patten didn't like you coming around," I said more sharply than I intended. "I couldn't afford to lose my place."

"You don't need that job. You don't even need to work for the Dickinsons. If we married, I would take care of you as your husband. You could have a home with me and our children. Henry could have lived with us too."

"You couldn't support all of us on your officer's salary. I know your wages are low."

He sucked in a breath as if I was the one who punched him this time.

"So that is why you refused me, because I didn't make enough money?" He didn't even try to hide the pain in his voice.

"No, that had nothing to do with it."

"Then why?" He was pleading now.

I closed my mouth because I wasn't sure it was a question I could answer for myself in the deepest part of my heart. Because I knew what a man could do to a woman? Because I knew how my father left my mother?

Because I was afraid that I would just take his offer for security and not for love, like my mother had. I didn't want to have the same fate as my mother. I had a nice place in the Dickinson home. Was I willing to give that up for a house of my own with a man I cared for but didn't know if I loved?

I couldn't say any of those things to Matthew. I didn't even want to admit them to myself.

"I have to get back to my compartment. If the Dickinson sisters wake up and find I'm missing, I could be in trouble."

It might have been a trick of the light, but I thought I saw tears in his eyes. "All right," he whispered. "Good night, Willa." He opened the door to the second-class car and disappeared behind it.

"Good night, Matthew," I whispered to the door.

THE JOSTLING AND bustle to get off the train was overwhelming. A Black man who said he was from Mr. Dickinson's residence in Washington met us with a carriage. He reassured the family that their luggage was already on the way to their hotel.

"There you are, Austin," Emily said as the family climbed in the carriage. "I'm happy to see that you made the train."

Her brother grinned at her. "There wasn't any chance that I would miss it, Sister." He lent his hand to his mother first and then his sisters, helping them into the large black carriage. To me, he said, "You can sit up front with the driver." He climbed into the carriage with his family and shut the door.

The driver folded up the step the family used to get into the carriage. "You just hop on the front seat, and we will be underway."

As I climbed onto the seat, I stared open-mouthed at everything around me. There were just so many people. Fine ladies and gentlemen walking into the station, servants running this way and that, people selling tickets for the next train right there on the street. And the chatter, the noise—I had never heard anything like it.

Matthew was nowhere to be seen. I would be lying if I said that I hadn't looked for him when we got off the train.

The driver hopped onto the seat next to me and smiled at me. "Your first time in Washington, I take it."

"It's my first time anywhere," I said in awe.

He laughed. "Well, this is an interesting choice for your first venture. The nation's capital is like no other city on earth," he said with pride. "I was born here and have lived here my whole life. I would never leave."

"That's what I think of my home in Amherst that I didn't ever want to leave."

"Leaving what you know is hard." He flicked the reins. "Betty Sue, let's go home."

"Your horse is named Betty Sue?" I asked, starting to feel at ease.

"Yes, after my dear sweet mother. God rest her soul." He looked to me as he expertly pulled into traffic between two delivery wagons. It was a tight spot that I didn't think any driver back in Amherst would dare try. However, I thought, when you lived in a big city like this, you had to take chances to get where you were going or you would be stuck in the same place forever.

"I'm Buford Buckley, by the way. I'm the driver for Mr. Dickinson while he's in Washington. He's a fair man. Perhaps a little stern, but I have driven for all sorts of men. I would much prefer to work for an exacting and honest fellow than for a crook. We have our share of those in this city, believe you me."

"I'm Willa Noble, and I'm the Dickinson family maid; well, second maid. I'm here to help the family any way that I can."

Of course, I didn't say a word about Mr. Johnson or my brother.

"What will you do when Mr. Dickinson goes back to Massachusetts for good? Are you worried about losing your position?" I asked.

"Oh, I'm not worried. There will be another representative coming in, and in a place like this, important men are always looking for skilled drivers such as myself. Now, pay attention, I'm going to point out all the highlights to you while we ride to the hotel where you will be staying."

He pointed out the sights: the half-built Washington Monument, the Smithsonian, and the Capitol. Then we traveled down Pennsylvania Avenue and passed the president's home. It was a grand white building with foreboding pillars in the front and a great green lawn that appeared to go on forever.

Buford flicked the rein again to encourage Betty Sue to pick up the pace. "President Pierce is in there right now, deep into the bottle if you ask me."

"He drinks spirits?" I asked.

He glanced at me. "In my opinion, all politicians do, but

not many like the president. Can't blame the man for that. He buried all three of his children. His wife is broken over it like any mother would be."

I stared at him. "How do you know all that?"

"You should know, Miss Willa; servants talk."

That was true.

"And here is where you will stay, Miss Willa. Right here on the corner."

I stared. It was a grand building that had a wide promenade in the front of it. Like the president's home it was white and striking against the blue sky and fluffy clouds. Black paint meticulously outlined each window, and there were more chimneys than I could ever possibly count.

"Oh my," I said.

"Wait until you see the inside of it," he said with a wink. He pulled up alongside the building, and young men in suits and small caps were there in a flash opening the carriage door for the family and helping the ladies out one by one.

"It's stunning," Miss Lavinia said.

For once, I wasn't the only one who was impressed with my surroundings.

"Your trunks and other luggage have already been delivered to your room," one of the porters said with a bow.

"Wonderful," Austin said and marched into the hotel without so much as a backward glance. His sisters and mother followed at a much slower pace.

I looked to Buford. "Thank you for the tour. It was very nice to meet you."

"Don't you worry, Miss Willa. You will see me again. I'll be driving you around this city while you're here. Be sure to enjoy yourself while you're in town, you hear me?"

"I will. I will see you soon," I said with a smile, and holding the carpetbag close to my side, I went into the hotel.

A uniformed porter stepped into my path. "Where do you think you are going? The Willard is only for guests and their parties."

"I—I—" I stuttered and looked around frantically for one of the Dickinson family members. I spotted them waiting to walk up the stairs, presumably to their rooms. Emily looked in my direction, and I waved at her.

"There. I'm with the Dickinson party."

"You? Likely story. Now, I think it's time for you to leave."

Emily walked over to us. "What is the problem here?" she asked the porter.

"This *woman* claims to be a member of your party," he said with something close to a sneer.

Emily stared back at him. "She is. She's our maid."

The porter scowled as if he didn't think much about that. It seemed to me that maids weren't held in high regard in the grand city.

There was a lot I would have to learn about life in Washington if I was going to survive the next two weeks.

CHAPTER EIGHTEEN

M UCH TO MY relief, the whole Dickinson family was so weary from travel that we had a light dinner at the hotel and retired for the night. As expected, I was in Miss Lavinia and Emily's room. While the sisters had plush beds to retire to, I was given the settee in the small parlor off of their room. As tall as I was, my feet hung off the end of it, but if I slept curled up in a ball it was quite comfortable. I imagined that I fell asleep before my head hit the pillow.

The next day, I was awake before the sisters, and was happy for my ability to rise early. My goal for the time in Washington was not to be a nuisance to the family, because I knew Emily was the only one of them who wanted me there. Mr. Dickinson still didn't know I had accompanied the family on their trip. I prepared for the day, taking extra care with my hair, putting away my bed linens in a closet, and tucking my carpetbag away there too.

I had everything settled before the sun was fully up, and

since I had the time, I finished *Jane Eyre*, which ended quite happily in my opinion.

The sisters woke a while later and had their breakfast. Along with their breakfast tray there was a note from their father. Miss Lavinia read it to herself and said, "Father has business today, so we won't see him until this evening. Mother would like to rest in her room, and goodness knows what Austin might be up to. Perhaps sowing wild oats before his wedding."

Emily frowned at her sister. "He would never treat Susan so poorly. Susan is a treasure and should be treated as such."

Miss Lavinia paused at this assessment as if she didn't completely agree with her older sister on that point. "In any case, we are free to amuse ourselves in the city. Father has given us the use of his carriage and driver."

"Excellent," Emily said with a smile. "I do have plans, you know."

After the sisters had a leisurely breakfast in their room and put on the new day dresses they had bought specifically for the trip, we left the hotel. When we walked up to Mr. Dickinson's carriage, Buford smiled at me. "Told you that you'd see me again, didn't I?" He then turned to the Dickinson sisters. "Where would you like to go, ladies?"

"We want to see the sights," Emily said.

"And the ice cream shop," Miss Lavinia said. "Our father told us there is a place that serves ice cream all year long."

"There surely is. We will go there first."

Ice cream—and before noontime? How extravagant!

He helped Miss Lavinia and Emily into the carriage. I climbed up onto what I was starting to think of as my perch on the driver's seat.

On a weekday, the streets were still bustling as men dressed in suits and ladies in their finest day dresses went to and fro about their day. There were plenty of servants and working people too. A boy stood on the corner selling newspapers. A girl on the opposite corner sold flowers. Both shouted at pass-ersby about their wares until their voices were hoarse.

"You will love the ice cream," Buford said. "It is so sweet that it will make your toes curl. Have you had ice cream before?"

"Homemade," I said, thinking of the time when I was about eight and my mother had been given cream and sugar from her employer. You would have thought he gave her a home. She was so proud of this gift. Instead of saving the sugar and using the cream to make something more practical like cheese, she made us vanilla ice cream. As the memory came over me, I could almost taste the cold, sweet treat.

Because she had made so much and we couldn't keep it cold enough to save it, we had to eat the whole lot of it that night. Henry and I went to bed with full and sour bellies, but it had been worth it, or so I thought the next day when my stomach had settled.

Buford pulled Betty Sue to a stop in front of a flat-faced brick building with a red-and-white pin-striped awning hang-ing over the large front window and door. "Here we are. Be sure to get the strawberry," Buford said. "You won't be disap-pointed." He hopped off of the driver's seat so he could open the carriage door for the Dickinson sisters.

Miss Lavinia's eyes were wide when she exited the carriage. "I can already taste it."

Emily glanced at her. "I will be surprised if it is as good as the ice cream that we make back home."

Buford tethered Betty Sue to a hitching post in front of the ice cream shop and caught me looking at him. "Go on now. You will like it. Trust me."

I followed Emily and Miss Lavinia into the ice cream shop and stared. The walls, ceiling, and floor were gleaming white. There were six small round ironwork tables surround by matching chairs and an ice cream counter that went from one end of the shop to the other. I guessed it had to be twenty feet long.

A line had formed in front of the counter as visitors one after another asked if they could sample the ice cream flavors. The shopworkers handed the flavors to the customers on tiny wooden spoons.

"I'm so glad they are giving samples," Miss Lavinia said, sounding more excited than I had ever heard her. "I don't know how I would choose otherwise."

The sisters made their way to the counter, and I hung back.

Emily looked over her shoulder. "Willa, get over here and try some ice cream." Emily pointed at the display case. "Choose whatever flavor you want."

I didn't know how I could ever decide. There were so many flavors. The ice chest ran the full length of the shop.

A freckled boy on the other side of the counter wearing a red-and-white-striped uniform smiled at me. "Would you like a sample, miss?"

I bit the corner of my lip. "The strawberry."

He nodded and grabbed the tiniest wooden spoon I had ever seen and spooned a bit of strawberry ice cream on it. He handed me the tiny spoon.

"Thank you," I murmured.

When I tasted the ice cream it was so cold, it was close to startling, and the berries were sweet like they had just been picked that morning in the strawberry patch. I knew they hadn't been. Whoever heard of having strawberries in February? They were a June berry to be sure. It was a wonder to have strawberry ice cream in the winter.

"I'll have the strawberry in a cone. It's delicious," I said.

"I'll have chocolate in a cone," Emily said.

Miss Lavinia also picked chocolate.

The boy at the counter nodded and began scooping ice cream. He set our ice cream cones in a holder on the counter. Miss Lavinia and Emily took their cones and went outside, chattering happily together.

Before he could turn to the next customer, I said, "Can I have a second strawberry cone?"

He glanced at me. "That will be another five cents, miss."

I stuck my hand into the satchel tethered to my wrist and removed the precious coin. I set it on the counter. He nodded and scooped a second strawberry cone. I took both cones and carried them out of the shop.

I found Miss Lavinia and Emily sitting on a bench enjoying their ice cream in the warm sunshine.

"How did you get two?" Miss Lavinia asked when she saw me.

Before I answered, I walked to the front of the carriage where I knew I would find Buford. I handed him an ice cream.

He stared at it like he had never seen anything like it in his whole life. "For me?"

I nodded.

"That's so kind of the Dickinson sisters to buy me an ice cream."

I didn't correct him as to who paid for his ice cream. Getting the credit for it wasn't the point. The smile on his face was.

Walking back to the sisters, I looked at my cone that was so perfectly crafted and prayed that I could always remember what it looked and tasted like. I wished there was some way I could bottle up this memory for those dark nights when I was missing my mother and brother, and when the world was drab and harsh.

This ice cream cone that might have only cost a few cents was proof to me that there was still joy to be found in the world.

"Aren't you going to eat your ice cream?" Miss Lavinia asked as she licked at her cone.

"Oh yes. I guess I was trying to savor it."

Emily looked at her own chocolate cone. "Savoring is one of the best things you can do. Taking a moment and realizing how special something is makes it that much more special."

I smiled and licked my cone.

Miss Lavinia sighed. "Where should we go now? I would like to walk by the White House. You never know who you might see strolling down Pennsylvania Avenue. You might find a suitor in this city, Sister. You might find yourself living here."

Emily wrinkled her nose. "I think not. I don't ever want to leave the comfort of Amherst. It is pleasant to be here in February, but the long summer months would be torture. Summer is the very best time for wandering the woods and thinking. I could not do that here in the heat."

"But what if your husband wanted to leave Amherst?" Miss Lavinia asked.

Emily lifted her chin. "I would not marry such a man."

Whether they were looking for suitors or just out for a stroll, Miss Lavinia and Emily agreed to go for a walk by the White House. I told Buford their intentions, and he promised to pick us up near the Washington Monument.

"That's fine by me," he said. "It gives me time to enjoy my ice cream." He winked at me. "It's a fine gift from you, miss."

"How did you know?"

He winked again but didn't answer the question.

Emily and Miss Lavinia were already making their way down the sidewalk, and I hurried to catch up with them. I fell into step behind the two sisters and rapidly finished eating my ice cream before it could melt.

We passed so many smartly dressed ladies on the way to the White House. They wore large hats with feathers, had impossibly small waists, and held parasols over their heads to protect them from the sun.

"We should have brought our parasols," Miss Lavinia said. "We will both have freckles by the time this trip has ended if we are not careful."

"I wear my freckles as a badge of pride," Emily said.

The sisters continued to debate the merit of freckles when they were interrupted by a man walking from the opposite direction. "My, this is something I never expected to find. The two Dickinson girls in the big city eating ice cream."

I stopped in the middle of the sidewalk. It was Mr. Arthur Milner, the Amherst postmaster.

"Mr. Milner," Miss Lavinia said. "What a shock to see you here in Washington!"

"I tell you that the shock is all mine." He raised his brow.

"And is that Willa Noble with you? I didn't see you there. How nice for me to see so many friends from home."

I didn't think he missed me. I might be quiet, but I was a tall woman, taller than most men, including Mr. Milner.

"We are here visiting our father," Miss Lavinia said.

He placed a palm to his cheek. "Yes, of course, I should have realized that the moment I saw you."

"What are you doing here?" Emily asked.

"Official postman business, I can assure you. There is a postmen's convention this week, and I was lucky enough to be invited. That is no small feat for a postmaster from such a small town." He smiled. "I am hoping to take back much of what I have learned from my time in Washington. The U.S. Postal Service is trying its best to make practices uniform across all of the offices. It's something that has needed to be done for a long time. We cannot guarantee that a piece of mail will travel from one part of the country to another without everyone following the same procedures and protocols. They're important. I run everything as it should be, but I am hoping to learn what other places are up to that might lead to delays."

"We know that no one could possibly have a better handle on the mail going in and out of Amherst than you," Emily said soothingly.

"Thank you kindly." He smiled. "Now, I best be on my way to the next meeting."

"Before you go," Emily said, "my father is having a dinner party at our hotel, the Willard, at the end of the week. If he knew you were in the city, I know that he would love for you to attend."

"I should love to, thank you." His cheeks colored with pleasure. "It would be an honor."

"I'll ask for an invitation with all the details to be sent to where you're staying," Emily said. "My father cares about Amherst first and foremost, and he would want anyone from back home to come to his event. Do you know of any other people from back home who might be here?"

Mr. Milner shook his head.

"That's odd," Emily said and tilted her head. "I thought I heard that Elmer Johnson, the stable owner, was also in the city."

Mr. Milner paled ever so slightly. "Johnson is here?"

"That is what I heard," Emily said. "I know my father would like him to be at the dinner party too if he's here. The last thing my father would want would be for anyone from Amherst to feel like they were unwelcome. If you see him, can you tell him about the dinner party?"

Mr. Milner pulled at the sleeves of his coat. I noted the sleeve was at least an inch too short for his arm. "That is not likely to happen. Now, I must leave. It was nice to see you ladies." He nodded to us all in turn and then hurried down the sidewalk.

"His reaction was odd," Miss Lavinia observed.

I thought so too.

CHAPTER NINETEEN

MISS LAVINIA AND Emily returned to the hotel chattering about all we saw that day. Sitting in the driver's seat of the carriage on the way back to the Willard on busy streets, Buford turned to me. "You seem deep in thought."

I smiled at him. "I suppose I am. I'm just taking it all in. It's a lot to absorb for a girl who had never left her home county before."

Buford nodded. "I guess if I ever travel to another place, I will do the same."

"You've not traveled either?" I asked.

He cleared his throat. "Being a Black man, it's not easy for me to travel. It's easier to stay in a place where everyone already knows my status."

"But you're free, aren't you?" I shook my head as the rudeness of my inquiry rang in my ears. "I'm sorry if that's the wrong question to ask."

"It's not. If you don't ask, you don't know. The truth is, I have a set of papers that I carry inside of my coat that prove I'm a freeman. I never leave my home without them for fear I will be asked by someone to see my papers and prove I'm free."

"Are you stopped often?" I asked.

"No, but I don't go places where folks don't know me either. I'm well-known around the city by dignitaries and congressmen as I drive them here and there. They know me, so they don't ask. I can't say I'd get the same treatment elsewhere, so I stay put."

The hotel came into view, and Buford pulled on Betty Sue's reins to let a group of finely dressed ladies with fringed parasols that matched their store-bought dresses cross the street. They looked like silhouettes in a painting.

I thought of Henry's friend Jeremiah back in Amherst and wondered if he dealt with the same challenges and fears. I guessed that he must.

Here I was feeling anxious about travel to new places, but at least I could do so without worry that someone would demand to see papers to prove I am who I say I am.

As Betty Sue began to move again, Buford said, "Someday, all that will change. Someday, I won't have to carry papers next to my heart proving I'm my own man. I just hope I live to see the day."

"I hope you do too," I said in a quiet voice.

The carriage pulled up in front of the hotel, and I noticed right away that Austin was marching back and forth in front of the entrance. Buford let the Dickinson sisters out of the carriage, and Miss Lavinia gathered up all their packages from shopping that afternoon.

She turned to her brother. "Austin, why are you bouncing about like you have a bee in your trousers?"

He glowered at his sister. "Because our father was here between sessions and meetings. He is wondering where his daughters are. He wasn't pleased when I said I didn't know when you would return."

Emily tilted her head. "And whose fault is that, Brother? When we left, you were nowhere to be found in the hotel, and Mother was fast asleep. Should we have awakened her after all the travel and told her our plans? You knew we had the carriage for the day."

Austin frowned. "Let's not argue any more about it now. Father and Mother are in the dining room planning the party for the end of this week. They would like your input."

"Oh," Miss Lavinia said. "Why didn't you say so? I would love to help plan the party."

Emily looked askance at the idea.

I took the packages from Miss Lavinia's arms and waved to Buford before I followed them into the hotel.

"See you tomorrow, Miss Willa," he called after me.

"Give the packages to the porter, and he will take them to the room," Emily said to me when I joined the brother and sister outside of the dining room.

"You want me to come into the dining room with you?" I tried my best to keep the squeak out of my voice. I didn't know how successful I was at that.

"Yes. Father will eventually know that you're here. It's best to get that surprise over with," Emily said.

I couldn't say that I agreed with her, but I did as I was asked. The porter took the packages with a bow.

By the time I made it back to the dining room, the Dickinson children were already in the room. The family of five sat at one end of a long dining table. A butler from the hotel showed Mrs. Dickinson the choices of china and silverware available for the dinner party.

"I want something fine, but not extravagant. We must show the frugality of the Whig party and the Commonwealth of Massachusetts," she told the butler. "We are not a flashy people, and we honor restraint."

"Yes, of course," the butler said and put the gold-rimmed plate with the intricate floral design back into its case. He opened a second china case and came up with a simple royal blue-rimmed china plate with a scalloped edge. They were plain in color, but their shape made them special, just what Mrs. Dickinson was looking for. She nodded. "This one."

"I will let the staff know your selections, ma'am," the butler said and left the room.

"Now that that is settled," Mr. Dickinson said in a tone that indicated he questioned the china selection's importance, "I would like to talk to all of you about the dinner party that will be in three nights' time. It is essential that we are all present and put on a good show."

"A show, Father?" Emily asked. "Are you going to parade us around like trophies?"

He scowled at his eldest daughter. "No, but I must finish my term here in Congress on a good foot. We are representing both the Dickinson name and the commonwealth. We cannot forget that."

"We won't, Edward," Mrs. Dickinson promised for herself and her children.

Mr. Dickinson glanced in my direction. "Who is this?"

"Father, it's Willa Noble. The new maid," Emily said.

"I can see that it is the new maid. What is she doing here?"

"I asked her to come." Emily lifted her chin. "She will be a great help to Vinnie and I while we are in Washington."

"Don't bring me into this, Sister," Miss Lavinia muttered.

Mr. Dickinson glared at me so hard it was like he was looking through me. "You're here now." It was a dismissive statement, as though the deed was done and didn't justify another moment of his time or thought. He turned back to his family.

I let out a breath I didn't even know I had been holding.

"Now, I went over the guest list with your mother. Is there anyone else you would like to add?" Mr. Dickinson asked his children. "We have a few spare seats, and it will be more pleasing to the eye if you have a full table."

"What about Mr. Elmer Johnson?" Emily said. "I saw him on the train."

Emily had not seen Mr. Johnson on the train; I had. However, I guessed she knew better than to bring my presence to her father's attention again.

"Johnson is here?" He frowned. "He is a property owner in Amherst, and should be included in the dinner," he said as if it pained him somehow.

"The man is brash," Austin said. "Do you really want him at a party with the elite of Washington? That can't look well on the Dickinson name or the commonwealth."

"I've made up my mind," Mr. Dickinson said. "I'll have a member of my staff find out where he's staying and extend the invitation."

"Then you will also want to invite Mr. Arthur Milner, the

postmaster," Emily said. "We saw him while strolling through the city today. He says he's here for some sort of post office conference."

"Yes, we will include Arthur then. I have the postmaster general also coming to the party, so that will be a nice opportunity for the two men to meet. It's odd that Arthur and Johnson would be here at the same time."

I bit my lip because I feared Emily would also tell her father that Matthew was in the city, but to my relief, she did not.

"That makes a dinner party of sixteen," Mrs. Dickinson said.

"Very good." Mr. Dickinson stood. "I will leave it to you, my dear, to make any final arrangements. I must return to the Hill. I have several committee briefs I need to review before tomorrow." He stacked his papers and tucked them into a black leather briefcase. "I trust that you will all be able to entertain yourselves until the dinner party on Friday."

"Of course we can, Father," Emily said, and then looking past her father's shoulder and directly at me, she added, "We have much to do."

CHAPTER TWENTY

THE NEXT DAY, Emily and her sister were eager to sightsee, and I began to wonder why I came with the Dickinson family to Washington. Emily had said that she wanted me to come because of my brother's death, but we had done little to find out who might have injured Terror and caused the horse to lash out and kill Henry.

By the time the two sisters emerged from their bedroom, I had already tidied up my bed linens and went to the kitchen to arrange their coffees and breakfasts.

Miss Lavinia poured coffee into a fine china cup. "If I can wake to coffee like this each morning, I think it was a fine idea after all that you came with us to Washington, Willa." She waltzed back into the bedroom to dress.

"We are headed to Mount Vernon, the home of George Washington, today. It's supposed to be spectacular. Can you make the arrangements for our departure, Willa?" Emily asked.

I glanced at the open door that Miss Lavinia had just gone through. "But what about . . ." I lowered my voice. "*The investigation.*"

She smiled. "Why do you think we are going to Mount Vernon?"

I folded my hands in front of me. "I don't know, miss."

"Last night, my father's aide sent a note that Mr. Johnson was staying at an inn by Mount Vernon, so it would behoove us to make due haste."

"You want to go to his inn?" I asked.

"Of course I do. I will become quite parched from walking the grounds of Mount Vernon. I can sit a long time and drink quite a bit of tea. How about you?" She smiled.

"I can sit and drink tea for hours if allowed."

She chuckled.

Buford and Betty Sue were ready and waiting for us when we left the Willard a little while later.

Miss Lavinia had asked their mother if she would like to come with us to Mount Vernon, but Mrs. Dickinson declined. She insisted she had much work to do for the dinner party. I knew that Mrs. Dickinson was quite anxious about it. The Dickinsons hosted guests often back in Amherst, but I would suppose in Mrs. Dickinson's mind, hosting friends who were traveling or people from the small town was quite different than hosting dignitaries and congressmen from the nation's capital.

As Buford drove us to the spot where we would get on the boat to cross the Potomac River, he told me, "Miss Willa, you are going to be amazed at what you see in Mount Vernon. I have been there a few times myself. The bowling green is magnificent."

The ferry ride across the river was another first for me. It seemed I was getting those "firsts" one after another since I started working for the Dickinson family. I clung to my seat the whole time. Emily tried to pull me away to catch a glimpse of Mount Vernon from the boat, but I was perfectly happy right where I was inside of the cabin.

A hired cart waited for us when we disembarked from the boat. On the ride to Mount Vernon, Miss Lavinia and Emily spoke excitedly over everything we were about to see.

We were close when I saw an inn on the side of the road called the Tortoise and the Hare Inn. It was the inn that Mr. Johnson was calling home while in Washington.

I tapped Emily's wrist and nodded at the inn as we went by.

"Oh! What a charming place," she said. "We will have to stop there for tea after we visit the mansion."

Miss Lavinia frowned. "You want to stop someplace for tea instead of going straight back to the Willard so you can write?"

"Why does this surprise you, Sister?" Emily asked.

"Because it's very much out of character for you. If you spend too much time around people, you withdraw. I imagine there will be many people at the president's home, and you will want to be alone after being around so many strangers."

Emily opened her mouth as if she was about argue more, but then the expansive bowling green and finally the west front of Mount Vernon mansion came into view. Behind it we could see just a bit of the great Potomac River.

The sisters fell silent. I felt the sight robbed me of words too. If I had thought the Dickinson home in Amherst was grand, it was nothing compared to Washington's estate. It was truly a mansion. It was cream-colored with a reddish-brown roof. Standing two stories high, the house was made to look even taller with a cupola tower and weather vane. As we drew closer, I saw the weather vane was a dove holding an olive branch. Had that been included because of the biblical story of Noah and the great flood? I wondered.

A male guide met us at the door. He wore a brown suit and had a long mustache that was turned up in the corners. "Welcome to Mount Vernon. This was the plantation home of our first president, George Washington. A truly great man."

I stopped looking at the house. "This was a plantation?"

"Yes, miss, a very busy plantation in its prime."

"He was a slaveholder," I said.

He pulled at his collar. "Yes, miss, but he freed all of his slaves in his will. It clearly stated upon his wife's death, they would all be free. He set quite an example for others to follow."

"Why did he wait?" Emily asked.

His mustache wobbled up and down. "Would you like to see the house?"

We nodded and followed the guide into the central passage. In front of us was a large staircase with a wide railing. The walls of the central passage were ornately carved and painted a cream color similar to the exterior of the house. To our right were two parlors, and to our left was a dining room and bedchamber. After the entryway, every room seemed to have a burst of color, either on the wall or in the carpets. The dining room's walls were a bright vibrant green.

"The bedchamber was for guests," the guide said.

We continued on our tour of the home and then visited the tomb at the guide's suggestion. We barely spoke throughout. I was so grateful to the Dickinson sisters for letting me share in this experience with them. They could have certainly left me outside of the house, as a servant.

The tomb for both the first president and his wife was behind a brick archway. The path into the tomb was blocked by an iron gate. We peered inside at the marble resting places.

Miss Lavinia and Emily held hands as they stared at the tomb. Emily's face had at times looked as if she slipped away to a place that could not be reached.

After a long moment, the sisters walked away hand in hand. I took one last look before I left. I thought of Henry and how much he would have wanted to be there. It was funny how after—and in many ways *because* of—his death, I was having the adventures that he always dreamed of having.

When we reached the mansion again, Emily murmured to herself. All I could catch her saying was "adjusted in the tomb." She said it three times in a row as if she tasted the words in her mouth, rather than just recited them. I didn't know where the words came from, but I thought perhaps they were her own.

"This was a lovely day," Miss Lavinia said. "I am glad we came. I'm only disappointed Mother missed it. She would have loved the parlors."

Miss Lavinia's words seemed to snap Emily out of her reverie. "Mother missed it because her duty is to her husband and throwing a party that will impress Father's colleagues. I would never put myself in that position."

Miss Lavinia laughed. "You say that now."

"I say it forever. Look what Mother gave up today for duty. I will never allow that to happen to me."

Miss Lavinia shook her head. "In any case, we should head back to the Willard and rest."

Emily nodded, and I felt my heart quicken. Had Emily forgotten why we were here?

I cleared my throat. "I thought you wanted to stop at that little inn on the way to the mansion for some refreshment. Being this close to Washington's home, they must be accustomed to serving tourists as they come and go from Mount Vernon."

Emily's brow furrowed and then cleared as if she just remembered why I brought this place up again. "You're right, Willa. Thank you for reminding me about that. It would be nice to have a bit of lemonade or tea before we get back on the boat. Don't you agree, Vinnie?"

I expected Miss Lavinia to argue with the idea because it seemed to me that she argued with everything and anything when I was involved. However, to my surprise she said, "I am thirsty. We have been walking and standing a long time. My head is full with so much information from the guide that it does sound nice to give my feet and my mind a little rest before we go back to the hustle and bustle of the city."

I let out a sigh of relief but then then fear gripped me. What would Mr. Johnson say when he saw us?

THE DICKINSON SISTERS and I walked into the Tortoise and the Hare Inn. In front of us was a simple reception desk for guests to check in if they were staying the night. To the left there was a large tearoom. The moment that I saw it, I felt charmed. I had never seen so many teacups and teapots in all my life. They sat on colorfully painted shelves and didn't seem to be organized in any way. There were glazed teapots with decorated rural scenes, teapots that appeared to be from India, and even teapots with cats dancing all over them. There were so many that it would be impossible to see them all.

"My word," Miss Lavinia said. "Why would a little tearoom like this have need of so many teapots and teacups? They couldn't even accommodate all of Congress. Why have so many here?"

"There you go again, Vinnie. Always being practical," Emily said.

"But really, Sister, this is excessive."

"I like it, and since this is my place, that's all that matters." A thin Black woman came into the dining room from a side door. As the door swung close, I just caught a glimpse of the huge iron stove inside. It was bigger than the one at the Dickinson home. Up until this time, the Dickinsons' stove was the largest that I had ever seen.

"*You* own this inn?" Miss Lavinia asked in disbelief.

The woman frowned at her. "Do you think I'm telling a lie?"

"No! No," Miss Lavinia said quickly.

"I know why you have your doubts. It's not common for a Black woman to own a business in Virginia, but I can assure you it's mine free and clear. When Miss Flora Macintosh, who started this place and ran it for forty years, died, she left it all to me, her most trusted employee. She was a good woman. Always treated me well and was my friend more than my employer." She looked at the three of us. "Now, are you here for tea?"

Miss Lavinia's face was bright red. I guessed it was from embarrassment over the questions that she asked.

Emily spoke up. "We certainly are, Miss . . ."

"Abigail. You can call me Miss Abigail. That's what Miss Flora always called me, and I like the sound of it, especially in your accent. Miss Flora was from up north too. She moved here to get married, but her husband-to-be died in an accident just before their wedding."

"That's awful," I said.

"She's a survivor. You have to be to be a woman nowadays. She scrapped together what she could, opened this place, and lived here alone the rest of her life." She pointed at the tearoom. "Sit wherever you like."

Emily led Miss Lavinia and me to a small table by the window. From here we could have a clear view of the front door and the street. If Mr. Johnson left the inn or he returned to it, we would see him.

Miss Abigail had so many teas to pick from, and she claimed they were from all over the world. I chose the black currant tea. Emily chose jasmine tea, and Miss Lavinia unsurprisingly went with a simple black tea.

With our teacups in hand, we sipped and waited for Mr. Johnson to appear.

Over two hours later, it seemed to me that Mr. Johnson wasn't coming. Miss Lavinia, Emily, and I sat at a table in the inn's small tearoom alone. Miss Abigail circled our table for the fifth time. "Is there anything else I can get you ladies?"

"We're fine." Emily sipped what had to be cold tea at this point. She had been nursing the cup for the last forty minutes. "We are enjoying this lovely room so much."

"Yes, well, I can understand that, miss, but the tearoom closes soon. We don't serve supper."

"We aren't here for supper," Emily said. "I adore your tea. I love the teapots and teacups too. I can't stop looking at them."

Miss Abigail's cheeks turned a light shade of pink. "Thank

you. Miss Flora had been collecting them all of her life. She always said she didn't have any children, so that gave her the liberty to spend her money on teapots. I have added a few of my own to the collection. As for our tea, we acquire the very best tea all the way from China. With our tearoom this close to President Washington's final resting place, we believe that we should only serve the very best."

"I agree," Emily said.

"Would you like me to warm your tea for you, then?"

"Oh no," Emily said. "I like it just like this."

Shaking her head, Miss Abigail walked away.

Miss Lavinia leaned across the table toward her sister. "Emily, I'm usually up for your little stunts, but what exactly are we doing here? Don't you tell me it's because you love the tea. We have the same tea back home in Amherst."

"It tastes different here," Emily said. "It must be the different water they have this far south."

Miss Lavinia made a huffing sound and threw up her arms. "Sometimes I feel like the older sister."

"I would think you would always feel like the older sister." Emily swirled her tea.

When Miss Abigail came back, Emily stopped her on one of her laps around the tearoom. "Miss Abigail, is there a man staying here by the name of Elmer Johnson?"

Miss Lavinia gasped as if she just put together why we were here. Emily would be hearing about that later. I likely would be, too, because Miss Lavinia would assume that I already knew this, and she would be right.

"Why yes. He has been here for a few days. Do you know him?"

"He lives not far from us," Emily said. "I heard that he was in town on business."

Miss Abigail sniffed. "If you don't mind me saying so, miss, I don't think young girls like you should be speaking to such a man."

"Why's that?" Miss Lavinia asked.

Miss Abigail looked at the door as if she expected Mr. Johnson to walk into the tearoom at any moment. "He just doesn't seem like a kind man to me. He is cordial and pays his bill in a timely fashion, but he doesn't smile. He has a terribly unfriendly demeanor. Also, he must be forty, far too old for you girls."

Emily made a face like she felt ill. "You think that we are asking after him because we consider him a potential suitor? Nothing could be further from the truth."

Miss Abigail blew out a seemingly relieved breath, and the single curl on her forehead fluttered into the air. "I'm quite glad to hear that. Quite glad. I would hate such nice girls like you, who love my tea so much, to be caught up with a man like him."

"Have you seen anyone with him since he's been staying at the inn?" I asked, speaking up for the first time.

Miss Abigail looked at me like she had just become aware I was there. It was little wonder why. Although I was wearing my very best dress and had set my hair with my mother's single hair comb with a pearl inlay in the back, it was clear of the three of us visiting the tearoom, being a guest anywhere wasn't something that I was used to.

After a moment of hesitation, Miss Abigail said, "He met two men here for lunch yesterday. It was during the busiest time of the day. Several large groups had stopped in the tearoom after visiting the mansion. I didn't hear much of what they were saying, but they all appeared to be very unhappy."

Emily sat up a little straighter. "What did you manage to hear?"

Miss Abigail's brow wrinkled. "I don't think I should talk out of turn about the men's conversation. I don't even know who the other two men were."

"What did they look like?" Miss Lavinia asked.

It seemed that Miss Lavinia either knowingly or just out of curiosity was joining in our investigation.

"One man was older than Johnson by at least ten years, I would say. He had silver in his hair. They both were dressed nicely, but in a way that made me think they didn't come from money. The younger man's coat sleeve had clearly been mended a time or two. There was a tear on the right sleeve just a few inches up from the cuff that still needed fixing. The silver-haired man had a deep Southern accent. I would even say he was from Georgia by the way of his speech. The first man with the mended coat had an accent much like yours."

Miss Abigail's description of the two men really could have been of anyone, and in such a large city, I didn't know how we would find either one of the mystery men. We hadn't even found Mr. Johnson yet and we were sitting in the tearoom of his inn.

"Did you hear their names?" Emily asked.

"I'm afraid I didn't," the inkeeper said, shaking her head. "And when I came to refill their coffees, Mr. Johnson didn't make introductions either. Not that I expected him to. As I already told you, he was quite a sour-faced man." She looked at each of us in turn. "I think it would serve the three of you young ladies well to stay as far away from him as possible."

"We won't be able to avoid him completely," Emily said. "My father is a congressman and is having a dinner party. Since Mr. Johnson is a constituent, he is invited."

"Mr. Johnson is not the type who strikes me as an enjoyer of dinner parties. I would be surprised if he goes." The innkeeper glanced at the clock on the wall. "I really must go clean the kitchen so that everything is ready for tomorrow's breakfast service. Was there anything else you girls needed?" She discreetly set the bill for our tea on the table.

"Not at all," Emily said.

When Miss Abigail had gone, Miss Lavinia scowled at her sister. "Are either of you finally going to tell me what's going on? I know something is happening, and Willa is not here with us in Washington because we need the extra help. There is plenty of staff in the hotel who could assist us if need be."

Emily and I shared a look. I shrugged. I would leave it to Emily to decide if she would tell her sister what we were up to. I would hate if this investigation became a wedge between the two sisters.

Emily set the still full and still very cold teacup onto the blue linen tablecloth. "If you really must know, we are trying to solve a murder."

"You're what?" Miss Lavinia shouted so loud that I would be surprised if Austin hadn't heard her back in the Willard Hotel.

CHAPTER TWENTY-ONE

EMILY ELIZABETH DICKINSON, you have had some outrageous ideas in your time, but this one is taking it too far. Who are you to believe you can solve a murder?" Miss Lavinia folded her arms and sat back in her seat.

"Logic," Emily said. "I have just as much intelligence as anyone at the Amherst Police Department, if not more."

Miss Lavinia rolled her eyes. "Now, I know what this is all about." She pointed at me. "And why you're here. This is about your brother who was killed at the town stables. That is why you are looking for Mr. Johnson and are so curious about his whereabouts. You both think he's the killer."

"We have not made that determination yet," Emily told her younger sister coolly, "but he is a suspect. There are rumors about him in the village, and you just heard the innkeeper. He's not a very nice man to anyone. Seems to me that makes him a prime suspect for the murder."

"Some would say Father is not *nice* because he is stern.

Does that automatically make him a murder suspect too?"
Miss Lavinia asked.

Emily rifled through her small clutch and set several coins
on the table for our tea. "You know Father's unfriendliness and
being a coldhearted killer are completely different." She stood
up. "It's time we went back to the hotel. If we did not find Mr.
Johnson today, we certainly will when he comes to Father's
party in two days' time."

I jumped out of my seat. I was eager to leave too. It was
never comfortable to be the third party of Emily and Miss Lavinia's verbal sparring matches.

It was a short walk from the inn to the boat dock where
were could travel back down the Potomac River to the city
proper.

Emily and Miss Lavinia walked ahead of me while I lagged
behind. It had been a lovely day, one that I never would have
expected to have. My mind was full of the fine furnishings and
well-designed rooms of Mount Vernon as well as the general
majesty of the house. I was so grateful that I was able to see it.
In all probability, I wouldn't see another home so grand in my
lifetime. But, the reason that I went there, to find out what
happened to my younger brother, had not been fulfilled.

I was beginning to wonder if coming to Washington had
been a waste of time for me. It certainly was for Margaret back
in Amherst who was cleaning the entire Dickinson home, top
to bottom, all by herself. I did hope that she took at least one
evening to put her feet up and enjoy sitting in the parlor with
a roaring fire with only Carlo and Miss Lavinia's many cats to
keep her company. That's what I would have been doing, if
only for an hour or two.

Emily stopped in the middle of the sidewalk. "He's here," she hissed.

"Who's here?" Miss Lavinia asked.

I wondered the same thing as I looked around the street to see if some crazy man was waiting to pounce on us from the shadows.

"Mr. Johnson," she said. "He's there at the dock. He's going to be on the same boat that we are."

Miss Lavinia shielded her eyes, looking in the direction that her sister pointed. "Looks to me like he's headed in the direction of the inn, not away from it. It is half past four. I'm sure that Mother is wondering what is taking us so long to return to the hotel."

"Should we go back to the inn and drink more tea?" Emily said.

Miss Lavinia cocked her head. "I think that would be very difficult for Miss Abigail to take. She was practically shooing us out the door when we left. She didn't even try to hide her relief. Not to mention how late it is."

The sisters stood in the middle of the sidewalk debating what to do. They were so engrossed in their conversation they didn't see that Mr. Johnson was marching right toward us with the most unpleasant scowl on his face. I thought Mr. Dickinson had an impressive scowl, but it was nothing close to Mr. Johnson's. There should be his daguerreotype in the dictionary next to the word "scowl" for the perfect example.

"Ladies," I said softly, trying to get the sisters' attention. They continued debating what to do next. "Ladies?" I asked a little more urgently this time.

At this point Mr. Johnson was only fifty feet from us.

"Emily!" I cried.

Emily jumped. "Willa Noble, what on earth?"

"Mr. Johnson is right there," I said in a hoarse whisper.

Emily and Miss Lavinia spun around. Emily recovered first. "Mr. Johnson, what a surprise to see you this far south."

The stable owner appeared to be lost in his thoughts; dark ones were my guess from his expression. "Hello? Do I know you?"

"I don't know if we have ever formerly met, but I'm Miss Emily Dickinson and this is my sister, Lavinia; we are Edward Dickinson's daughters. As you must know, our father is serving out his term as a representative from the great Commonwealth of Massachusetts. We are in Washington visiting him and just had a lovely visit to Mount Vernon. Is that where you are headed now?" Emily finished.

I had to admit I was impressed that she was able to say all of that as if she were just having a normal chat with a neighbor and not with a man she thought could be a killer. I knew it was something that I wouldn't be able to do. Just looking at Mr. Johnson made my stomach twist into a horrible knot. Could this be the man who killed my only brother? Did he take Henry's life? For what exactly? And was he really working with a slave catcher to return runaways to the South? All of these thoughts ran together in my mind, and I felt my face harden.

Mr. Johnson looked in my direction, and for a split second, his angry mask slipped in surprise as if he was taken aback by how much fury and something very close to hate was flowing from me.

His scowl was firmly back in place when he answered

Emily's question. "I have not been to Mount Vernon. I'm in Washington on business."

"Oh, what kind of business?" Emily asked.

Miss Lavinia standing next to her groaned just loudly enough for me to hear.

"I do not know why it's your concern, miss." He made a move like he wanted to step around Emily.

Emily pretended she didn't see it. "I just know that my father will ask when we mention seeing you this close to Mount Vernon. If you have business in Washington, it's odd that you would be this far down the river away from it. Is your business more closely related to Virginia? Perhaps having something to do with the Southern states?"

I winced. Emily might as well ask him if he was working with slaveholders. At least that is how it sounded to my ears. I hoped that I was wrong, and Mr. Johnson wouldn't see it that way.

However, Miss Lavinia must have had the same thoughts as I did, because she said, "It was nice seeing you, Mr. Johnson, but we must go to catch the next boat up the river. Our family is expecting us back within the hour."

He looked from Emily to her sister. "It is not my intent to keep you. Good day, ladies." This time, he stepped out into the street to get around Emily should she jump into his path again.

"My father's aide sent you an invitation for his dinner party on Friday. We very much want you to be there. There will be several men from Amherst in attendance," Emily called after him.

He turned and looked back to her. "Please give your father

my apologies, but I have much more important work that needs to be done than sitting at a dining table with people I neither know nor like."

Miss Lavinia gave a quick intake of breath, and I have to admit, I was a little shocked, too, by the sharpness of his words.

Emily, however, was undeterred. "Very well. I will give my father and the others from Amherst your apologies then."

He hesitated. "Who are these *others* from Amherst?"

"My family, of course, and Mr. Milner, the postmaster from town."

He frowned. "Milner will be there?"

"I'm sure he will," she said. "We extended an invitation to him as well. Good etiquette would tell him that it wasn't an invitation that he could possibly turn down. At least that's what people of good breeding know."

"I'll be at your party, miss. Good day." He spun around and clapped his heels together in the process before he marched back in the direction of the Tortoise and the Hare Inn.

CHAPTER TWENTY-TWO

THE FOLLOWING DAY was a flurry of activity, and Mrs. Dickinson thought it was time to put me "to work" while I was in Washington and help her with the final preparation for the next evening's party. So while Emily and Miss Lavinia had another day to explore the city, call upon acquaintances who were in town, and go back to the ice cream shop, I was at the Willard painstakingly writing out name cards for each and every one of the Dickinsons' guests for their dinner party.

When Mrs. Dickinson learned I had such good penmanship, she immediately gave me the task.

"This is usually a job for a daughter in the family, but Vinnie hates writing and Emily's handwriting is atrocious. I find little scraps of paper that she's written on around the house at times. They are written all over with words scratched out so no one could possibly ever read them, not even her. I just toss away those little scraps when I find them outside of her room. What she does in her room is her business."

My heart ached when she said that. I knew Emily would not want her words to be carelessly tossed aside. I had heard her say once that she wanted to be a writer, so those little scraps would be very important to her, would they not?

Mrs. Dickinson stood up from the small desk in the parlor off of the sisters' room. "I will leave you with this task. I'm going to lie down. I'm supposed to have tea with some other congressmen's wives this afternoon, and I know I will need my strength for those conversations."

I wondered what she meant by that. Why did she need strength to speak?

She left the room, and I found myself alone for the first time since coming to Washington. At this point, I had only finished three of the sixteen place cards that I was supposed to write. I was taking much care with each one, and I realized it might take me another two hours to finish the lot. I should work on them so they were ready by the time Mrs. Dickinson returned from her tea.

But I didn't do that. My head was still too full of the conversation that the Dickinson sisters had with Mr. Johnson. Emily seemed to be confident on the matter, but I remained unconvinced that he killed my brother. However, I believed he knew who did.

I needed to clear my head. I decided to take the risk and sneak out of the hotel for a few minutes for a short walk. Then, I promised myself, I would return to the place cards, and the place cards would be better for it too.

I stood up from the desk, grabbed my small satchel and straw hat, and went out the door. As soon as I was outside of the Willard, the scent of spring surrounded me. There were daffodils and tulips in stone planters in front of the hotel. When I went back to Amherst, I wouldn't be seeing flowers like those for another four weeks at least.

However, the most overpowering scent was that of the blue and pink hyacinths that encircled a tree by the sidewalk. The sweet fragrance always reminded me of my mother. Every fall she would plant hyacinth bulbs in front of our little house just outside town, and when they bloomed in spring, it was such a joy.

I bent down to inhale the scent of the flowers more deeply.

"You have always been fond of flowers," a man said.

I jumped and looked up to find Matthew smiling at me. "What are you doing here?" I asked and took a quick glance around. I knew that all from the household but Mrs. Dickinson should be away from the Willard that day. However, I wasn't going to take any chances and let Matthew and me be seen together. I could be in serious trouble if it appeared that we were too familiar with each other.

"That's not the nicest greeting in the world." He chuckled.

"I'm sorry, Mat—Officer Thomas."

"Please, Willa, let's not be formal. That hurts me too much."

I bit the inside of my lip. "Are you here to see the Dickinsons? Because only Mrs. Dickinson is in her room right now. She's resting."

"I was just out for a walk, and I will admit that I came this way because I knew you were staying at the Willard."

"How did you know?" I asked and wondered if Matthew had been spying on me. Perhaps I was just becoming paranoid with all this investigation business.

"It was in the society pages that Edward Dickinson's

daughters were staying at the hotel. I guessed you would be in the same place."

Ladies out for a walk moved around us as they made their way down the sidewalk, and guests and the bellman went in and out of the hotel with suitcases and packages.

"I think we are in the way here," I said.

"Yes, let's walk a bit, and we can talk about what you've been up to in the city."

"I haven't been up to anything."

He laughed. "That's not what I've heard."

The knot in my stomach tightened a bit more. What exactly had Matthew heard?

He maneuvered down the sidewalk, and with one more glance over my shoulder, I fell into step next to him. Because of my height, Matthew didn't even have to adjust his stride to meet mine. There was a small park at the end of the street, and just at the front there was a bench. "Would you like to sit?" Matthew asked.

I shook my head. "I have to think about my reputation, Matthew. I don't know who might walk past us that will be connected to Mr. Dickinson. It might be an aide or someone who works in Congress alongside him. We are completely innocent, but I can't take the risk of being seen as guilty of anything improper. Suspicion is all it would take for me to be dismissed, and you know that."

"I was going to suggest that you sit and I stand," he said.

"I don't think that's much better. Meeting briefly on the street to trade pleasantries like it appears we are now is fine."

"Very well. What luck are you having finding Mr. Johnson?"

"How do you know that I'm looking for Mr. Johnson?"

"You said as much on the train. He's not a kind man. It would serve you well to stay away from him." His tone became more serious.

I gripped my satchel tightly. "And let my brother's killer get away?"

"Mr. Johnson is not the killer," Matthew said with much more confidence than I would expect.

"How do you know that?"

He pressed his lips together in a thin line.

I straightened my shoulders. "If you don't tell me your reasoning, I can't believe it."

"Can't you just take my word for it, Willa, as your friend and a friend of Henry's, and as a person who has your best interests in mind?"

As much as I wanted to believe Matthew, I couldn't completely. However, I did give his opinion weight. Perhaps Emily had been too quick to conclude that Mr. Johnson was behind Henry's death. Yet I still had suspicions about him. "What about the rumors running through Amherst claiming he's working with a slave catcher?"

"I don't know anything about that," he said and looked down the street.

I knew by the way he wouldn't look me in the eye when he said it that he was lying to me, and it broke my heart just a little.

Matthew sighed and faced me again. "It's clear that Henry knew something he shouldn't, and it is likely to involve the Underground Railroad. This is why it is important that you stay out of it. This is a very dangerous game that both sides are playing. I don't want you to be caught in the middle of it."

"It does not sound like a game to me, Matthew. It sounds like life or death for many, and in my brother's case, death."

"Which is exactly why you should drop it and leave the inquiry to the police. My theory is that Henry learned the identity of the informant for the slave catcher and that got him killed."

"And who is the slave catcher?" I asked.

"I—I don't know."

"Please don't lie to me, Matthew. If you were really my friend, you would not lie to me." I looked him in the eye.

He turned away. "I'm not lying to you. If I am holding back information it is only to protect you. Your safety is my number one concern before anything else."

"Who is the informant?"

"We don't know, and I can't say the police department is putting in much effort to find out. I'm here of my own accord, as you know. It's legal to take runaways back to the South if it can be proven they ran away."

"How do they prove that?" I asked.

"By name and physical description."

I frowned. "If you're right and this informant killed my brother, I deserve to know everything that you do about him. Henry was the only family I had." My voice caught, and I swallowed the lump in my throat. "I deserve to know."

He sighed. "There are mentions on the railroad that if you want to travel through Amherst on your way north, the person you need to talk to is the Reader."

"Who is the Reader?" I asked.

"That's what we don't know, but it seemed to me that he was the one who told which runaways to go to which places.

Sometimes, he told them places that would deliver them directly into the hands of the slave catchers."

"Sometimes?" I asked.

"From what we can tell he didn't do it every time. Perhaps that was so he could stay under the radar. He would pick and choose which runaways would go back south and those who could continue their journey to freedom."

"He was playing God," I gasped.

He nodded. "That is one way to look at it, yes. Perhaps he got pleasure from having power over people's lives. As far as we can tell, there is no pattern to who he saved and who he damned."

I shivered and then something he said struck me. "You keep saying *we*, but you told me that you are here in Washington of your own accord."

Again, he didn't meet my gaze.

"Are you part of the Underground Railroad?" I asked.

"No," was his curt reply.

I frowned. "And you keep referring to the Reader as a man. If you know nothing about this person, how can you be sure it is not a woman?"

"This work is far too dangerous for a woman," he said, as if even making the suggestion was insane.

I didn't agree with this at all, but I didn't think it was worth arguing the point with Matthew. "What compels the Reader to do this? Is he a Southerner? Does he have a connection to a plantation?"

"Greed. It is simple as that. From what we have learned, the Reader is paid handsomely by the slave catchers a portion of their fee every time he assists in apprehension."

"So could it be that the runaways that he lets get away have bounties on their heads?"

"It's possible." He nodded as if he had not thought of this before.

"If the runaways are in contact with the Reader to find the next safe house, then it makes sense to me that they would have seen him. One that got away has to know what he looks like."

"He is always wearing a mask when he tells them. He tells them also that his mask is for their safety because knowing who he is could be dangerous to them."

I sighed. If Matthew and whoever the *we* he was working with had not been able to find the Reader by now, I didn't know why I thought that Emily and I might be more successful.

"Will you be at the dinner party?" he asked, changing the subject.

I had been deep in thought. "What?"

"The Dickinsons' dinner party. I ran into Austin Dickinson and he asked me to join."

"You know Austin?" I asked.

He laughed. "Amherst isn't that big, you know, and we had played together some as children. Boys' games."

I couldn't help but wonder what those boys' games had been.

"No, I won't be at the party, and your comment reminds me that I have been away from the hotel for far too long. I am supposed to be writing the place cards for the event. If I don't finish them in a timely manner, Mrs. Dickinson will be cross with me."

"You should be there if I am. We are of the same class," he argued.

"We may be of the same class, but it is not our decision. Austin invited you as a friend. I'm just a servant, Matthew. You know that."

He looked me in the eye. "You're more than a servant to me, Willa. You are a compassionate and strong woman that any man would be lucky to have at his side no matter his class."

"Matthew," I gasped, looking around for anyone who might have overheard us. "You shouldn't say things like that."

"Why? My feelings for you have not wavered. I want you to know that."

I looked down and my gaze fell to his coat sleeve. "There's a thread that is hanging from your jacket. Don't pull on it or the whole arm might come undone."

Matthew pressed his lips together as if he was disappointed with the change of subject, but then his expression cleared as if he was accepting the sudden turn that I had made. "Oh, this jacket. I have mended it so many times over the last year, but I must say I'm a terrible tailor."

"I could mend it for you," I said. "If you give it to me, I can mend it this afternoon and give it to you at the dinner party. I won't be attending, but I will be nearby in case the Dickinsons need anything from me."

"Would you? It's a warm day and I can do without the coat for now. I would like it to be mended before I leave to return home. Who knows what state it will be in by the time I arrive in Amherst if it's not attended to?"

I accepted the coat and folded it in such a way that it appeared I was carrying a wool blanket. That might get some curious looks when the sun shone too brightly and when it was so warm, but it would have piqued people's curiosity much more if I had walked up the street with a man's coat hanging from my arm. "It's the least I can do. Even though I know you're not telling me everything, I know that telling me anything at all about the investigation into Henry's death is difficult for you. It's kind of you to tell me what you could." I paused. "But I do wish you would say more."

He smiled. "And your need to know every detail is one reason that I care about you so much. Can I walk you back to the hotel?" His face was hopeful.

I hated to disappoint him, but I shook my head. Hotel staff at least saw us walk away together. I didn't want them to think that I had been alone with Matthew this whole time and report that to Mr. Dickinson.

"It's a short walk. I can see the top of the hotel from here." I clutched his coat. "It's best if I go back alone."

He nodded. "I do hope that I see you at the hotel tomorrow, Willa, even if it's in passing."

I didn't say a word, but I hoped so too.

CHAPTER TWENTY-THREE

I GOT BACK TO the room and finished the place cards before anyone in the family realized I was gone. Something that I knew from my conversation with Matthew was that I would finally have to gather the courage to read the rest of my brother's journal. Henry wrote that he would not be naming names, so I knew the name of the Reader would not be in those pages, but there could be other clues to the Reader's identity that I might be able to glean. As painful as it was to see and read my brother's thoughts, it was something I could no longer avoid.

But when I read his words, it would be done. There would be no more Henry. He would be over. Because I had not read his diary yet, I knew there was more of him to discover. There was more to learn about my younger brother. When I read the words, I could not unread them. It would be a great loss to know that he was truly gone from my life.

I finished the place cards and went to find my cloak in the wardrobe in the parlor. The cloak was right where I left it. I slipped my hand inside until I found the secret pocket I had sewn into the fabric that was just big enough for my brother's tiny diary.

The diary was gone.

All of the air left my body, and my hands began to shake. How could I have been so foolish as to leave the diary unattended? I should have taken it everywhere I went. However, since coming to Washington and enjoying the fine weather and spring temperatures, I had not needed my heavy winter cloak. I had told myself the diary would be fine in the wardrobe with the cloak because it was locked in the hotel room that I shared with the two Dickinson daughters.

I took a breath. The diary must have fallen out of my pocket. Yes, that is what happened. All of the Dickinson girls' cloaks, coats, and hats were in the wardrobe. I removed them each one by one. Every time I took a garment out of the wardrobe, I searched it thoroughly and then laid it on the floor.

I did this to piece after piece and never found the diary. I sat in the middle of the carpet with dozens of coats, cloaks, and hats all around me. I checked my cloak pocket for what must have been the thirtieth time. I looked for any tiny tear in the hidden pocket. There was none. Henry's diary was utterly and truly gone, and someone stole it.

Tears rolled down my cheeks. I had put off reading my brother's words because it had been so painful the first time. Now, I cried because it was very likely that I would never read his thoughts again, and that was so much worse.

"Willa Noble, what in heaven's name are you doing?" Emily asked as she and Miss Lavinia walked into the parlor.

I wiped tears from my eyes. I didn't want the sisters, especially Miss Lavinia, to see me cry. I scrambled to my feet breathing heavily. "I'm so sorry, Miss Dickinson. While you were away, I got it into my head that I could organize the luggage in the parlor closet. I just wanted to make sure everything was in order for when you travel to Philadelphia since I won't be there to help you unpack. As you can see, it got a bit away from me."

"A bit?" Miss Lavinia asked as she scanned the room. "It looks like a tornado came through here."

"I'll be sure to clean up the mess in no time. When you return from your evening meal, the parlor will be well in order," I promised.

Shaking her head, Miss Lavinia carried their shopping baskets into the bedroom.

I began to pick up the coats and hang them back in the wardrobe.

Emily set her small satchel down on a table and began helping me gather the garments.

"You don't have to do that," I insisted. "I made the mess and now I will have to clean it up."

"Yes, but the question remains: Why did you make the mess?"

I hung up another coat. "I have just told you."

She cocked her head. "Willa, I saw you put all those coats, cloaks, hats, and gloves into that wardrobe with such care the day we arrived. Everything was perfectly aligned. There was no need to reorganize the closet."

"Maybe I just needed something to do after I helped your mother with dinner party preparations. I'm not used to sitting down. If we were back home, Margaret would have given me a long list of tasks to keep my hands and mind busy. A maid sitting still is the root of trouble, she says."

"Or maybe," Emily said as if she were just having a thought for the very first time, "you are organizing the wardrobe to recover from your walk with Officer Thomas?"

I glanced at the closed bedroom door. "How did you know?" I didn't see a purpose in denying it.

"One of the bellmen told me when I came into the hotel that my maid went for a walk with a young man. I asked him to describe the young man, and he described Officer Thomas down to the smallest detail. I told him that he was so good at it that he should work for the police and describe suspects to them. If he saw a crime being committed the culprit would surely be caught."

I felt my face grow hot. "Yes, I went on a walk with Ma— Officer Thomas. He wanted to talk to me again about my brother's murder."

"I see." She sat on the settee and removed her hat with a large dry flower on the brim. "And what did he say?"

I quickly told her about Matthew saying Mr. Johnson didn't kill my brother and what he knew about the Reader.

"And was that all?"

"Yes, of course." I held my hands behind my back and twisted my left wrist with my right hand. I wanted so much for this conversation to be over so that I could go back to searching for my brother's diary.

"I don't think so." Emily brushed at the sleeve of her dress. "When are you going to tell me about your relationship with the young police officer?"

I blinked at her. "My relationship?"

She looked up at me. "Yes, Willa. It is clear the two of you have a history together. He said that he knew you and your brother."

I blushed. "Henry had a way of finding trouble, as I have told you. Ma—Officer Thomas had arrested him in the past. He was lenient on Henry, and since then, he kept an eye on him. I met Officer Thomas through Henry. Because he was so kind to my brother, he is curious about what happened to him. I believe the two were friends in their way."

She nodded. "Maybe. But that is not the whole story. It does not tell me why he looks at you the way that he does. I may not have much experience in such things, but I do know love when I see it. He has love"—she paused—"for you."

"I don't—"

"Please, Willa, don't lie to me about this. We are partners in finding your brother's killer. To be that, we have to trust each other. If you keep talking around my questions, I will lose trust in you."

"He asked me to marry him," I said in a rush. "It was a year ago."

"And what did you say to that?" she asked, keeping her expression neutral.

"I said no." My answer was barely above a whisper, but Emily was a good listener and I knew she heard it.

"You said no. You surprise me, Willa," she said with a bit of awe in her voice. "Many young women in your station and even in mine would be elated at the chance to be the mistress of their own home, with children and the trappings of being a wife and mother. But you said no?"

"I'm not saying that I don't want those things someday," I said quietly.

"Then why did you not take them when they were offered to you?" she asked as if she really wanted to know, not to pry but because she was curious.

"I have my work . . ."

"And keeping a home is not work?" She leaned back on the settee. "I would say it's the hardest work there is. Other than gardening and being in the kitchen, I detest everything about it. Vinnie is sure to be better at the occupation than I ever will."

"Maybe it is more work than I am ready to do then," I said, hoping that our conversation would come to a natural end.

She smiled when I said that. "To think of domestic things is to give up internal thoughts. A new life would come at great cost."

I had never thought of it that way. The more time I spent with Emily, the more she showed me there are different ways of thinking. In that way, she was like Henry. When I had looked at life as hard work and a list of rules to follow, he had seen it as something completely different. Henry had seen the world as a place of adventure and new opportunity. I was just plodding along trying to keep myself on the straight path. There was quite a bit I could have learned from Henry if I had been willing to listen. There was still quite a bit that I could learn from Emily.

"I have had suitors," Emily went on to say. "Some would have wanted to marry me if given the right encouragement, but it is hard to find in the boys of Amherst more than a passing distraction. Why should I marry at all? I am comfortable with my family. Tell me how marriage can improve my life."

I didn't have an answer for that. "I can't, miss."

"In your case, the one improvement I see is love. He loves

you. But love"—she paused—"it leaves little time for anything else . . ." She trailed off, and for a moment, she had that faraway look in her eyes again. "It leaves little time for anything else," she repeated.

I took a breath. "I don't know if he loves me. He might think he does, but that's not the same thing. I—I think more than anything, he feels sorry for me because of my mother's death and for the trouble that Henry has gotten into in the past. He feels sorry for me even more now that Henry is dead. He wants to rescue me, but that is not the same thing as love."

She looked at me thoughtfully. "And do you need rescuing?"

I thought about her question. "I need to know who killed my brother."

Emily nodded. "And that's exactly what we are going to find out."

CHAPTER TWENTY-FOUR

I COULD NOT SLEEP at all that night. I twisted and turned on the settee that was too short for my long limbs. My mind was so occupied with the lost diary. How could I be so careless not to keep it with me at all times? What was I missing from its pages? I wasn't just thinking of the murder or what Henry might have been up to in the final days of his life, but what little pieces of Henry I could have winnowed out of those pages to learn more about him and the man he was in the process of becoming. He was only eighteen when he died. He was gone far too young.

The next morning when the sisters came out of their shared room, I'd already had their breakfast and coffee ordered and delivered by the hotel kitchen.

Emily rubbed her eyes. "Willa, we are so grateful that we brought you here. I love walking into the parlor and being greeted by these delectable smells." She poured herself a cup of coffee. Tucking the cup under her nose, she inhaled deeply.

"This is just what I need for today. Mother is going to be very anxious about the dinner party tonight. Instead of sightseeing, Vinnie and I are staying at the hotel to help any way that we can."

Miss Lavinia buttered a piece of toast. "Mostly, we are staying to keep Mother calm. We won't be doing any of the heavy lifting."

I had expected as much. I didn't say this, of course.

"I'm sure there will be plenty for all of us to do today," was my diplomatic response. Maybe I was getting better at speaking like a politician since working for the Dickinsons.

As it turned out we were all right. There was much to do to prepare for the dinner party. Where the sisters were concerned, it was a matter of going ribbon shopping for the perfect velvet ribbon for their hair, and I had to take Mrs. Dickinson's dress to a seamstress at the last minute. It seemed that a small tear happened just beside the seam in the bodice. Only an expert seamstress would have the ability to mend it to the point that it could not be seen.

The tear in the dress reminded me that I hadn't yet mended Matthew's coat, and he would be at the dinner party expecting to get it back. I had no idea how I would give it to him without being seen.

While the sisters were out on their errand, I removed the small mending case from my carpetbag. I thought I had some navy thread that would be a perfect match to his coat. Most of the thread I had was in masculine colors. Henry had the odd ability to tear a sleeve or pant leg every week. We could never afford to buy replacements for the clothes he harmed, so it was up to my trusty sewing kit to save the day.

Sewing was a skill that I had struggled with as a young girl. As a child, I hated to sit still, and that was what sewing required. I preferred the tasks of cleaning, fetching water, and cooking; anything that involved movement was welcomed.

As I grew older, I found that if I sat still too long, I gave time to my thoughts. Sewing was a skill in which my mind could wander, and I didn't like that. It was too easy to dwell on hardship and what I didn't have. If I kept moving, it was much more difficult to do that.

My mother insisted that I learn to sew though. She said it was a skill that all women needed no matter their class.

"I can assure you, the president's wife can darn a pair of socks. It is a required skill. I cannot send you into the world without knowing how to thread a needle, place a button, and mend a seam at the very least. If I don't I will have failed you as your mother."

"Why doesn't Henry have to learn to sew?" I had asked. My voice had been especially whiny because I knew on this occasion Henry was traipsing through the woods with his friends while I was trying and failing to sew a button on straight.

"Henry is a boy. Sewing is women's work." My mother had opened her sewing box and was removing all the buttons, needles, and thread that we were going to use for that day's lesson.

I looked at the window. It had been a Sunday afternoon. One of the few times that there was free time outside of school or cleaning for one of the rich families in Amherst. I wanted to be out tramping about like I knew Henry was. It wasn't fair that I was stuck back in our tiny home while Henry was having a fun day.

"Mama, it's Sunday. Can we have the lesson another day?"

"You know Sunday is the only time that I have any hope of teaching you children anything at all. Now please return your attention to the task at hand."

I wasn't ready to do that just yet. "You said that sewing is women's work, but then why is the village tailor a man?" I asked defiantly. I thought that I had really pinned my mother into a corner there.

"Mr. Roscoe the tailor is European. That is different. An American woman needs to learn to sew, not an American man."

I scowled. That logic had not worked for me, but ultimately, because I was an obedient child, I learned to sew, and now as an adult I even enjoyed it. Perhaps that is going too far. I didn't hate it, which was a vast improvement from my childhood.

I laid Matthew's coat across my lap and threaded my needle. I had been right; the navy thread was a perfect match.

I flipped the coat over and looked for the tear in the sleeve. It was in the right sleeve just a few inches up from the cuff. I stared at it with a sinking heart. Hadn't Miss Abigail said that one of the men who was meeting with Mr. Johnson at her inn was younger and had a tear in his right sleeve in that exact spot?

I shook my head. I knew that I couldn't be right about this. It was just a coincidence. And who is to say that Miss Abigail's description was accurate? She said they were there when the tearoom was busy. She was the only person waiting on the tables. It was very possible that she remembered the details incorrectly. It could have been the old man with the tear on his sleeve, or maybe the tear was on the young man's left arm. She was frazzled; she could have misspoken.

But in my heart I knew that wasn't the case. Matthew, my Matthew, was one of the two men who met with Mr. Johnson. This meant that he wasn't here to investigate Mr. Johnson or find my brother's killer. Instead, he just might be helping him.

CHAPTER TWENTY-FIVE

I HELPED THE DICKINSON sisters prepare for the dinner party. Both of them wore the finest dresses they brought with them to Washington. Emily's emerald ball gown offset the red in her hair. Her dark eyes sparkled as if she knew how lovely she was. Around her wrist there was a black velvet satchel that matched the black velvet ribbon in her hair. She smiled at me when she saw me admiring the satchel. "I do like the black velvet, but the most important detail is it is just big enough for paper and pencil. I'm sure I will meet some very interesting people tonight, and I want to jot them down. You never know what can be amusing for a letter to friends back home."

I smiled. "Then that satchel is not only fashionable but practical."

"Emily, are you ready?" Miss Lavinia came into the parlor. She wore a royal blue ball gown that looked as lovely on her as Emily did in hers. She didn't carry a satchel. I supposed that was because she didn't need paper and pencil wherever she went. Instead around her wrist there was a piece of fine lace. I guessed that it came from another dress at some point.

Before my realization over Matthew's coat sleeve, I had wanted to accompany them to the dinner party. What would it be like to be in the room with all those witty and intelligent people and their varied conversations? Just to be around a group like that would have to lend itself to making the listener wittier and more intelligent.

Miss Lavinia frowned at me. "I hope that you will stay here and out of trouble for the night. We don't need any more episodes from you."

"Vinnie, that is not fair. Willa didn't have an episode," Emily said.

Miss Lavinia eyed her sister. "She tore the wardrobe apart."

"Making a mess is not an episode. You're as bad as Mother's doctor who labels her days when she can't get out of bed as episodes. Don't you just think that makes it worse for her?"

Miss Lavinia huffed. "I wasn't talking about Mother. There is no point in talking about any of this now. We have to go. Father wants us there to greet the guests."

"Of course he does," Emily muttered. "Sister, do you ever feel like we are supposed to be dolls on display for our father's guests? We're there to make witty conversation and amuse old men who are embittered by years in politics."

Miss Lavinia arched her brow. "That is a very dark perspective on the evening. Maybe it is just a dinner party to celebrate Father's time in Congress. Why does it have to be anything other than that?"

Emily looked like she wanted to retort, but Miss Lavinia was faster. "Besides, Father would never see you, Sister, as just a doll. You've always pushed back too much."

Emily grinned. "Well, that's a relief."

Miss Lavinia put her hands on her hips. Because she had so many petticoats under her blue skirt, her stances seemed even more formidable. "Now, can we please leave?"

"I've been waiting for you all this time," Emily said.

Miss Lavinia threw up her arms.

Emily smiled, and then she turned to me. "Enjoy a night off, Willa. There are a few more books in my room. You're welcome to them."

I smiled and wondered if she had a volume with her that I would like as much as *Jane Eyre*.

There was a knock on the door, and Mr. Dickinson came into the room. "Emily and Lavinia, it's time to go down and greet our guests. Remember that tonight you're not only representing your family but the entire Commonwealth of Massachusetts. I trust there won't be any embarrassing missteps." He gave Emily a meaningful look.

Emily pressed her lips together. I guessed that she wanted to say something in return to her father but thought better of it.

Mr. Dickinson left the room, and the sisters followed him out. No one so much as looked back at me.

As much as I wanted to read another of Emily's books, Henry's diary was so much more pressing. I let out a breath as I put away the sisters' discarded ribbons and packages from their ribbon shopping trip earlier in the day. I had to search for the diary, and the time while the family was at the dinner party was my best chance. I bit my lip. As far as I knew, the only people who had been in our rooms were the five members of the Dickinson family and the hotel staff.

I couldn't for the life of me think of why a member of the staff would want to take the diary. There were so many more valuable things in our rooms to steal. Both the Dickinson sisters had a piece or two of fine jewelry and nice fans. They weren't much compared to what I had seen on many of the women in the city who seemed to be dripping with jewels, but they would still get a good price with a dealer who was willing to buy without asking too many questions.

I walked to the closed bedroom door and hesitated. I would be a fool not to think that the most likely person to take the diary was Emily or Miss Lavinia. This might be my only chance to search their things.

I opened the door. The bed had a white lace duvet over it with lace-lined pillows leaning against the ironwork headboard. The floor was covered with an ivy-patterned carpet of greens and creams. Those colors were mirrored in the wallpaper, which also had an ivy pattern, but in between the leaves were roses with blossoms in full bloom larger than my hand.

There was a chest of drawers in the room, a writing desk, and a wardrobe just like the one in the parlor.

When we arrived several days ago, I had helped the hotel maid unpack the girls' belongings. I knew where everything should be.

I started with the chest of drawers. I went through it quickly. In it, I found underclothes, stockings, and petticoats. There was also a small metal box. I opened it and found medicine. The brown glass bottles and jars were labeled with a piece of paper that said things like "headache," "stomach," and "sleep."

I closed the box with a frown and put it back where I found it.

After the chest of drawers, I moved on to the wardrobe. Inside were the sisters' dresses. I carefully removed each dress and looked for a pocket or hem where the diary could be placed. Again, I didn't find it. I was beginning to believe that I wasn't going to find my brother's diary. The pain that I felt in my chest the moment I realized that it was gone came back worse this time.

I moved on to the writing desk. It was a small desk just large enough for one person to write letters. It reminded me of the desk Emily had back in her bedroom in Amherst. The top of the desk was clear except for a small oil lamp, matches, a stack of fresh paper, and a writing set. The set was perfectly in line with the paper. I smiled at this. I guessed that Miss Lavinia had lined up the paper and pen set just so. It would not have been Emily; I knew that.

There was a single slim drawer in the desk. I opened it. Inside there were scraps of paper with scribbles on them. I recognized Emily's handwriting. Her penmanship was difficult to read. There were lines drawn through words where I could guess what might have been written there, but other words were scratched out so completely that it was impossible to know what they might have been.

I picked up one piece of paper.

> *Because I could not stop for Death—*
> *He kindly stopped for me—*
> *The Carriage held but just Ourselves—*
> *And Immortality.*

There was a knock on the parlor door, and I jumped. Quickly, I tucked the papers back into the desk drawer, left the bedroom and closed the door behind me, and went to the parlor door.

I opened the door, and a young girl no more than fifteen stood on the other side. She wore a maid's uniform. "I brought fresh towels for the ladies, miss."

I stared at her. My mind was still preoccupied with the missing diary and the bit of poetry that I found. Had she been inspired to write that poem over Henry, who died at the stables?

"Miss?" the young girl asked nervously.

I took the towels from her hands. "I'm so sorry. Yes, these are wonderful. Thank you for bringing the towels."

"You're welcome, miss," the girl said as she backed away. By the look in her eye, I guessed that she worried that something was wrong with me.

I thanked her again and shut the door. Holding the towels to my chest, I leaned against the closed door. My chest heaved up and down. I glanced back at the sisters' bedroom. There was one more place to search.

I opened the bedroom door a second time and went to the bed. I stuck my hand under the mattress. I felt nothing. I tried the other two sides away from the wall. Nothing still. Finally, I peeked behind the headboard and found a small leather book, my brother's diary.

CHAPTER TWENTY-SIX

I TUCKED THE DIARY into my satchel and left the room. I had to get out of there. My heart was pounding. I thought that I could trust Emily, but she stole my brother's diary. My thoughts raced. It might not have been Emily at all. It could have just as easily been Miss Lavinia. In any case, one of the sisters—or both of the sisters—had taken the diary. They had stolen something precious from me. I wasn't sure how I could go on with them.

Did I leave my employment? How would I afford a train ticket to return home? Where would I work when I got there? My thoughts were so jumbled together. I couldn't make any sense of them.

I had to get out of the hotel. A walk would clear my mind. That's what I needed. I hurried down the stairs to the main floor of the hotel.

Just as I reached the door, Matthew came inside. He looked

distressed. If he was just arriving now, when the dinner party began almost an hour ago, something must be amiss.

We saw each other at the same time, and we both froze. All I could think about was the tear on his sleeve that I had mended. I hadn't thought to bring the coat with me. It was still in the room.

"Willa," Matthew said.

His voice broke me out of my trance. "Officer Thomas," I said as formally as I could when I felt every vibration in my chest.

"Willa, I—"

"You must be looking for your coat. I did mend it, but I left it upstairs. Let me go grab it for you. Are you headed to the dinner party? I can give it to the coat check man under your name, and you will be able to take it when you leave. I think that is the best plan."

A pained expression crossed his face. "What's wrong? I can tell that something has happened."

"I mended your coat. I'll go get it now." I spun on my heels and fled back up the stairs. If only I had left the hotel a minute or two before, I would not have seen him so soon after knowing that he was involved with Mr. Johnson.

I let out a breath as I went back into the room. I did not *know* that he was involved with Mr. Johnson. At the same time, I didn't *know* he wasn't. I supposed asking Matthew was the only way of knowing for certain.

I found Matthew's coat where I had hidden it in the bottom of the wardrobe and left the room again. Letting out a breath, I walked up to the bellman at the coat check. "Please check this coat under the name of Matthew Thomas. He will pick it up this evening."

The bellman nodded and took the coat from my hands.

"What I want to know is how you got Officer Thomas's coat?"

I spun around to find Emily standing in front of me in her ball gown.

"Emily! What are you doing here?"

"I needed a break from the table. All those men want to do is complain about politics and gossip about their colleagues. It was interesting for the first thirty minutes." She removed her pencil from her satchel and held it in her hand. "Are you going to answer my question?"

I didn't say anything.

"Would you be the reason that Officer Thomas was late to the dinner party? That would be interesting to know."

"I'm not."

"Then how did you get his coat?" She rolled the pencil back and forth in her fingers.

"He gave it to me after his walk. He had a tear on the sleeve. I promised to mend it."

This piqued Emily interest. "On which sleeve?"

"The right."

Understanding filled Emily's eyes. "Was he the man who met Mr. Johnson in the tearoom at the inn?"

"I—I don't know."

She stopped moving the pencil. "But I can tell from your face that you are afraid that he might be."

I dropped my head. "I am."

"You need to come to the dinner party and observe what is going on. Officer Thomas and Mr. Johnson aren't anywhere near each other, but since you know Officer Thomas well, you might see something that I would miss."

"I can't come to the dinner party."

"Not as a guest, no, but as a servant you can."

"How?"

A butler was hurrying by with a tray of coffees, presumably for a group waiting for their rooms to be ready.

"Excuse me." Emily stopped him.

He smiled. "Yes, Miss Dickinson, how can I be of service?"

"I would like my maid Willa here to assist with the dinner party."

"But miss, we have everything well in hand. We don't need any help at all. I must tell you the waiters at the Willard are the very best in the world. I trained them myself. I wouldn't let a subpar servant on my staff."

"I'm sure that is true. However, it would be a great help to me personally to have Willa in the room. Her presence will steady me."

His forehead creased in concern. "Miss, is something wrong that you need your maid's support?"

"Well, yes, you don't know what it is like being a young woman in search of a husband. The pressure is intense. Willa's kind face will be a great comfort to me when I have to speak to those potential suitors."

Understanding dawned on the butler's face. "Say no more. I'm sure the pressure to marry well is heavy on your shoulders. Your father will expect you to find a successful husband just like himself." He put his free hand to his chest. "Washington might not be the very best place to find a sincere husband. The men here are politicians and because of that are well versed in the art of lying."

"I will keep that in mind, sir, but for my peace of mind, I would like to continue forward with the evening. My father went to a great deal of trouble to make it possible."

He bowed. "I will find something less complicated for your maid to do." He looked at me as if seeing me for the first time. "She's not homely, which is a great help. I have found that guests do not respond well to unattractive waiters. It upsets their appetite."

I ground my teeth at the comment but said nothing more. I felt like I was caught on a train and there was nothing I could do to keep it from barreling down the tracks. I didn't want it to stop completely, just slow down.

The butler, who was still holding the coffee, turned to me. "Come with me. We will have to find a uniform for you if you are going to be in the dining room."

Emily smiled at me. "Perfect."

Perfect wasn't the word I would have used. I didn't think it was perfect at all.

Emily went back to the dinner party, and I followed the butler through a hidden door in the wall. He looked over his shoulder. "Don't look so afraid, miss."

"I'm not afraid." My wavering voice betrayed my fear.

"My name is Dexter. I have been a butler here at the Willard for over twenty years. Nothing happens at this hotel that I don't know about." He paused.

"Oh," I said.

"Nothing," he insisted. He stopped in front of a closet. "There are extra uniforms in there. I trust you will be able to find your size. There is a changing room at the end of the hallway. When you have finished, come back to this spot, and I will give you your duty for the evening." He walked away.

I stepped into the closet and saw a line of black-and-white maid dresses and caps. There were shoes as well, but I opted to wear my own shoes. I still remembered how my toes ached from wearing those too-small shoes when I first arrived for my interview at the Dickinson home weeks ago.

I gathered up the dress and walked down the cold hallway. There was a scraping sound behind me. I jumped and looked over my shoulder. A gray mouse froze in the middle of the hallway. We stared at each other for a moment, and then he scurried away.

I let out a breath and continued down the corridor. In the changing room, I found a number of ladies' clothes on hooks. It seemed that several of the hotel maids changed into their uniforms for work here.

I quickly put on the borrowed dress. The sleeves were a little too short for my long arms. I pulled at them and sighed. The skirt was a little too short and brushed the top of my ankles when it should have reached my heels. I hoped that Dexter and the Dickinsons wouldn't notice the ill fit of my clothing.

I smoothed my hair in the broken looking glass on the wall and went back into the hallway. Dexter stood outside of the dress closet where I had left him.

He scrunched up his forehead. "The dress is a bit short."

"I'm tall. It was the best fit I could find."

He sighed. "I hate to imagine what my mentor would think of me allowing a maid in the dining room with a dress too short in the skirt and sleeve." He shook his head. "If it can't be helped, it can't be helped. Miss Dickinson wants you in the dining room, and our goal at the Willard is to fulfill all the guests' wishes that we possibly can. That is what we are going to do." He turned around. "Follow me."

Instead of taking me back through the hidden door in the lobby, I followed Dexter through a weaving trail of servants' passageways in the hotel. When he came to a stop, he pointed at the door. In a low voice he said, "The dining room is through there."

"And what do you want me to do when I go in the dining room?" I asked in an equally low voice.

"Nothing. My staff is well trained. You are there to support Miss Dickinson. Stand in the corner and be quiet." His tone was stern.

I frowned.

"Now go. I have much work to do."

I went through the door. I found myself in the same dining room where I had met Mr. Dickinson for the first time when the family had planned the party. The two gas chandeliers sparkled above in the carved ceiling, and a golden cloth covered the tables. The dishes adorning the table were the white and blue-lined plates and saucers with the scalloped edges that Mrs. Dickinson selected at the planning meeting. The table was set for a party of sixteen, and the only women at the table were Mrs. Dickinson and her daughters. The rest of the attendees were men and seemed to be from all walks of life. I recognized the people from Amherst, but my eyes went to Matthew immediately. I noted that he looked quite nervous sitting with so many learned men from Washington.

Next to Matthew sat a balding man with blue eyes and a

long face. He nodded at something Matthew said and seemed to be engaged in the conversation.

I couldn't catch what they were saying as another man was giving a passionate speech. He wasn't directing his conversation to anyone in particular. He was a young man with a dark beard and piercing eyes. He said, "The Whig party has no future if it does not take a stand one way or the other on the issue of slavery. It has to pick a side to survive. It's all but been torn apart from it. So many of our members have left for the Republican or Democratic Parties because there is no official stance. Some even have declared the party dead."

"Mr. Allen, the party is not dead," Mr. Dickinson said. "Am I not still a Whig in the eyes of Congress?"

"But for how long? I tell you the Whigs are all but gone, and it's over slavery. The nation is being ripped in two because of it. Those who are left standing in the middle are the ones who will be torn to bits when this all blows up," a red-faced man said from the other end of the table. Perspiration gathered on his forehead as he spoke.

Mr. Dickinson set his wineglass back on the table. "There are other issues that my party is more concerned with. Economic stability is at the forefront."

"How can the economy or any of these other so-called issues be more important than this one?" Mr. Allen wanted to know.

"All topics of the law are given their due," Mr. Dickinson said. "I agree that this issue of slavery seems to be coming to a head. Every time a new state or territory is added to the Union we have to ask if this new addition will be slave or free. It's a ridiculous question to ask. What we should be asking is how this new territory will increase the wealth and power of the United States of America."

"When you do that," a second young man spoke up, "you are displacing the Indians who live in those places."

"Let's not get into that," the red-faced man harped.

The young man looked like he wanted to argue more but pressed his lips into a thin line.

"Where are the Indians going to go if we continue to push them west?" Emily chimed in. "Will we push them into the ocean?"

"This is not a discussion to be had at the dinner table in mixed company," Mr. Dickinson said. "Politics is men's work."

"Men's work, women's work. I can scream the number of times I have heard that. What if my interests are supposed to be reserved for men? What am I supposed to do with those?" Emily wanted to know.

"They can't be your interests," the young and bearded Mr. Allen said.

"How can you tell me how I can and cannot feel?" Emily asked. "If you stub your toe and experience pain, what should I say to you? Well, as a man you should be stronger than that. That should not hurt you. I don't think you would like that."

"That is not the point I'm making."

"I see, but it is the point that I'm making, which is the difference," Emily said archly.

"Mr. Allen, it seems that you have met your match in Miss Dickinson here," a man with sandy-colored hair that was going gray at the temples said.

"Westward expansion is not the main concern," Mr. Johnson spoke up in his gruff voice. "Our country is being torn in two over the issue of slavery as Mr. Allen said."

Everyone at the table looked at the stable owner.

"And what is your view on it?" Emily asked, holding her glass in the air.

"My view is of no importance," he practically growled.

Emily set her empty glass on the table. "I think your view is very important, Mr. Johnson. Is it not true that a young man was killed in your stables a few weeks ago? There are murmurings in Amherst that he was in some way involved in the Underground Railroad. Is that not true?"

I froze in my spot against the wall. How could Emily just come out and say that? She had to know that it would send Mr. Johnson over the edge.

Mr. Johnson glared at her. "I had a stable hand that was killed by a horse because the stable hand was careless. That's all there is to it. When people are around horses they forget that they are large and powerful animals. That's what my employee did and now he is dead. It's no one's fault but his own."

I gave a quick intake of breath. When I did I grabbed the attention of Matthew. His head turned in my direction, and his eyes went wide as if he realized that it had been me standing there the whole time. In the hotel uniform, I had been overlooked by everyone at the dinner table, including Matthew. It was far too easy to see servants as fixtures in a room instead of the real people that they were.

"You seem to be very determined to blame young Henry for his own death," Emily said.

Mr. Johnson's jaw twitched, but he didn't say anything back.

"Emily," Mr. Dickinson spoke up. "That is enough."

Emily frowned but did not argue with her father. She knew that she had pushed the conversation as far as it would go.

Mrs. Dickinson cleared her throat. "Mr. Campbell," she addressed the balding man who had been speaking to Matthew when I first came into the room. "Have you had an opportunity to speak to Mr. Milner? He's our postmaster in Amherst." She gestured at Mr. Milner who was sitting across the table from her next to Matthew. Mrs. Dickinson smiled at Mr. Milner. "I'm sure you already know that Mr. John Campbell is the postmaster general for the nation."

Mr. Milner pulled on his collar. "I do."

"Oh!" Mr. Campbell said in a friendly voice. "How nice to meet one of our postmasters from a small town. Every member of the postal service is important. We are making so many vast improvements because of the hard work of the men on the front lines of delivering the mail."

Mr. Milner's face turned red. "Thank you, sir. We all try to deliver the mail in a precise and timely fashion."

Mr. Campbell nodded. "I know this very well."

"Mr. Milner told my sister and me that he was in Washington for a postal conference this week. Were you at that conference as well, Mr. Campbell?" Emily asked.

The postmaster general wrinkled his brow. "I don't know anything about a postal conference happening this week in Washington. Usually, I'm notified about such events. I do hope that my secretary did not make a mistake and leave this off my calendar for the week."

"No, sir." Mr. Milner took a sip from his wineglass and then set it back on the table. "The conference was a small regional affair. As much as we would have been honored to have you be a part of it, sir, we know your duties are far too demanding for our small gathering."

"Yes, that must be it," Mr. Campbell said absently.

"If it was a regional meeting," Emily said, "it does not make much sense that you meet so far from home. There are many big cities in New England to meet."

"Emily," Mr. Dickinson said in a measured tone.

Mr. Campbell opened his mouth as if he wanted to say more on the matter, but Mr. Johnson stood up from the table. "Thank you for the kind invitation this evening, but it is time for me to leave. I have pressing business that I must attend to."

Mr. Dickinson's face turned red. "Please stay, Mr. Johnson. I hope my daughter speaking out of turn has not caused you to leave."

"It hasn't," Mr. Johnson said, but I believed that everyone knew that it had.

I noticed then that Mr. Milner stared at the table and his arms were pressed closely to his sides. It was almost as if he was trying to make himself as small as possible.

"Good evening." Mr. Johnson stomped out of the room.

When he was gone, Mr. Milner looked up and seemed to visibly relax.

Mr. Dickinson cleared his throat. "I want to apologize for my guest's behavior. I was hesitant to invite him here tonight with so many esteemed guests at my table, but he is a businessman from Amherst. I invited him out of duty. I regret that decision now."

"Yes, that was quite rude to leave the dinner party like that," Emily said.

Mr. Dickinson glared at her. I would say that Emily was in a whole heap of trouble as far as her father was concerned.

Without taking the time to think about it, I went through the door after Mr. Johnson. By the time I made it to the lobby, he had his coat and hat in hand and was striding out of the hotel.

I hesitated. What did I do now? Follow him? By myself? Was I crazy for even thinking it?

Outside of the hotel I watched as Mr. Johnson climbed into a carriage and a moment later the carriage was underway down the busy street.

"Miss Willa, you look like you're lost."

I turned and found Buford standing on the sidewalk. "That man who just came out of the hotel. I—I think he's up to something."

"I do too. That's why we need to follow him." I looked over my shoulder to find Emily standing in the middle of the sidewalk in her ball gown.

Buford began to untether his horse from the hitching post. "Then we better go before we lose sight of him."

Emily ushered me to the carriage. I climbed inside and she came in after me. The wide hoops of her skirt took up most of the space between us. Buford called to Betty Sue the horse, and the carriage rolled into traffic.

I stared at Emily. "How?" I couldn't even think of the best way to ask the question.

"How did I get here?" she asked with a smile.

"Yes, did you walk out of your father's dinner party too?" My eyes were wide.

She looked out the window of the carriage. "Not exactly. I

said I had a headache and needed to lie down. I'm sure my father is using that right now to explain my behavior to all of his guests. I helped him by leaving. He will say something to the effect that women don't know what they are saying when they have a headache or some such nonsense. The key to the nonsense that men say about women is to use it to our advantage as I did in this case."

She opened the window and stuck her head out. "Buford is good at following. He is keeping a delivery wagon between our carriage and that of Mr. Johnson's. I'm sure Mr. Johnson has no idea we are behind him."

I folded my hands in my lap. I was alone with Emily in the carriage. I went along with her like I always did, but how could I trust her when I knew either she or her sister stole my brother's diary? I considered saying something about it, but it seemed the more pressing issue at hand was the fact that we were following Mr. Johnson. I asked, "And what are we going to do when we catch up with him?"

"I haven't settled on that part yet."

I bit the inside of my lip. She had better settle on it soon, because I had a feeling that Mr. Johnson would not like it if we showed up unannounced.

The small window between the driver's seat and the carriage opened, and we heard Buford's voice. "It looks to me like he's stopping at the Washington Monument. You want me to follow him?"

Emily's skirts made a ruffling sound as she scooted closer to the window to be heard. "Yes, don't lose him!"

The wagon jerked as Buford snapped his switch in the air to encourage Betty Sue to trot faster.

A moment later, the carriage rocked to a stop. I peered out the window and saw the foot of the Washington Monument twenty or so yards away. I could only make it out because of the gas lampposts throughout the public grounds. The sun had long set.

"What do we do?" I asked in a hoarse whisper.

She opened the carriage door. "We get out, of course." Without waiting for Buford to help her, she hopped out of the carriage.

Even with my trust in Emily waning, I groaned and followed her.

CHAPTER TWENTY-SEVEN

EMILY STOOD UNDER a lamppost in her beautiful gown, and the black velvet ribbon in her hair caught the light. My heart seized, for in my mind, for just a moment, she looked like a ghost.

"Willa, do not stand there and stare. Come on," she said.

I looked back at Buford and Betty Sue.

"We will wait right here for you, miss. Don't you worry about that."

I nodded and ran over to Emily. When I reached her, I said, "I don't know if we should be out here at night. Being out after dark can be dangerous, especially in such a large city." I glanced around as if someone was going to jump out of the trees at any moment.

"Buford is here. We'll be fine." She picked up her skirts. "This is not the best outfit for tracking a killer, but there's nothing to be done about that." She started toward the Washington Monument. The marble gleamed in the moonlight. The stone tower that had meant to be an obelisk and the tallest structure in Washington stopped at 156 feet in the air.

I had read about the monument in the paper when construction stopped last year because there was no money left to build it. After seeing the majesty of his home in Mount Vernon, it felt like an insult to Washington that the monument to his greatness would go on unfinished. Perhaps in this way it was a symbol of where the country was at the moment, half finished.

"Come now, Willa. The monument will be here to admire during the daytime. We have to find Mr. Johnson." She disappeared around the base.

With fear gripping my heart, I ran after her. If anything happened to Emily, I would never forgive myself, and I doubted her family would be very forgiving either.

On the other side of the monument, two men stood under a lamppost. I immediately recognized the larger of the two men as Mr. Elmer Johnson.

There were still piles of dirt and debris around the monument as if the men who had been constructing it just walked away from the build site when the money ran out. Emily hid behind a metal barrel just ten feet from the two men. How she got there without being seen, I didn't know.

I knew why she moved. I couldn't make out anything the men were saying from where I stood at the base of the monument. I grimaced. Emily might have been able to sneak over to the barrel in her crinoline and hoop skirts, but there was a good chance that I would trip over my own two feet when I tried.

Emily waved at me to join her. The two men turned away

from us and were facing the Mall. I took that to be my chance. Lifting my skirts again, I ran to Emily's side and ducked behind the barrel next to her. I caught my breath.

"Shh," she whispered. "Stop breathing so hard. They'll hear you."

I put a hand to my chest and willed myself to calm down. I thought that I was breathing hard due to my anxiety about what we were doing rather than from exertion or running. The itchy wool from the hotel maid's uniform felt rough against the palm of my hand.

Emily peeked around the barrel in one direction. I looked around it in the other. The men had turned again, and I saw that they both faced the monument. To my surprise, the man next to Mr. Johnson was Black. He wore a brown suit with a black scarf tied at his throat. His beard was trimmed and grizzled with gray as was his hair.

"You have done good work for us," the man with Mr. Johnson said. "But the death of the boy has brought too much attention to our work. We will have to leave Amherst."

"You can't change course now. There are too many who know Amherst is the place to come. It would be impossible to reach everyone running north."

"I have to think of the safety of these men, women, and children. That boy brought to light that there is someone in your local network who is betraying us."

"Let me find out who the traitor is, and we can return to normal," Mr. Johnson pleaded.

I glanced at Emily, and she sat riveted watching the argument between the two men.

"No. I can't risk any more lives while I wait for you to sort this out. The cost is too great. It is beyond great. It is death itself. There are other towns that are ready and willing to help. Northampton among others."

"But—" Mr. Johnson started to argue again.

"No. If you can clean up the mess in Amherst we will try again there, but going forward, no conductors will be taking anyone through Amherst." The finality in the man's voice was palpable.

"Yes, sir," Mr. Johnson said grudgingly.

"Good, Johnson. I know you came to Washington hoping for a different result, but this is the way that it has to be. Saving lives is our focus, and above that, abolishing the stain on the world that is slavery." The man put on his hat. "The decisions have been made. Go back to Amherst and do what you can as an observer of the movement if not a true participant." He strode away.

Beside me, Emily tried to shift her position, but in doing so she caught the heel of her shoe on the last hoop of her skirt. She flopped over like a fish on a line and landed with an "Omph."

I scooted over and helped her up. There was dirt all over the back of her dress. I didn't know how we would get it out of the delicate fabric. I prayed the dress wasn't ruined. It was the only ball gown that she owned.

Just as I got her to her feet, Mr. Johnson loomed over us. "What are you two doing here?"

Emily dusted off her hands and didn't appear to be the least bit concerned over her tumble. "We were about to ask you the same thing, Mr. Johnson. It seems quite late for a nighttime meeting with a mysterious man by the Washington Monument."

"You need to go back to your hotel and forget about everything that you have seen here tonight."

"That's very unlikely to happen," Emily retorted. "Who was that man with you? You appeared to be in deep conversation."

Mr. Johnson scowled at her. "I can't answer that question."

"Are you double-crossing him? Everyone in Amherst knows that you are the one who hands runaways over to slave catchers."

Mr. Johnson glared at her. "I do no such thing."

Emily folded her arms and looked up to him. "Well, from the conversation that I just heard it sounded like he caught you doing it and put a stop to it," Emily baited.

Mr. Johnson clenched his fists at his sides. "You heard nothing of the kind."

I found myself taking two small steps back away from him.

Emily, however, held her ground. "Isn't that true?"

"No, it's not true. In fact, it could not be further from the truth. I'm a conductor on the railroad. I'm saving runaways, not harming them."

Emily and I stared at him.

He looked at me. "I hired your brother to work for me. He had heard about the railroad and had interest in helping. I was also in need of a stable boy, so the timing was perfect. He was hired to care for the horses, but more important, he was hired to be a spy for the railroad. For months, we had been plagued with slave catchers, all of whom seemed to know what we were up to. I run a very tight operation. The only people that could have known were from my circle. I hired Henry to find out who the person was."

My heart beat faster in my chest. Could what he said be true, that he was on Henry's side, not against it?

"What proof do you have?" Emily asked defiantly.

I had the proof, I realized. The proof was in Henry's diary, but I didn't have it in my hands. A sinking feeling fell over me.

The diary was back in the maid's dressing room at the hotel. I had left my satchel with my dress. I kicked myself. How could I lose it again after finding it? I had been so preoccupied by the idea of going into the dining room and facing the Dickinson sisters and Matthew that I just left it on the peg with my dress. Surely, someone would have stolen it by now. I felt ill. That diary might have all the answers that I was looking for, the proof that Mr. Johnson's story was true or not.

"The stories about me were planted with a purpose," Mr. Johnson said. "And under my direction. They were meant to trick the enemy, and they worked for a time."

"How can we believe anything you say?" I asked. "My brother is still dead. I can't ask him to verify the story."

"That's none of my concern. My concern is that you girls don't mention anything that you saw tonight to anyone. Do you understand me?" The whites of his eyes caught the reflection of the flame in the lamppost.

I gasped.

"If you do, the cause will be ruin. Slavery needs to be obliterated, and if I have to do that single-handedly, then I will. I will find a way even if it's not being a conductor. The Reader has ruined Amherst. We will no longer be able to help those trying to make it to Canada. It's not safe." He scowled at me. "Your brother has fault in this too."

The Reader? That was the name that Matthew mentioned as well.

"Is that why you killed Henry, because you think he failed you in finding the Reader?" I asked.

"You think I killed Henry?" He glared at us.

I shivered. Even though I was tall for a woman, Mr. Johnson was still taller than I was. It wasn't often I felt small, but next to Mr. Johnson, I did.

I was frightened, but I held my ground just like Emily had done. "I do."

Some of the fire went out of his eyes. "I tell you I didn't. Losing that boy was a great tragedy. I saw a future for him in this. He was passionate about the cause."

I stared at him, confused.

"If you didn't kill him, who did?" Emily asked.

"The Reader did, of course. Henry knew he who was. He told me as much, and he was going to tell me more the night he died. I was moving a young mother and her child to safety. I told him that I didn't have time to discuss it the last time I saw him alive. I regret that now. I could have at least learned the name."

I remembered something Jeremiah said about being away from the stables the night Henry died. "Was Jeremiah York with you when Henry died?"

Mr. Johnson's eyes went wide. "How did you know that?"

I shook my head and felt an odd mix of relief and betrayal. Jeremiah had known that Henry's death was tied to the Underground Railroad, and he knew that Mr. Johnson was innocent, but he told me neither. In fact, he had led me to believe that Mr. Johnson might be the killer. Why? Why didn't he tell me the truth?

"Jeremiah was helping me move the mother and child that night. They were unwell and the child needed to be carried."

My heart ached for that mother and child. Did they make it to safety? I wasn't sure that Mr. Johnson even knew. After they left Amherst, they would have been in another conductor's hands.

"Now, I will ask you two girls to stay away from this business. Henry was killed because he got too close. That could very well happen to you." He marched away into the dark Mall.

We had to return to the hotel. My skin crawled at the thought of my brother's diary being in someone else's hands.

As promised, Buford and Betty Sue waited for us just where we had left them. Buford helped Emily into the carriage and then offered me his hand to assist me as well. He smiled at me. "Did you find the answers you're looking for, Miss Willa?"

I gave him a wan smile. "I found answers to questions that I hadn't known were there, but no, I didn't find the answer to my question, my biggest question."

The question I spoke of was who killed my brother.

Emily and I rode back to the Willard in silence. We were both lost in our own thoughts. I watched as Washington at night traveled by the window. There were a few people out walking briskly here and there. Carriages and wagons made their way down Pennsylvania Avenue. There were countless lights ablaze inside of the president's house, and I wondered if there was some sort of formal function at the White House that night.

When we reached the hotel, Emily did not wait for Buford to open the carriage door but opened it herself. "This was a striking turn of events, wasn't it? Who would have thought Mr. Johnson wasn't the villain?"

"And Matthew," I said quietly. "Matthew was helping Mr. Johnson, too, so he is also innocent in my brother's death."

Emily studied me and then said, "Let's go inside and discuss it." She hopped out of the carriage.

I stepped out of the carriage more slowly. "I have to go back in the maid quarters and return this dress for my own."

She nodded. "Don't be long; we have a lot to talk about."

I nodded. We had more to talk about than she even knew.

"Miss Willa," Buford said.

I turned and saw him standing under the lamppost next to Betty Sue.

"Will you tell me why we followed that man tonight?"

I glanced back at the hotel. I was eager to go inside and find my brother's diary. It had to be where I left it in the changing room. It just had to be. I turned to face Buford again. His kind face studied me, and I knew that I owed him an answer. He had followed Mr. Johnson no questions asked. He'd done it, I knew, because of the friendship we had built in the last few days.

"I lost my brother recently. I thought he knew how he died."

He crinkled his brow. "And did he?"

I shook my head. "No." I licked my lips. "But I am determined to find the answer."

"Then I know you will find all the answers you seek."

I wanted to hug him, but instead I gave Betty Sue's nose a pat before going into the grand hotel.

CHAPTER TWENTY-EIGHT

THIS LATE IN the evening, the lobby was all but empty. The two bellmen waited at attention at the door, and a new butler stood at the base of the stairs ready to assist guests to their rooms. While Emily headed for those stairs, I put my head down and went to the hidden door. Much to my relief, it was unlocked. I slipped inside the dim servants' hallway that was simply lit with candle sconces on the wall every three paces.

Not wanting to waste any time, I hurried down the corridor. With cold stone an arm's length from me on either side, I felt like I was walking around the inside of a medieval castle, not in a modern hotel.

The dressing room was empty and my dress was just where I had left it. I hurried toward it and found my satchel hanging behind the dress on the hook. The book was there. I could feel it. A crude bench was against one stone wall, and holding the satchel to my chest, I slid down onto the seat. With shaky hands I opened the bag, and my brother's diary was, in fact, inside. Relief flooded through me.

I knew that I promised Emily I would return quickly to our rooms, but I had to see what the pages said. I opened the book to the very last entry, which had been written the day before my brother died.

January 30, 1855

I know who the Reader is, but I won't write the name in these pages. There is far too much of a risk that this diary could fall into the wrong hands. If I had the will, I would throw it into the fire. It would be much safer if no one ever read a word that I have written here. But I don't have the will to do that. Perhaps I hope that this diary will fall into the right hands someday and be a testament to the good work that we have done.

I am the only one who knows the Reader's identity. I will tell Jeremiah and Elmer when they return from their work tomorrow night. Until then, I will stay close to the barn and away from town. If I see the Reader in town, there is no telling what I will do. Both Mother and Willa have told me that I don't think before I act, but in this case, I am thinking. I will stay in safety until all can be revealed.

The entry ended. Those were the last words my brother ever wrote. I knew when I combed through the diary later page by page and sentence by sentence, there still wouldn't be any hint to the Reader's identity. Henry would have been too careful for that. I thought of him, that last day of his life.

Knowing Henry, he would have been buzzing with excitement with his discovery. He would have paced and had trouble sitting still. Anyone who saw him would have known that something was on his mind and whatever it was, it was big.

He had been wise to hide out in the stables that day, but what he hadn't expected was for the Reader to come to him. He thought he was safe when in actuality he was trapped. I shivered.

I finally made it back to our rooms in my own dress. I knew I had taken much longer than Emily had anticipated. I had every expectation that Emily would be waiting for me tapping her foot in the parlor. When I opened the door it was Miss Lavinia who was sitting on the settee with her arms folded, not Emily.

"Where is Emily— I mean Miss Dickinson?" I asked.

Miss Lavinia scowled at me. "Do not put on a facade that you and my sister are not close enough friends that you call her by her Christian name."

"With her permission," I said. "I would never call her that if she didn't suggest it."

Miss Lavinia's delicate features settled into her scowl, and for a moment, I could see a clear resemblance to her father. Mr. Dickinson had the strongest will in the Dickinson family, but I would put Miss Lavinia second. When their father was gone one day, it would be Miss Lavinia who would hold the family together, but I couldn't help but wonder what the personal cost would be for her to fill that role. Would she forgo a life of her own to care for the Dickinson legacy?

"What you need to know about my sister is she is not like the rest of us. She thinks differently. She speaks differently, and she acts differently too. She does not care for conventions, church, or expectations. She makes up her own mind and makes her own way. She is more than a sister to me. She is my closest friend. She is this to me when I know that she would much prefer Susan's company and now perhaps yours as well. Even so, I understand her best, and I will protect her fiercely." Her gaze narrowed. "I will not let a *maid* lead her into trouble. I am sorry that your brother was killed, but that is your issue. It had nothing to do with the Dickinson family. Your hardship is not our hardship. It is separate from us. Stop dragging my sister, who is just looking for a little passing entertainment, into it."

I swallowed as she finished her speech. I bit back the words that gathered on my tongue. The reason that Miss Lavinia could think my brother's death was passing entertainment was because she personally had not retained such a blow. And she could speak to me as she did now with her father's wealth and importance, two things that I would never have.

In the back of my mind, I heard my mother admonish me for my envy. She had believed that the good Lord provided for all in his way. We never went without a dry place to sleep and without food and water. She would remind Henry and me when we were young that we had more comforts and blessings than many other souls. "Have you not seen the Black men and women who move through town on their travels farther north?" Mother would ask us. "You do not know the hardship they have felt. I pray you never do, but do not complain that you have stale bread for another night with no butter. You have bread. That in and of itself is a blessing."

It was hard to accept that when Miss Lavinia was speaking to me in this way though.

"Vinnie," Emily said as she came into the room in her dressing gown. "Please do not speak to my friend Willa like that."

Miss Lavinia spun around. "Sister, I am just trying to protect you."

"Protect me from what? Myself?" Emily scoffed. "It was my idea, not Willa's, to investigate her brother's death. It was my idea to chase after Mr. Johnson tonight too."

"Sister, you can't be running all over a strange city after a man you don't know. I'm not just thinking of your safety, I'm thinking of your reputation as well. You could be ruined."

"Ruined for what? Marriage? What loss would that be to me?" Emily folded her arms.

Miss Lavinia frowned. "What about the fact that Willa has been lying to you all this time?"

"I have not," I cried, coming to my own defense for the first time.

"Oh, really? Have you told her about the diary?" Miss Lavinia's eyes bored into me. "Have you?"

My heart sank.

Miss Lavinia nodded. "I can tell from your expression that you have not." She turned to Emily. "Did she tell you about the diary? Did she tell you that she has her brother's diary?"

Emily turned to me. "Willa?" There was hurt in her voice. "Is there a diary?"

I didn't say anything. I didn't know what to say. How could I say to her that I kept the diary to myself because it was the last piece of my brother, of my family, that I would ever have? And if that is true, how could I say to her I have had it for all this time but have been too frightened to read it from beginning to end for fear of being overcome by memory? Sometimes memories, even good memories, were better left buried in the far reaches of the mind for the pain they caused in the present.

"Willa?" Emily asked again. Her voice was sharper this time. "Is this true?"

I bit the inside of my cheek. "It's true."

Miss Lavinia smiled, pleased that she outed me this way.

"I want to see it," Emily said.

"She doesn't have it now." Miss Lavinia stood up from the settee. "I hid it." She left and went into the bedroom.

"Emily," I said.

Emily frowned. "Why didn't you tell me about this?"

"It's the last thing that I have from my brother. I—I just wanted to keep it to myself for a while. Maybe I kept it secret for a little too long, but I always intended to show it to you after I read it myself."

Her face softened. "If it were my brother, I would have felt the same way."

Miss Lavinia ran back into the parlor. Her face was red. "The diary is gone."

I looked her square in the eye. "That's because I found it hidden behind the headboard in your room." I removed the diary from my satchel. "You had no right to take it. It was left to me from my brother."

Miss Lavinia pointed at me. "Do you see how she is behaving, Emily? She's a maid and she's keeping things from you."

"Vinnie," Emily said gently. "I know at some point in your life you gave yourself the job of protecting me. I'm grateful for that. There will be times I need protection, but I do not need protection from Willa. She is my friend."

Miss Lavinia folded her arms. "She lied to you."

"No, she omitted."

"What is the difference?" Miss Lavinia wanted to know.

"Everything. Everything has secrets, even the skies," Emily said. Again, she spoke in such a way as if she were testing the words on her tongue and deciding if they were sweet or bitter to her.

Miss Lavinia threw up her hands. "Very well. Even though I have misgivings, I will trust your judgment, Sister, when it comes to Willa. You leave me no choice." She went into the bedroom, slamming the door after her.

Emily nodded to the diary. "Are you ready to share it now?"

I pressed my lips together. "I am."

Emily and I pored over the diary for most of the night. In each day's entry, Henry detailed how he spent his days. It seemed that most of his time was spent caring for the horses at the stables, but he was able to find time to slip away and continue his investigation. It seemed a favorite place for him to gather information was from the old men who sat day after day by the Amherst post office and then also outside of the town bakery and butcher shop.

"He was going to the places where people gossip the most," Emily said. "But I wonder if this was his undoing. After so many times loitering around the post office, bakery, and butcher, people would start to ask questions about why he was spending so much time there."

"And knowing Henry's reputation, they would assume that he was there to steal something," I said reluctantly.

"But the killer might not. Somehow the Reader realized what Henry was really doing. It might have been the questions he was asking. People talk."

I nodded. "I wished he had told me what he was up to."

She leaned back in her chair. "What would you have said to him if he had?"

"I would have told him to stop because it was dangerous."

"And so you know why he didn't tell you," she said gently.

Near the end of the diary there was a list of names of prominent men in Amherst and in Massachusetts.

Emily stared at the page. "My father's name is on this list. So are many of his friends. These are all names of businessmen, politicians, and educators."

"His list of suspects before he narrowed it down to one person?" I asked.

"I can tell you that my father has nothing to do with this. He's a Whig. He wants peace and has not taken a public stand on slavery in either way. He would not put himself in this conflict."

I frowned.

"You need to go back to Amherst. Tomorrow. And see what you can learn."

I stared at her. "But we were to be here another week."

"I know, but if we are going to solve your brother's murder, there is no time to waste." She sighed. "I wish that I could come with you, but I'm expected to stay here and then go on to visit friends in Philadelphia. Believe me when I say I wish I could go home with you and continue in the investigation. I will give you the address of where we are staying in Philadelphia and ask that you write me with a full report every few days."

"But I don't have a ticket to get home."

"Leave that to me. Father will purchase the ticket. I will tell him that Margaret has written me asking for your speedy return to help with the house. There is truth to that. She will certainly welcome the help. She will have been cleaning the house from top to bottom by herself all this time. An extra set of hands will be welcome."

I nodded as my mind whirled over going back to Amherst early. A large part of me was homesick for the familiar, but a smaller part of me wanted to stay. I knew it was unlikely that I would ever be in a place like this again. I did not have the means to get here or the lodging when I arrived, without the Dickinsons. However, when it came down to it, I worked for the Dickinson family, and if they wanted me to return home, that is what I would do.

Emily worked quickly, and by midmorning the next day, I had a train ticket in hand and I was saying goodbye to Emily outside the front door of the Willard Hotel. Buford and Betty Sue waited patiently for me a few feet away.

Emily handed me Henry's diary. "You should take this with you. We have both read it cover to cover, but Henry would want you to keep it close."

I accepted the diary and held it to my chest. "Thank you." I paused. "I'm sorry if I have caused conflict between you and your sister."

She shook her head. "Vinnie will come around. She always does. She didn't care for Susan when we were first friends. This was before Susan had any relationship with our brother. Now, she loves her like a sister." She looked thoughtful. "Vinnie feels the weight of the world on her shoulders. She carries the burdens so that I can fly. Sometimes, I have to remember what she carries is too heavy for her slight build."

I nodded, knowing that Emily was speaking again from the

special place in her mind that I never would quite be able to comprehend.

"I will be home in less than a month. Gather information, but don't do anything rash until I'm back in Amherst. I want to be there when we catch the killer."

"Are we going to do rash things when you do return home?" I asked, unable to keep the concern from my voice.

"It's always possible," she said with a smile. "Now, go." She gave me a little shove in the direction of Buford. "You don't want to miss your train home."

I told Emily goodbye and walked over to the carriage. Buford took my carpetbag from my hand and set it in the carriage. "I have to say, Miss Willa, I hate to see you go."

I scratched Betty Sue's nose. "I'm sorry to be going, but there are things I must take care of at home."

He nodded. "We all have responsibilities. It's good that you are going home to face them." He opened the carriage door for me.

"Can I sit up with you in the driver's seat?" I asked. "Just one last time?"

He grinned. "You bet." He closed the carriage door, climbed into the driver's seat, and scooted over, making room for me.

A moment later, he guided Betty Sue into the morning traffic of carriages, wagons, bicycles, and carts. And people of course. I doubted I would ever be in a place again where I would see so many people of all kinds. It was quite different than Amherst.

"A penny for your thoughts," Buford said.

I smiled at him. "I was just thinking about how different

this place is from my home. I hope that I will be back someday, but I don't think that is likely to happen."

He nodded. "It's impossible to know what the future holds, but I do hope that we see each other again. You are a kind girl, Miss Willa."

I smiled. "I think you would have really liked my brother." And then, I found myself on the ride to the station telling Buford everything from Henry's death to the diary to learning Mr. Johnson hired him to be a spy to help the abolitionist cause.

As I spoke we passed the White House. I took in all the sights and committed them to memory as the words spilled out of me.

Finally, we reached the train station and people ran this way and that as they departed and arrived in the capital.

Buford pulled back on Betty Sue's reins and jumped from the driver's seat like he was a spry young man, not a gentleman with gray in his beard. He tied off Betty Sue at a hitching post and removed my bag from the carriage as I climbed down from the driver's seat.

Buford handed me my bag. "Your brother was doing good work, and he lived up to his name Noble as he died for a noble cause. Don't you forget that."

Holding tightly to my carpetbag, which held my brother's diary, I promised him I wouldn't.

"We might not see each other in this life, Miss Willa, but I will be seeing you someday at our good Lord's feet. It's hard to know who will be there when the day comes, but you, you, I am sure will show up there someday."

Tears gathered in my eyes, and I held my hand out to him.

He squeezed it briefly in both of his own. "You're train is waiting."

"I'm glad I can call you my friend." I turned and walked toward the train station.

I looked back one more time before stepping through the door, and both Buford and Betty Sue were watching. Buford held his hand in the air in a motionless goodbye.

CHAPTER TWENTY-NINE

WHEN THE TRAIN came to a stop at Amherst Station, I let out a sigh of relief. The trip back home had not been as pleasant as the one down. Due to a spring storm and trees falling on the tracks, the trip had been delayed by a day. All the passengers had to wait on the train until the tracks were cleared. I had never felt so trapped in my life and I had ridden in third class. The woman who sat next to me snored and drooled most of the trip. She was also in the aisle seat, so anytime I had to get up, I had to wake her. She was not pleased by that, to say the least.

With my carpetbag in hand, I jumped off the train. It may not have been the most ladylike exit, but it felt like an escape. I hurried from the station set on going to the post office to bring home the Dickinson family mail.

I had just walked out of the station when someone called my name. "Willa!"

I spun around and saw Catherine Dwight walking toward

me. She was in a light blue dress as if spring was just around the corner. After being in Washington D.C., the Massachusetts air felt cold to me.

She walked up to me. "How dare you?"

I stared at her. "Catherine, is something wrong?"

"Yes, there is something wrong. My father is now convinced that I planned to run away and marry your brother. I cared about Henry, but I would have never done that. However, multiple people who are friends with the Dickinsons have asked him if I was betrothed to Henry. He's furious with me, and there is nothing I can say to convince him I was not secretly engaged."

"I don't . . ." I trailed off because I remembered the letters Emily sent to her friends about Henry and Catherine. I closed my eyes. "This is just a misunderstanding."

"A misunderstanding that you and Emily Dickinson caused!" she shouted.

Several people coming out of the station glanced our way.

"To make matters worse, others are asking if my brothers would have hurt Henry to stop our elopement! My brothers would do no such thing. They are good and upstanding Christian men."

"I'm sorry, Catherine." I couldn't think of anything else to say.

"Don't say you're sorry. Think about what you are doing working for a woman like Emily Dickinson. She doesn't care about you. Your life and everyone's life is just an amusement to her. You should remember that." She burst into tears and marched away.

I felt my heart racing. Shaking, I continued on my way to

the post office. As I walked through the door, the dried lavender wreath sent a burst of fragrance into the air.

"Good afternoon, Willa," Mrs. Milner said.

"Oh!" I said. "I didn't expect you here."

She smiled. "I've been filling in for my husband while he is
away on business. What can I help you with?"

Mrs. Irene Milner was a short, plump woman with the
brightest golden hair I had ever seen. It was the perfect color
for a cheerful woman. I didn't believe I had ever seen the postmaster's wife so much as frown.

"I'd like to pick up the Dickinson family mail."

She nodded. "It will just take me a second. Most people
don't believe it, but I know this post office just as well as my
husband does. Who do you think keeps it so clean and tidy?"
she asked with a chuckle and disappeared into the back room.

While Mrs. Milner was gone, I peeked out the window. The
old men on the benches were there chatting away, but they
were the only ones I saw. I half expected Catherine, or worse
her brothers, to be waiting outside to reprimand me again.

"I just have one letter for you. It's addressed to a Miss
O'Brien and appears to be in Miss Dickinson's hand. It came
all the way from Washington." She smiled and handed me the
letter. "I did not know until Arthur left that the Dickinson
family would be in Washington the same time as my husband.
I asked him in a letter if he ran into the family, but in the following letter, he said he did not."

I frowned, but we had seen Mr. Milner in Washington. I
shook my head. He must have received the letter and replied
before he saw any Dickinsons in the city.

"I just got back from Washington myself. I went to help the

family but came home early to help Miss O'Brien with the spring cleaning."

"I can imagine that is a big job in such a large home." Her cheeks pinkened. "I can barely care for this office and our tiny house behind it. I could not do the cleaning that is required of you and Miss O'Brien."

I smiled. "While I was in Washington, the Dickinsons had a dinner party and invited everyone from Amherst who was in the city. Mr. Milner was there as were Mr. Johnson and Officer Matthew Thomas."

She raised her eyebrows. "My, that must have been an interesting group. Arthur must have replied to my letter before the party. I will be sure to ask Arthur about it when he gets home. I love hearing about his travels. I wished that I could go with him, but someone must always stay back and care for the mail. The mail doesn't stop for travel."

"Does he travel often?"

"Just a few times a year, and it seems to me he always goes south. He says there's a lot of work to be done in the postal service in Southern states. I really don't know much about it. Arthur is always tired when he gets home from his trips and doesn't speak much on them."

I nodded and thanked her for the letter.

"Willa, before you go."

My hand was on the doorknob, and I turned to face her.

"I just wanted to say that both Arthur and I are so sorry about what happened to Henry. It's such a terrible loss. There were many times I would hear he and my husband talk about their plans of moving west. They were both dreamers in that way and had that dream in common."

"Mr. Milner wanted to move west?" I asked.

She nodded. "Very much so. I am not keen on the idea. I like the civilized life here in Amherst, but when the time comes I will have to follow my husband, won't I? I don't have any choice in the matter."

My heart constricted. I supposed that she didn't.

"Anyway, I wanted to share my condolences and tell you I know that Arthur misses talking to Henry about their dreams. Henry was a fine young man. A bit of a troublemaker." He eyes smiled at me. "But a fine and good young man."

"Thank you," I murmured and slipped out through the door.

I arrived back at the Dickinson home with the letter from Emily telling Margaret that I would be coming home early. I went into the house through the servants' entrance and found Margaret in the dining room polishing every single vase that the Dickinsons had in their collection. The entire table was covered with vases in every size and color.

Margaret jumped when I walked into the room. "Good heavens! You gave me a shock. What are you doing here?"

Carlo hopped up from his spot on the rug and looked behind me. He whimpered.

"I'm sorry, Carlo. Miss Dickinson didn't come home with me."

The large dog sighed and shuffled back to his spot on the rug, lay down again, and flopped his large head onto his crossed paws.

Margaret put the vase she was holding down. "Why are you here?"

I held out the letter. "This will explain things, but I believe all it says is that they sent me back early because they knew you needed help with spring cleaning."

She looked surprised. "They thought I would need help?" She put a hand to her chest. "I never thought that would occur to them. I never thought they would ever think of what I might need." She blinked back tears as if she was truly touched. I would never tell her Emily's true motive for sending me back early.

My heart swelled with compassion for Margaret. She had been left behind to work day and night while the family and I were gone. Had she taken any time to rest at all? How would anyone know if she snuck in a nap here or there while the house was empty?

I set my carpetbag on the floor, removed my cloak, and hung it on the back of a chair. "Let me finish here. You go make yourself a cup of tea and put your feet up."

"I—I don't know what to say . . ." Her Irish accent was thicker than ever with emotion.

"Say yes. You can come back and check my work before we put the vases away."

She stood up and hurried out of the room as if she was afraid I would change my mind. And with Carlo by my side, I got to work.

By the time Margaret returned, I had polished all of the vases until I could see my face in them, and Miss Lavinia's four cats were lying around the dining room each in their own ray of sunshine. Carlo's large head was on my feet.

"My," Margaret said. "You work quickly." She picked up a vase. "And well. These are ready to be put away. The ones we use in the winter months can be packed right away. We will not use them in this house again. The family will be moved before winter comes. After you do that, you can get yourself settled from your travel until it's time for supper."

I thanked her, and after I put away all the vases in various chests and cabinets around the house and packed the few winter vases into a crate to move to the home on Main Street, I went up to my little room in the servants' quarters. I sighed with relief when I sat on my bed. It had been a very long trip from Washington and an equally long day when I arrived back in Amherst.

The first thing I did was remove Henry's diary from my carpetbag and tuck it between the wall and the bed for safekeeping. I didn't know what else I could glean from the little book, but I wanted to keep it close. Tomorrow, under Emily's direction, I would begin my investigation.

I'D HOPED TO go to town and start asking questions the next day, but Margaret had other plans. She put me through my paces as I removed everything from the kitchen cupboards, scrubbed them out, and polished the wood with oil soap before putting all the dishes, pots, pans, and countless utensils back where they belonged.

Part of me wished that I could just put them all in packing crates right then to move to the house on Main Street, but it would not be for several months that the house, in the middle of renovations, would be ready for the family, so back into the cupboard everything went.

On the third day I was home, Margaret sent me to the general store for more lye so that we could make soap. I was relieved to be given the task and the ability to go outside.

In the time that I had been in Washington, the weather in Amherst had taken a turn. There was still a chill in the air, but there was also a freshness to the breeze. Trees began to bud, and crocuses at the edge of gardens and around the base of the trees bloomed. While the small crocus blossoms came into their full bloom, the daffodils and hyacinths just began to poke their bright green heads out of the ground. Spring was on the way.

As spring brought new life, it was difficult for me to fathom that my brother had been gone for well over a month now. And other than knowing that our prime suspect, Mr. Elmer Johnson, was actually Henry's employer and had nothing to do with my brother's death, Emily and I had learned very little that would give us answers.

I decided that before I bought the lye, I would go to the post office and see if I could learn anything from the old men who sat outside of it.

Emily asked me to write her and tell her how the investigation was going, but as of yet, I had nothing to report. I hoped that I would be able to change that this afternoon and send her a letter.

As I walked down the sidewalk, I heard the old men's laughter long before I saw them on the benches outside of the post office. It seemed that they were enjoying the turn in the weather to more springlike days.

"Well, if it's not the great traveler who is back in our midst," a gravelly voice called.

I looked over my shoulder to see if the old man sitting on a makeshift bench outside of the Amherst Post Office was speaking to me.

"Yes, Willa, I'm talking to you. Don't go looking over your shoulder like there is someone else there."

I stopped in front of the three men. "You know my name?"

"Course we do," the second man said. "Amherst is really a small town."

I recognized him as the man with the yellow mittens I had seen when I came to the post office with Emily weeks ago. "And what is your name?"

"I thought you would never ask," he replied. "I'm Holden, and my esteemed friends are Salinger and Beard."

Beard had a long silver beard and brought the story of Rip Van Winkle to mind, so it wasn't difficult to know where his name came from.

"We were all fond of Henry," Beard said.

Tears sprang to my eyes, and I turned toward the street to blink them away. "Did you know my brother well?"

"Quite well," Holden said. "He stopped by often to collect all the news of the day from us. He knew we were the ones who were really aware of what was happening in Amherst. We know you have been to Washington. There are no secrets in this town as far as we are concerned. We especially know the comings and goings of the Dickinson family. They will be in Philadelphia for several weeks, is that not true?"

I didn't answer his question. I would not gossip about my employer.

Besides, Holden and his friends might like to think they knew about the Dickinson family, but the longer I worked for the family, the more I learned that they were champions at keeping their own secrets and they were much more complicated than anyone outside of their household could ever possibly know.

"You said my brother enjoyed gossip. What did he ask you about?"

Beard folded his arms. "He was always trying to learn what he could about the slave catchers in town. I can't say we ever knew enough to satisfy him. He was always looking for more."

"I think he was concerned because he was good friends with the Black stable hand Jeremiah York. Somehow he got it in his head that Jeremiah was in danger."

"But Jeremiah is free," I said.

"Doesn't mean he's out of the woods," Holden said with a shake of his head. "I hate to say it, but he will always have to be on his guard. It's just the way of the world."

"Then the way of the world is wrong," I said with folded arms.

"Not much you can hope to do about it. You are a servant and a woman."

I dropped my hands to my sides and then let out a breath. "Was there anything in particular that he was asking pertaining to the slave catcher?"

"Who he was in contact with. That was the main concern. Henry wanted to know who was welcoming to the catcher and who chased him off."

"And did you have an answer for that?"

"Not to his liking."

I frowned and wanted to ask more about this, but Beard spoke up. "Your brother's ways got him in trouble. Do you think the slave catcher or his employer would sit by while a young man asked prying questions?" He clicked his tongue.

Holden frowned at his friend. "It's not right to blame Henry. He did nothing wrong."

I swallowed. "Thank you for saying that. I'm afraid that Henry will be remembered as being a troublemaker, which he could be from time to time, but my dear brother was much more than that."

"He was a visionary," Holden said. "He should not have been born in this time. He was meant for a much later date in this world. Perhaps that is why the good Lord took him so early. He knew he put Henry in the wrong time and place."

I bit down hard on the side of my cheek to keep myself from crying. When I had composed myself, I asked, "Did you ever tell Henry who the slave catcher was talking to?"

"We told him what we knew, which wasn't much. The slave catcher was definitely bankrolling someone for information. I saw him drop money near the Amherst Library," Salinger said.

Holden folded his arm. "You never told us that."

"You never asked, and it's difficult to get a word in edgewise where you're concerned."

Holden grunted.

"How do you know it was money he dropped?" I asked.

Salinger turned to me. "Because I looked. I saw him drop the bag and I wanted to see what was inside of it. After he left, I walked over and inspected the bag. It was full of cash."

"Did you take any of it?" Beard wanted to know.

"Are you insane? I don't want a slave catcher with my name on his list. Those men are a different kind of mean."

I bit the inside of my lip. It sounded to me with the dropping of the money that the slave catcher didn't even know who the Reader was. I guessed that this would make it even more difficult to find my brother's killer.

I thanked the men and decided to go into the post office.

Perhaps there were packages or letters for the Dickinson family that I could take home after I stopped at the general store for Margaret's lye.

The bell above the door rang when I went inside. Mr. Milner looked up from a box he was tying with string. "Willa, it's so good to see you."

I smiled. "Is there any mail for the Dickinson household? I was walking by and thought I would stop."

"There is, in fact, some," he said. "The mail carrier was going to take it out this afternoon, but I will give it to you and save him the trip. Wait right here." He went into the back room.

A moment later, he returned with a sheath of letters and a small box. "This is all I have for them."

I accepted the letters and box. "Thank you."

"It was quite interesting to see you in Washington. Did you have a nice time?"

I thought about the trip to Washington. Overall, I would have called it a unique experience. "I did enjoy seeing the city, and Mount Vernon was very impressive."

He laughed as he organized a stack of letters on his counter. He worked so fast, he barely looked at them. It was almost as if by feel he knew where the letters were headed. "That was a very political answer of you. It seems that you learned quite a bit in the capital. Please tell Miss Dickinson when she returns that I look forward to seeing her again."

I turned to go, but then I stopped myself. There was a question that was nagging at me, and with no one else in the post office, this might be my only chance to ask it. "Mr. Milner, did you enjoy the Dickinsons' dinner party?"

"Very much, but I had to leave early. My conference ended

early, so I decided to take the next train home. There were many things I learned during the lectures that I want to implement here in Amherst, so I was eager to get back."

"Did Em—Miss Dickinson have a chance to speak with you at all the evening of the party?"

His face turned red. "I'm afraid not. She had left the dining room and had not returned by the time I had to leave."

That was becuase she was with me following Mr. Johnson, but I made a point of not saying that aloud.

"Please give her my apologies. The last thing in the world I want to do is insult such a prominent family. Edward Dickinson has been a great champion of the town and of the post office in particular."

"How?" I asked.

"Without him, we would only have mail delivery once a day from outside the town. Now, we have it twice a day. Citizens receive this mail quicker because of him, and I'm grateful for that."

I held up the stack of letters. "Thank you for the mail."

"You're welcome, Willa. Remember, working for the Dickinsons is an honor. Do not ruin it."

I nodded and left the post office. How did he think I would ruin working for the Dickinson family? I felt more confused leaving the post office than I had when I'd entered it.

I was so perplexed over my conversation with Mr. Milner, I didn't even wave to Holden and his friends when I walked by. I vaguely heard their complaints about my not saying goodbye. They would remind me of the slight when I saw them again, this much I knew. Even so, I was too distracted to give it much thought.

I wished that Emily was home, and that I could tell her what I learned. I seemed to be very good at gathering information. And she was very good at deciphering what I gathered to find out what it really meant. When we were apart, the investigation was quite challenging. It would be another fortnight before she was home.

I was so lost in thought that I must have wandered out into the street on my way to the general store. A cart driver yelled at me, "Get out of the road!"

I yelped and jumped back on the sidewalk.

CHAPTER THIRTY

I STOOD ON THE sidewalk with a hand on my beating heart.

"Willa, what were you doing? You could have been killed."

My heart flipped as I recognized Matthew's voice. It was the first time I had heard or seen him since leaving Washington.

"Matthew?" I held the Dickinsons' letters and package close to my body. What did I think would happen, that Matthew would try to take them from me?

"You can't just wander into the street like that. If that cart driver had not been watching, he would have hit you," he admonished.

The hair on the back of my neck stood on end. "I'm glad that you were here to remind me of that."

His face fell.

"I'm sorry," I said. "I should not have snapped at you. I was distracted."

"You seem to be distracted a lot lately."

I didn't see any reason to respond to that. "I have to make

a purchase for Miss O'Brien and get back to work." I left him on the sidewalk and hurried into the general store for Margaret's lye.

Much to my surprise, Matthew was still standing on the sidewalk outside of the general store after I bought the lye. He was in uniform and watched the street with care. It was evident that he saw everything all at once, including me while I tried to sneak by him.

"I will walk you back to North Pleasant Street."

I frowned at him. "People will talk."

"I know," he agreed. "But there are things I need to tell you."

I sighed and let him fall into step with me. "Are you going to tell me what you were doing with Mr. Johnson at the tearoom when you were in Washington last week?"

He looked down at me in surprise.

"You are helping him, aren't you? On his abolitionist crusade? And you knew Henry was also helping him. You tried to mislead me that Mr. Johnson was dangerous. You told me that Henry was hired to spy on him. He hired Henry. Are you going to tell me that you lied to protect me?"

Matthew's jaw twitched as if he was trying to control his emotions. "Is that wrong?"

"Yes. I would not want the man who professed to lo—care about me to lie to me."

He closed his eyes for a moment. "You're right. I should have told you the truth from the beginning. Jeremiah and I agreed to spin the tale that Henry was spying on Johnson to keep you safe. While you concentrated on Johnson, it kept you from getting too close to the real culprit. We also wanted to protect the cause. If the Reader knew we were looking for him, he would be more difficult to find. I should have known you would figure it out in the end. I am sorry."

I searched his eyes, which were so full of regret. "I see why you did it, but you have to promise me something. Promise me you will never lie to me again no matter the cost."

"I won't lie to you again. You have my word."

I let out a breath. "I thought as a police officer, you weren't supposed to be involved in politics like that. Can't you get in trouble?"

He stared straight ahead as we walked. "I could," he admitted finally.

"And you went to Washington on your own time, not at the request of the department. Why? Are you an abolitionist too?" I asked in a voice so quiet I wasn't sure that he heard me.

However, he must have heard me, because he said, "I am. As a police officer, I am acutely aware when the law can harm and not protect. I have always been against slavery, but when things became worse, I stepped forward."

"Stepped forward how?"

"I joined the movement when the law changed in 1850. As an officer of the law, I would be required to put men, women, and even children back into the hands of slave catchers. I couldn't bear it. I became a police officer to serve and protect, not to hurt and enslave."

I stopped in the middle of the sidewalk. A wagon full of squawking chickens in wooden cages in the back rattled by us. The sounds of the chickens' clucks were deafening. When they were gone, I asked, "Are you a conductor like Mr. Johnson?"

He removed his policeman's cap and held it in his hands. "No. As a police officer, it would be too noticeable if I were.

However, I have been an informant for the railroad. The police department would receive tips when the slave catchers were in town, and I would pass those on to the conductors."

I was silent. It was so much to take in. Both my brother and Matthew had been involved in something so important, and I had no idea. What would I have done if I'd known? Joined? Or asked them not to participate for their own safety? I was ashamed to realize that it would most likely have been the latter of the two.

Matthew let out a deeply held breath. "I can't stand the idea of you thinking that I was in any way involved in Henry's death. I was on his side. I went to Washington to meet with Johnson and others in the movement. I wanted to make the loss of Henry mean something. I loved him like a brother. I want to know what happened to him just as much as you do."

I nodded and tried to take this all in. "I can understand why you had to keep your involvement secret. The movement would be at risk, and you would be at personal risk of losing your position with the police, but why are you telling me all this now?" I asked.

"Because you're an important person to me, Willa. I even . . ." He trailed off.

I studied his face. "You even what?"

"I even admire you too." He said "admire" like he choked on the word. As if it wasn't the word he had planned to say from the beginning. "You're unlike any other woman—person—that I have ever met. You were fiercely loyal to your brother even when he made mistakes. You're loyal to him still as you put yourself at risk to find out what happened to him."

His tone changed. "But I don't think you understand what a dangerous game it is you're playing. The men on both sides of this issue would not have a second thought about hurting a poor woman who found herself in the middle of it."

I pressed my mouth closed because I was afraid of what I would say. How could I not try to find out what happened to my brother? He was all I had.

"You don't have to do any of this," Matthew said. "You don't even have to work for the Dickinson family. I know that you are upset about Henry's death. I am too. For all the trouble that he got into, I knew his heart was always in the right place. He and I were fighting for the same things. He would think it was more important for you to be happy than to find his killer."

"Maybe I can't be happy without out knowing what really happened."

"I know you can. I can make you happy if you let me."

"Is it right to go about my life when Henry's life has come to an end? What right do I have to that?"

"You have been a good daughter and a good sister. You deserve happiness."

Tear sprang to my eyes. That's where he was wrong. I hadn't been a good sister. If I had, Henry wouldn't be dead. I should have paid more attention to what he was up to. I should have asked more questions. How could I know that I wouldn't fail Matthew too?

"I can see that you are close to telling me no again to my offer of marriage. I will not accept that answer."

"I do not accept something offered in pity."

"It's not pity, Willa."

I looked him in the eye. "Then what is it?"

Instead of answering my question, he said, "I'll wait. I will wait for as long as you need."

"Don't throw your life away for me," I whispered. "It could be a very long time, maybe even forever."

"Then forever it will be."

CHAPTER THIRTY-ONE

BETWEEN THE WORK that Margaret expected me to do around the Dickinson home and the errands that she asked me to run around town, I used every free moment to ask questions about the Underground Railroad and what people in Amherst knew about it. The truth was there was surprisingly little the average person knew.

It was a very secretive operation, and the people involved were skilled at keeping its secrets. I didn't even fully know Matthew's involvement in all of it, and I had the feeling he wasn't at liberty to tell me either. However, I kept trying to learn more with the hope it would solve the mystery of Henry's death. Since my brother had gone to the bakery and butcher shop in search of information, I started there too.

In the bakery, Mrs. Cutter gave me a chocolate chip cookie for my trouble, but she didn't have much information to share. She dusted flour off of her hands after she placed a lattice-topped apple pie in the display case. "I really have not heard of a slave catcher being in town. It's not my business. I try to stay out of the fray, you see. As for Henry—goodness, I was sorry to hear what happened to him—I'd seen him around here, yes. He was always asking questions just like you are now, and his questions were quite similar. What is going on with the Noble siblings asking such questions?" She studied me.

I bit into my cookie, so I had some time to think of an answer. It was divine. The chocolate melted in my mouth, and I was delighted that she had also included walnuts in her recipe. There was nothing that I loved more than the delicious crunch of walnuts in cookies and cakes. They cost extra and they weren't something that we baked with often at the Dickinson home as Mr. Dickinson was a frugal man.

I swallowed the bite. "I suppose in my case, it's because I miss my brother. I just want to know what he was up to those final days of his life." Tears gathered in my eyes.

"Oh, you poor girl." She reached into the glass cookie jar on the counter. "Here, have another cookie."

I wasn't above taking it.

I was eating my second cookie outside of the butcher shop when the door opened and Reverend Dwight came out. He glared at me, and the last bit of cookie lodged in my throat.

"Miss Noble," he said in his deep baritone voice. "I have been told by my children that you are causing trouble for them."

"I'm not, sir." I swallowed, praying the cookie would move down my throat.

"I surely hope you're not. Because I would not want a sister of one of the best men in our operation to ruin things."

I stared at him. "Excuse me, sir?"

"Henry and I had similar sympathies, let me say. This was one reason I would not let him court my daughter."

With a sharp intake of breath, I realized Reverend Dwight was telling me that he was also part of the Underground Railroad. How little did I know about the people of Amherst before my brother's death? Who else was caught up in the cause? I looked up and down the street.

"I did not want my daughter to have to worry about the man she loved or be in danger herself. If I had let her fall in love with Henry, that would have happened. What he was doing for the cause was dangerous, and that was proven when he was killed."

I wanted to ask him how he could stop his daughter from loving someone, but I realized that the question would be in vain. Worse yet, it would keep me from learning what he might know about Henry's death.

"You believe Henry was killed for the cause?" I asked.

"I know that he was. Everyone in the network knows it too. We've all been very careful since. There has not even been a whisper of the Reader." He looked around as he said the name, as if he was afraid that someone might overhear us.

I loosened the ribbon on my bonnet. It felt very tight on my throat after I swallowed that last bite of cookie. "Do you know who the Reader is?"

"No." The word came out harshly. "No one does."

That wasn't true. Henry did.

"It would serve you well not to ask about it any longer. Things are changing in the network here. The Reader seems to have gone underground himself. The more questions you ask, the more dangerous it will become for you."

I wasn't that worried about being in danger. I lost Henry. I didn't have that much more to lose.

As if he could read my mind, he said, "The more questions you ask, the more dangerous it will become for the whole Dickinson family. You are their maid. As such, they are responsible for you and your behavior. Do you want to put the family that has been so kind to you at risk?"

My heart clenched. I had not thought of the danger that Emily and her family might be in if the Reader realized what Emily and I had been up to. And here I had been the last few days, walking uptown every chance that I got to ask more questions about Henry, the Reader, and the Underground Railroad. That was bound to attract some negative attention.

"I can tell by your expression that you have not thought about it up until now. You should think of it, Miss Noble. Think on it long and hard." With that, he turned on his heels and walked up the street way from me.

After my conversation with Reverend Dwight, for the next two weeks, day to night, I washed the windows, dusted the floorboards, and chased cobwebs from the corners. I stayed at the Dickinson home and did every task that Margaret requested of me, and I watched my back. I jumped at every knock on the door and creak of the house.

I knew that Emily would be disappointed that I stopped asking questions, but it was what I had to do. Reverend Dwight's warnings to me about putting the entire Dickinson family in danger rang in my ears, and it wasn't the first time I had been warned. There was also the letter I received just days after Henry died. The letter had said, "Tell your brother to stop poking his nose where it doesn't belong. If he keeps at it, he will come to a bad end and so will you." The writer, who I could only assume had been the Reader, had been true to his word. Henry did come to a bad end. I couldn't let that happen to Emily or any member of her family too.

So instead of asking questions, I buried myself in the act of cleaning, something I was far better at than investigating murder. I put the finishing touches on the parlor and stepped back. The room was spotless, and I couldn't help taking some pride in that.

There was commotion at the entry of the house.

"Home!" I heard Emily cry. "I thought I would never see it again."

"Emily," her sister said.

Carlo, who was in the parlor keeping me company while I cleaned, galloped into the foyer. There were shouts and barks of jubilation as the dog and his mistress were reunited after so many weeks.

One of Miss Lavinia's cats that napped on the windowsill in the parlor yawned. She would wait to greet her owner when the owner came and found her.

I smoothed my skirts and touched the white cap that covered my hair to make sure it was pinned in place. Then I went into the entry to welcome the family home.

In the entry, I found Margaret helping Mrs. Dickinson and her daughters with their bags.

"The porter will bring our trunks soon," Mrs. Dickinson said. "I was so eager to return home that I didn't want to stay at the station while they got the luggage sorted." She sighed.

"It is good to be home. I have missed it so." She placed a hand on her cheek. "The travel has worn me through. Lavinia, can you help me to my room?"

Miss Lavinia nodded. "Of course, Mother." She nodded at me as she passed.

I wondered if the nod was Miss Lavinia's attempt at a truce between us. I could never be sure with her, so I planned to keep my guard up where the younger Dickinson sister was concerned.

"Margaret, would you be so kind to take my bags to my room?" Emily asked.

Margaret nodded and shot a look at me. I knew she must be wondering why Emily asked her to carry her bags and not me since I was the lesser maid in the household. However, she didn't say a word. Instead she picked up the three bags and left the room.

When she was gone, Emily smiled at me. "It is so good to see you, Willa, and I did appreciate your letters with updates about our investigation. How much I longed to be here when you were questioning everyone."

"I wrote to you everything that I learned. I'm sorry to say it's not much."

"It confirms what we have thought though. The slave catchers were paying the Reader for information about the railroad."

"But we are no closer to finding out who the Reader is."

Emily eyed me. "That could be because you stopped your search."

I licked my lips and lowered my voice. "I wrote to you about what Reverend Dwight said. He said if we continued that your family might be in danger."

"We are the Dickinsons," Emily said with the confidence of her class. "No one can harm us. There would be a great uproar if someone even tried." Her face softened then. "But I do appreciate the concern even if it was unwarranted. Now that I am home, we will redouble our efforts. It could be that since you have been quiet the Reader will become complacent and slip up, making him even easier to catch."

My brow knit together with worry, but I knew that Emily was determined to carry on, so I had no choice but to carry on as well to protect her the best that I could in this dangerous game we stumbled into.

"I have a feeling deep in my bones that it is just a matter of time before we discover the Reader's identity." She stretched. "Oh, how I loathe being cooped up in a train like that and with so many people. Let us take Carlo for a walk. I know he's dying to go, for I can sense he has missed our daily walks as much as I have."

I glanced at the doorway Margaret went through. "But Margaret will want me to start preparing meals for you all now that you have returned."

She waved away my concern. "Margaret can start the meal and you can help her after the walk." She opened the door. "Carlo."

That was all the big dog needed to hear and he galloped out of the front door with a wide doggy grin on his face.

Emily laughed and followed him.

I shook my head and went out the door as well knowing that I was jeopardizing my rapport with Margaret by leaving with Emily so soon after the family had returned.

Emily headed south on North Pleasant Street in the direction of town. "Father was staying in Washington while we were in Philadelphia. His term is up in a few days, and we expect him home shortly after that. Sadly, Austin had to go back to Boston before we even went to the next city, and it is so hard to see him go. I know it's harder still for Susan, as she didn't get to travel with us to Washington. By the time Austin returns to Amherst, she will not have seen him for several months. I will have to make a call to her tomorrow to make sure she is all right. It must be very hard to be living with her aunt. I know that she is looking forward to starting a life with our family, and so are we."

We made it to the other side of Main Street before I realized where we were going. I stopped in the middle of the sidewalk. "Are we going to the stables?"

She grinned. "Of course we are. It's always good to visit the scene of the crime."

"Wouldn't another visit to the stables bring more attention to what we are doing?" I asked.

She shrugged. "I need to get back into the investigation. Oh, I was itching to work on it while I was with the Hollands. They are lovely people, but by the end of the visit I was more than ready to return home. Five weeks was far too long to be away from Amherst. When I told you that we would discover what happened to your brother, I meant it. We need to see this through."

When she said that I realized that despite the dangers, I needed to see it through, too, for Henry, for Emily, and for myself.

As usual when we walked into the stables, no one stopped us. Emily, Carlo, and I marched up to the main stable with no trouble. When we stepped inside, the smells of the barn hit me. I inhaled deeply thinking these were the last scents my brother had before he died. There was an ache in my chest. I wondered when that ache would subside or if it ever would.

"Carlo, stay," Emily said, leaving the big dog by the door.

The curly-haired Carlo didn't appear to be happy about it as he lay by the threshold, but he was an obedient animal and did his mistress's bidding.

"It doesn't look like anyone is here," Emily said. "I would have expected Jeremiah to greet us at the door."

"I haven't seen Jeremiah since I have been back in Amherst, but I haven't come to the stables either," I admitted. An uneasy feeling fell over me. "Let's go back and see Terror."

She glanced at me. "You have a thing for that horse, don't you?"

"I think he was used like a pawn in all this. I know that he wasn't responsible for what happened to my brother."

Terror's back was to the stall door. He stared into the corner and didn't move. On his flank, I could see the outline of his ribs. He was losing weight by the day because he refused to eat much since my brother's death. An animal of this size had to eat often to be in the best physical shape.

"Terror?" I asked in a small voice.

The only indication I had that the horse heard me was the slightest twitch of his right ear.

"I'm going in the stall."

Now his left ear twitched.

Emily grabbed my arm. "I don't know if that's a good idea. You could be hurt."

I looked at her. "He won't hurt me. I know it." I unlatched the gate and slipped inside. I latched the gate after me. In his feed tray there was a carrot that looked like it had been sitting there for a long while since it was starting to whiten around the edges. I picked it up. "Terror, you have to eat."

He buried his head in the corner of the stall.

I placed my left hand on his neck. "Terror, please."

His left eye rolled back and looked at me.

I held the carrot out to him. "Please take it."

Gingerly, he took the carrot in his teeth. He held it in his lips for a moment and I scratched his forehead. "I'm Henry's sister, and I know that he would want you to eat and be well. I know it's hard—" My voice caught. "I know it's hard to go on without him, but it's something we have to do. It's hard for me, too, but Henry would want us to take care of ourselves, to have a long life."

Then the horse walked over to his feed trough, dipped his head in, and began to eat.

Emily stared at me. "You have a way with animals."

"Maybe, but not like Henry."

"What did you do to him?" a male voice asked.

I stepped through the gate to find Jeremiah staring at Terror with his nose in the trough. He pointed at the horse. "How did you make that happen? He hasn't eaten for days."

"I asked him." I closed the gate.

Jeremiah pushed his glasses up his nose. "You asked him?"

I nodded. "Yes, I asked him to eat, and he did."

Jeremiah shook his head. "Johnson was talking about having the horse put down because he would not eat. You might have saved his life." He studied me. "And you saved his life after knowing what he did your brother?"

I petted Terror's mane. "It wasn't his fault. It was the Reader's."

Jeremiah gasped. "How?"

Emily folded her arms. "Yes, we know about the Reader. We also know that you and Henry were working with Elmer Johnson to find out his identity since he was directing runaways into the slave catcher's hands. And we know that you have lied to us. You said it was a wealthy man who paid Henry to spy on Mr. Johnson, when in fact, Mr. Johnson hired Henry as a spy within the railroad to find the Reader."

He hung his head. "I felt like I had no choice but to lie. I needed to throw you off to protect you." He looked at me. "Henry spoke highly of you, Willa. I knew that he would have wanted me to protect his sister any way that I could even if I had to lie."

Emily lifted her chin. "Well, the lies didn't work. They rarely do. We know everything but the Reader's identity. Do you know it?"

Jeremiah swallowed hard. "We don't know who the Reader is, and it's eating me up inside. Henry knew, and it got him killed." He looked over his shoulder. "I can't sleep at night. I'm afraid that I will have the same fate because the Reader will believe that Henry told me, but I tell you that I don't know. Henry didn't tell me."

"I know. The package you gave me was Henry's diary."

Jeremiah nodded. "I thought as much."

"He didn't reveal the Reader's name in the diary. He was too afraid the diary would fall into the wrong hands. However, he did say he knew who it was."

"I expected that. Henry would be far too smart to write down the Reader's name, but oh, how I wish that he had. I wish I knew it."

"He was going to tell you and Mr. Johnson that night he died," Emily said.

Jeremiah's shoulders sagged. "Do you know how many times I have wished that I hadn't left the stables that night? It's constantly in my thoughts. If there had been two of us here, he might have had a chance, a real chance."

A door slammed somewhere in the stable.

"You both had better leave," Jeremiah whispered. "Mr. Johnson is coming, and he will not like to see you here."

I glanced back at Terror. He continued to eat like he was afraid that he would never be fed again.

Mr. Johnson came around a neighboring stall. "You got the horse to eat. Good work, Jeremiah."

"It wasn't me, sir. It was Willa." Jeremiah pressed his lips together as if he was afraid of what Mr. Johnson might say to that.

Mr. Johnson turned to Emily and me. While I shuddered under his angry gaze, Emily seemed to gather power from it. She stood up straighter and lifted her chin a little bit higher. "Mr. Johnson."

"What are the two of you doing here? I told you to stay out of this," he said angrily.

"We can't until we know what happened to Henry Noble," Emily said.

"What happened to Henry Noble does not matter. What matters is protecting the people traveling north. Henry died for the cause. That should be the end of it. We are grateful for what he has done, but we must continue forward and save as many lives as we can."

"But don't you want to know who the Reader is? Henry knew that and was killed," Emily said.

"I have given up on this. I have already been told that people are being directed away from Amherst for their safety. In time, the Reader will move on and we will be able to resume our work."

Terror lifted his head up from the trough and shuffled back to the corner of his stall.

"That horse may have eaten a little, but he will never be able to race again after all the weight he's lost. I want you to put him down tomorrow." Mr. Johnson pressed his mouth into a thin line.

"You can't do that," I cried. "He's a good horse. He just needs some extra attention."

Mr. Johnson glared at me. "He's a racehorse, not a pet, and I'm not running a petting zoo; this is a working stable." He pointed to Jeremiah. "You heard what I said about the horse."

"No," Emily said. "Do not have the animal put down. My father will buy the horse," Emily said. "We have need of a new carriage horse, and Terror will do nicely."

Mr. Johnson put his hands on his hips and glared at her. "What makes you think you can come here and buy my horse like that?"

She glared back at him. "Because you want money not just for the stables but for the work you really care about." She pointed to Terror. "And he needs a new home."

He scowled.

"Wouldn't you rather make some money off the sale of the horse than to lose all of its value by putting it down?" Emily asked. "What difference is it to you if the horse is dead or living in another place? My father is in the process of updating the old family homestead. We have the space and the stables to care for this animal."

"Fine. I will give you a week. If your father doesn't buy the horse in that time, I'm having him put down." Mr. Johnson stomped away.

Jeremiah stared at us. "Will your father buy the horse? Because Mr. Johnson is always true to his word. He will have Terror destroyed."

I wondered the same thing. "How do you know that Mr. Dickinson will agree to this?" I asked anxiously.

Emily lifted her chin. "My father can be a cold man, but to his children he wants to give us all he can. If I ask him for this horse, he will buy it."

Relief washed over me. I couldn't bear the idea of Terror being killed.

"I will send a letter to him in the morning asking permission. We will know in a week's time."

I walked over to Terror's stall. "It's all going to be fine. I promise."

Terror looked over his shoulder at me and slowly blinked his eyes.

"We should return home," Emily said. "Even though we didn't learn anything new, I'm glad we came here to save Terror. The only thing I'm certain about when we get him home is my sister will want to change his name." She walked toward the stable doors.

Carlo jumped to his feet when he saw his mistress coming.

"Willa?" Jeremiah asked me. "How did you get Terror to eat?"

There were tears in my eyes. "I told him that it was what Henry would want. We are both going to continue on for Henry."

Jeremiah studied me. "Then I shall continue for him too."

Emily and Carlo waited at the stable door. "You were a good friend to my brother. If you ever need help, get word to me, and I promise I will come."

He nodded. "Thank you."

CHAPTER THIRTY-TWO

T HE NEXT MORNING, Emily and I walked to the post office to mail her letter to her father asking him to buy Terror.

I wrung my hands the entire way.

"Don't be so nervous about this, Willa. I know my father, and he will have a soft spot for this horse. If there is one thing I am gifted at it is writing appealing letters."

I wished that I had Emily's confidence.

Holden and his friends were sitting outside of the post office.

"Well if it isn't Willa with Miss Dickinson in tow. You two are up bright and early this morning."

Emily held up her letter. "We have much to do."

"Yes, like finding a killer," Salinger said. "You two are the talk of Amherst for the many questions that you have asked about Henry's death. Do you really think that is wise? You could be gathering some unwanted attention."

Emily looked down at him. "In my opinion all attention is unwanted."

The men laughed as Emily walked into the post office, and I was close on her heels.

The bell over the door rang just like it had the last time I was there.

"We open in thirty minutes," Mr. Milner called from the back room.

"We are just dropping off a letter."

Mr. Milner pushed a cart into the room. "Miss Dickinson, I didn't realize that it was you out here. I'm sorry to make you wait."

"I thought you opened in thirty minutes," Emily said.

"For the general public, yes," he said with a red face. "But we are always open for a member of the Dickinson family."

Emily nodded as if that was the only acceptable response he could have given.

Mr. Milner nodded to me as well. "Willa, it's nice to see you again too."

I nodded.

"Let me have that letter and make sure it gets off safely."

Emily held it out to him.

"I see that it's going to your father. His last letter in Washington, perhaps."

Emily cocked her head. "My father receives a lot of correspondence, so I doubt it. I'm telling him about something happening at the stables that needs his attention."

Mr. Milner's eyes went wide. "Oh, and what is that?"

"It's none of you concern, Mr. Milner. Please take care of that letter. It's urgent that it makes its way to my father in today's mail."

He nodded. "Of course."

Emily and I left the post office.

I tried not to worry about Terror for the rest of the day, and I prayed Emily's letter would make it to her father in time. In many ways, saving Terror was an attempt at saving Henry, too, because I knew that's what my brother would have wanted. I couldn't let him down.

When we arrived home, Emily went to her room to write, I was certain, while I went through my daily duties around the house. After I washed the dishes from the evening meal, there was a knock at the back kitchen door.

I opened the door to find a boy no more than ten standing on the back step. The boy handed me a note.

"Wait? Who are you?"

He ran away without looking back.

Willa, I need help.—JY

I stared at the note. "JY." Jeremiah York.

It was already dark outside. What did Jeremiah expect me to do?

The kitchen door opened and Emily came inside. She smiled at me. "I thought I would bake a cake tonight for Father's return. He always liked my black cake. It's quite an undertaking, so I will start . . ." She trailed off when she saw my face. "Willa, whatever is wrong?"

I handed her the note.

She read it. "This means only one thing."

"What's that?" I twisted the hem of my apron.

"We have to go, and we have to go now." Her tone left no room for argument.

"We should call the police and send them over to the stables. If Jeremiah is in serious danger, the police need to know."

Emily frowned as if she didn't like this idea at all.

"We can at least tell Matthew," I said.

"Fine, I will have the neighbor boy run a note to your Matthew, and then we will leave."

"He's not my Matthew," I said.

She gave me a look that said I was kidding myself. Maybe I was.

Emily sent the note as promised, and she and I snuck out the back door of the house. As we ran through the backyard, I looked up at the clapboard home. I could clearly see Miss Lavinia watching us from her bedroom window. I would hear about that later, and even though our nighttime adventure was Emily's idea, her sister would blame me for corrupting her again.

The streets of Amherst were quiet. We only passed a wagon making an evening delivery on Main Street. All the shops and businesses were closed. Even the college with all those students was silent.

When we reached the stables, they were even darker than I remembered. With dense forest on one side of the property, a wall of shadows seemed to fall over every inch of the place.

"I wish we had brought Carlo," Emily whispered.

I wished we had too.

We stepped into the barn, and it was pitch-black inside. There was a lantern hanging from a nail and a matchbook on a board. I struck a match and lit the lantern. It gave off a small four-foot ring of light. Everything beyond that was cloaked in darkness and shadows.

The nearby horses blinked at us.

I held the lantern high. "Jeremiah?"

No one answered.

My stomach tightened. "Emily," I whispered, "I think we should go to the big house and talk to Mr. Johnson. Let's find out from him what's going on before we go too far into the stables. We don't know who is in here."

"Mr. Johnson won't be happy to see us," she whispered back.

"I know, but that's better than—"

A staff or a handle of a rake knocked the lantern out of my hand, and then all I saw was blackness.

CHAPTER THIRTY-THREE

I GROANED AND TOUCHED the back of my head. There was light coming somewhere from my right. I tried to prop myself up on my elbows, but even that small motion caused my head to spin.

My eyes adjusted to the dark, and a large mass came at my head. I gasped and rolled over to protect my face when I felt something soft and wet blowing on me. I reached back and touched a hoof.

"Terror?" I whispered.

The horse blew hot breath on my neck.

Even though my head continued to throb, I sat up on my knees and hugged the horse's neck. His skin was slick with sweat, and I wondered if he was ill. "It will be all right," I told the horse even though I knew nothing of the kind.

I shook my head, and it felt like my brain was set loose and sloshed back and forth in my skull. I bent forward and held my head in between my hands. My palms were caked with dirt and smelled like horse and worse.

Terror pressed his wet nose onto the back of my neck. I had to get out of this barn for him and myself. And for Henry. I had to escape for Henry most of all. He would not want this fate for me.

The trouble was I didn't know what my fate was. Who had hit me? I touched the back of my head and felt a bump there. And where was Emily? Had she been struck too?

All at once, a lantern swung back and forth from a man's hand, and a face loomed over me.

"Ah, good, you're awake," a man said.

In the wavering light of the lantern, I saw a familiar face, a face I had known since I was a child, a face that I had thought belonged to a friend.

"Mr. Milner?" I gasped.

"And who did you expect the Reader to be, Willa, but the reader of mail? All the mail. I know everything that happens in this town."

I tried to get to my feet, but my head spun. "I don't understand why you would hurt people."

"That's the most surprising part of this. I thought you would understand. You of all people who have been a servant all your life. I had the opportunity to make extra money so I could leave this thankless town and head west. Do you think my salary from the postal service allows that? I can assure you it does not."

My heart raced. Where was Emily? Was she hurt?

"And just like your brother died, you will meet the same

fate by the same horse." He held up a red-hot piece of iron. This was how Terror got those burn marks on this flank.

I held my hands in front of me. "But why would you hurt runaways? If you're angry about being a servant then why would you want to hurt someone who also lives a life of service?"

"Slaves, you mean? What use are they? They are no more important than that worthless horse in the stall with you."

I felt sick as thoughts rushed through my mind. Emily's letter to her father about something happening at the stables must have tipped Mr. Milner off that we knew too much. His wife told me he made frequent trips to the South. Why would he need to do that as a postmaster from a New England town? And he must have written that threatening note to scare me away. It would be so easy for him to put it in the mail. He *was* the mail service in Amherst after all. Only, he didn't know I had moved to the Dickinsons, so I received the letter too late. Henry was too close, and threats would no longer work. He made the choice to kill my brother. And now, he was going to kill me.

The postmaster waved the hot piece of iron at Terror. Terror backed into the corner of the stall and his eyes rolled back in his head.

"Leave the animal alone and just deal with me," I shouted. It pained my head to cry out like that, but I had no choice.

He glared at me.

"Where's Jeremiah?" I asked, fear gripping my heart. I knew better than to ask after Emily. I prayed that she had gotten away and was safe.

"He and Johnson are out there saving runaway slaves or so they think. They might save a few here and there, but they will never really win. Slavery is a national institution. It's not going anywhere. There is too much money at stake. The almighty dollar is the true ruler of this country."

"You killed Henry. You claimed you cared about him," I accused. "You told me you were sorry he was dead. How could you say that to me knowing full well you are the reason I no longer have my brother?" My fear was turning toward anger. This man stole everything from me.

"I am sorry he's dead, but he brought it on himself. I did not want to kill Henry. He forced me to do it. If it got out what my involvement was as the Reader, I would be ruined. There are too many sympathizers to the slaves in this town. I blame the college that there are so many abolitionists here. I would have been run out of my position as the postmaster in Amherst. Even if I was within my rights of the law to help a slave catcher reclaim his property, I would be ruined. I can't be run from town yet. I don't have money enough for the property I need. There is a piece of land that I have my eye on in Nebraska Territory. I almost have money for it. I was planning to leave in July. By then, I would have enough if everything had gone to plan."

"But Henry ruined that plan," I said, remembering what Mrs. Milner said about her husband's dreams of moving out west. She had said that was the dream he and Henry had in common. It was the only thing they had in common, I realized. Henry and Mr. Milner could not be more different in their thinking.

"I suspected that Henry figured out it was me the night

that I went to the stables. That morning before light, I received word that slaves were to come to the post office for direction to the next station. They never came, and by midday, I learned they had gone another route. Someone had gotten the word to them that the post office should be avoided. I knew it must be Henry. I knew he was asking questions around town. I was furious. If I didn't direct them to the slave catcher, I was paid nothing. I had worked too long and too hard for Henry to take this from me. I thought my best choice was to get rid of him before he could tell anyone else."

I struggled to my feet and rested my hand on Terror's side for support as I stood.

Mr. Milner didn't even seem to notice as he was too wrapped up in his story. "Getting rid of your brother was harder than I expected. He was never alone. My only option was to see him at night in the stables. To say he was surprised to see me that night is an understatement. He greeted me warmly like we were old friends, but I saw the wariness in his eyes. He knew who I really was and he was afraid."

My heart thundered in my chest, and it pained me to hear how devious Mr. Milner could be. In my mind, for so long, he had been a friendly face. He was a person who chatted with the townspeople on a daily basis, appearing to be the congenial postmaster of a small town. All the while, he had been trapping runaways by guiding them into the slave catchers' grasp for the money so he could start a new life. He stole their chances at a new life for his own? There was nothing redeemable about what he had done.

Mr. Milner leaned over the stall holding out the hot poker. He pointed it at Terror. Frantically, I looked around the stall for something to throw at him. The only thing in the stall was Terror's food trough, and I knew I would not be able to pick it up.

Mr. Milner leaned farther into the stall. The hot poker was just inches from Terror's shoulder now. As foolish as it was, I stepped between the horse and the poker. I would not stand by while this animal that had endured so much already was harmed again. I could not stand by while any innocent life was endangered if I had the power to stop it.

Suddenly, Mr. Milner jerked and cried out.

The poker fell to the ground in the stall with Terror and me just inches from my feet. I kicked dirt onto it, and then I threw open the gate. I grabbed Terror by the bridle and walked him through. The horse was breathing heavily, but other than that he appeared to be all right.

In the dim lantern light, I saw Emily holding a shovel over Mr. Milner's unconscious body.

"He hit you on the head," she said. "It seemed only right for me to return the favor."

I stared at her. "But . . . what? How?"

She laughed. "When you were struck and pulled into the barn, I jumped back. I don't think he realized that I was there. I ran to the big house for help, but no one was home."

"Jeremiah and Mr. Johnson were conductors tonight."

She nodded. "That's what I surmised, so I believed I had no choice but to take saving you into my own hands." She shrugged as if this was the obvious conclusion. "And I have." She looked down at Mr. Milner. "I hit him quite hard. He will be out for a little bit."

There was yelling outside the stables.

"Police!" a voice cried.

"It seemed that your Matthew got my note after all," Emily said with a grin. "It's always amusing when the menfolk run in ready to save the day."

I groaned and held tight to Terror's bridle. "He's not *my* Matthew."

She leaned on the handle of the shovel and laughed.

EPILOGUE

S PRING GAVE WAY to summer, and Emily had been able to convince Margaret to let me help her in the garden more often. I was grateful for the chance even if it meant more dusting around the home under Margaret's direction.

I deadheaded a row of zinnias so that they would bloom again that season. I glanced at the back pasture behind the garden and smiled as I saw Terror nibbling on the grass. Emily had convinced her father to buy the horse after all. Although Mr. Johnson was so grateful that we captured the Reader that he practically gave the horse to the Dickinson family. He asked for little more than the cost of a case of flour for the creature.

He was a beautiful horse and fully recovered from his troubles. He ate with gusto again and filled out to his once majestic size. His sides, though scarred, were healed. I wasn't completely healed myself from what happened to Henry or in the barn that night with Mr. Milner, but my own scar was beginning to form.

Mr. Milner was in prison awaiting trial for my brother's murder. I was happy about that. I had sympathy for his wife. She left Amherst soon after her husband was arrested. I heard she went to live with her sister in Boston. I hope that she could find the happiness she always had again.

Emily walked through the garden with a pair of scissors as she collected blossoms for a bouquet and nodded approvingly at me. "You always know what needs to be done when it comes to the garden, Willa. I must say that it comes as a great relief that I don't have to train you."

"My mother loved to garden, and I learned from her." A happy memory of my mother filled my mind instead of a sad one for once.

She nodded. "She was a good teacher. I think she was a good teacher to you in a great many things."

I stopped snapping off dead, withered blossoms. "What do you mean?"

Emily considered this for a moment. "My opinion about a person rarely changes, and that is true in you as well."

I put a hand on my chest. "Me?"

"Yes, when I first met you, you had just learned that your brother had been killed. You were broken and devastated, but not fragile. A fragile woman is one that cannot rise to the challenge before her. Even though you were clearly and rightly upset by what had transpired, there was a determination to your posture that I noted. I knew you were stronger than you appeared. I guessed that your mother gave you that."

"I think many people think that because I am so tall and sturdily built," I said.

"No, your appearance had nothing to do with my opinion

of you. People's physical appearances rarely do. And your brother, Henry, must have been the same way. Strong and determined."

"He was even more so."

She nodded. "I wish I'd had a chance to meet him."

"I wish you had too," I murmured.

"After this, let's take Carlo for a walk uptown."

I made a face. "Miss O'Brien—"

"I've already told Miss O'Brien my plans, Willa. You should know that by now."

As she waltzed away, I considered my first impressions of Emily. I found her to have a wandering mind as if she was somewhere other than in the room with me. I had since learned at other times she was decidedly present and almost overly aware of everything going on around her. I wondered what it must be like to have that level of aloofness or that level of concentration. I said none of this to Emily, though, and I noted that she did not ask what my first impressions of her had been. Because in truth, I don't believe that it was important to her. She was secure in what she believed of herself, whatever that might be. Her own opinion was the only one she truly required.

There was much I could learn from Emily Dickinson.

AUTHOR'S NOTE

EMILY DICKINSON IS one of the most well-known names in poetry. She is world-renowned and studied with the same intensity today as when collections of her poetry were first posthumously published. She is even more popular today than she was then. To write a novel starring Dickinson is a daunting task, but one I had dreamed about for a very long time. Since I am a mystery author, a mystery was the story that I was able to tell.

When I set out to write *Because I Could Not Stop for Death*, I already knew that Dickinson's father, Edward Dickinson, served one term in the U.S. House of Representatives, and in 1855, Dickinson and her sister visited him in Washington D.C., at his request. I wanted to include that trip in the novel because it's not the common perception of Dickinson. Many only think of her as the tortured poet who wore a white dress, never left her home, and feverishly wrote night and day. Dickinson became that at a point later in life, but that was many years after the time of this novel. I included several true anecdotes about Dickinson's visit to Washington. She did visit Mount Vernon, enjoy ice cream from an ice cream shop, and socialize throughout the town.

Knowing that I would be sending Dickinson and her fictional maid, Willa, to Washington, I felt the need to tie my novel to the politics of the 1850s, and nothing was more prominent at the time than the events leading up to the American Civil War. When the Fugitive Slave Act of 1850 was passed, it allowed "slave catchers" to come into the North and physically take runaway enslaved people back to the South. After 1850, there truly was no real safety for runaways until they made it to Canada. Where Emily lived in Massachusetts the Underground Railroad was active in helping runaway enslaved people on their journey north.

In Massachusetts, most of the stationmasters and conductors on the Underground Railroad were white like many of my characters are in the novel, but there were free Black citizens, like my character Jeremiah York, and former enslaved people who also helped.

Now Dickinson herself makes little mention about slavery or the Civil War in her letters and in the poetry that she left behind, but it would be impossible to believe that the time period in which she lived did not affect her. Her father was a member of the Whig party, which was noticeably unwilling to take an official stand on the issue of slavery. The party was most concerned with stability and infrastructure improvement. Ultimately, by 1854, the party was all but torn apart over the issue of slavery because it did not take an official stance, but Edward Dickinson did finish his term in 1855 as a Whig.

As daunting as the task to write about Emily Dickinson is, the idea of writing a story involving the Underground Railroad was even more overwhelming, but I believe to not include it would be a disservice to the history of the brave men and women who saved so many lives at great personal risk. To be as true to the time period as possible, I thoroughly researched the topic, and authenticity readers have read the novel before publication in order to give valuable feedback. My goal and my hope is that I have written this story with historical accuracy and with the utmost respect and care for all who lived through that tumultuous time and for Emily Dickinson as well as her family. And I also hope that it's an enjoyable historical mystery that kept you guessing to the very end.

ACKNOWLEDGMENTS

To write this book is an actual dream come true. I have been a fan of Emily Dickinson since I was fifteen and was assigned the poem "I heard a Fly buzz - when I died" to memorize in high school. Ever since I have been fascinated with the poet and her work, and considering the content of the poem, it's not surprising I was destined to write mysteries.

Emily has inspired me as a writer, but as a mystery novelist, not a poet. The unanswered mysteries of Emily's work and life are what I find more interesting. The first novel I wrote inspired by Emily was a contemporary cozy mystery, *Crime and Poetry*, where the sleuth interprets Emily's poems to solve the crime. *Because I Could Not Stop for Death* is the first time I have written Emily as a character, which has been exciting and challenging. So first and foremost, I want to thank Emily Dickinson for her life and work, without which this novel would not exist.

I would also like to thank the countless Dickinson scholars who helped me with this work by making their analysis and research available in books and articles. I read so many accounts of Dickinson's life for this one novel. It would be impossible to share them all. However, most noticeably I would like to thank the following: Richard B. Sewall, the author of *The Life of Emily Dickinson,* and Aífe Murray, the author of *Maid as Muse: How Servants Changed Emily Dickinson's Life and Language.*

In addition, I thank my agent, Nicole Resciniti, for supporting this book from the moment I pitched the idea to today, and to my editor, Michelle Vega, and the team at Berkley. I'm so grateful for everything you've done for this novel.

Special thanks to librarians and friends Suzy Schroeder and Alexandra Coley for research assistance, Kimra Bell for her comments on the novel, and the handful of other readers who commented on the novel before publication.

Thanks to my husband, David Seymour, for being a great partner and friend and encouraging me to write this book even when I was scared to be taking on such a beloved historical character and an emotional story line involving a difficult time in American history. My hope is that I have written this story with historical accuracy and with the utmost respect and care for Emily, her family, and others who lived through the tumultuous 1850s in the United States.

Finally, gratitude to God in heaven for the bravery to take this next step on my journey as a writer.

David M. Seymour

Amanda Flower is the *USA Today* bestselling and Agatha Award-winning mystery author of more than forty novels, including the nationally bestselling Amish Candy Shop Mystery series, Magical Bookshop Mysteries, and, written under the name Isabella Alan, the Amish Quilt Shop Mysteries. Flower is a former librarian, and she and her husband, a recording engineer, own a habitat farm and recording studio in Northeast Ohio.

CONNECT ONLINE

AmandaFlower.com
AuthorAmandaFlower
AmandaFlowerAuthor
AFlowerWriter

Ready to find
your next great read?

Let us help.

Visit prh.com/nextread

Penguin
Random
House